The Bulgarian Exclusiv

The Bulgarian Exclusive, sitting right on the edges

This book has a strong se sharp humour. . . I recom

It is an intricately plotted, cries out for filming. *Grimsby Evening Telegraph*

Chilling, unnervingly plausible. *She Magazine*

An exceptional novel of high-level intrigue behind the Iron Curtain. . .The reader is almost as easily misled as the hero. . .who winds up a fall guy. A dandy! *Booklist USA*

The story moves along at a breakneck pace. The terse, journalistic style makes the clever twists of plot perfectly clear. Grey is a highly placed journalist who seems to be writing from seasoned experience. A sure bet. *Library Journal, New York*

A gut-tensing, meal-missing, masterpiece of thriller writing. . . Brilliantly conceived, meticulously executed. *Huddersfield Examiner*

Grey knows how to keep the story going. He has the necessary staying power for the novel. John Braine, *Surrey Advertiser*

Only a journalist could have written such a well-documented and authoritative story. *Bolton Evening News*

The Bulgarian Exclusive

Anthony Grey, the author of seven novels to date, is a former foreign correspondent in Eastern Europe and China. His enduring epics, *Saigon* and *Peking*, have won international critical acclaim in the Far East, Australasia, Europe and America. His first book, *Hostage in Peking*, is an autobiographical account of two years' solitary confinement in China during the Cultural Revolution.

Books by Anthony Grey

Autobiography
Hostage in Peking (1970)

Short Stories
A Man Alone (1972)

Nonfiction
The Prime Minister Was a Spy (1983)

Novels
Some Put Their Trust in Chariots (1973)
(Now published by Pan as *The German Stratagem*)
The Bulgarian Exclusive (1976)
The Chinese Assassin (1979)
Saigon (1982)
Peking (1988)
The Bankok Secret (1990)
The Naked Angels (1990)

Anthony Grey

The
Bulgarian
Exclusive

PAN BOOKS
London, Sydney and Auckland

First published 1976 by Michael Joseph Ltd
This edition published 1990 by Pan Books Ltd,
Cavaye Place, London SW10 9PG
9 8 7 6 5 4 3 2 1
© Anthony Grey 1971
ISBN 0 330 31196 4

Typeset by Selectmove Ltd, London
Printed and bound in Great Britain by
Clays Ltd, St Ives plc, Bungay, Suffolk

To Lucy
and
Bernie
with love

Contents

PART ONE: Ingress   9

PART TWO: Congress   111

PART THREE: Egress   165

PART ONE

Ingress

However much the reactionaries try to
hold back the wheel of history, sooner
or later revolution will take place
and will inevitably triumph!

MAO TSE-TUNG – in a speech to the
Supreme Soviet, Moscow, November 1957

However much the revolutionaries try to
hold back the wheel of history, sooner or
later, reaction will set in and will
inevitably triumph – if I have anything
to bloody do with it!

JONATHAN ROBSON – in the Hotel
Balkan bar, Sofia, February 1976

One

'Get that purple leg of yours round me, sweetheart, it's cold.' He had his back to her. His voice was muffled by the pillow and he was still half asleep. Since she'd been dead to the world too for the last four hours, it wasn't surprising she didn't hear him. She began to stir only when his hand, groping blindly behind him, located her right knee. She grunted sleepily and, knowing the routine, shifted obediently towards him. With his eyes still closed, he dragged her thigh up and over his hip like an extra blanket.

'Be even colder in bloody Bulgaria.'

Even through heavy layers of sleep she recognized that this grumbling tone begged a sympathetic response. So she mumbled inarticulate consoling noises as she hooked her leg hard round him and wound herself tighter into his back.

'That's better.'

Slowly her burning female warmth began to spread upwards from the concentrated glow at the base of his spine. He pulled the thin covers closer round his exposed ear to keep out the wintry chill of the room and edged deliberately back towards the brink of sleep.

Outside in Battersea Park the sleet that had been falling steadily all night was finally hardening into the real thing. The rising wind drove the first frantic flurries of white flakes low across the lake then spun them high again for a moment like great pivotless galaxies before dashing them against the wall of gaunt, black tree-trunks along the avenue.

Under these same bare trees a polished grey Mercedes wearing CD plates switched on its windscreen wipers to clear the vision of the swarthy man sitting in its passenger seat beside a uniformed driver. In his hands the swarthy man held two polaroid colour photographs taken with a telephoto lens. In close-up, against the red brick and sandstone entrance to the Victorian mansion block of flats that he was watching fifty yards away, they showed the full face and profile of a dark-haired man. The swarthy man relieved himself of a short stream of low Slav curses as he flung the photographs like a defeated hand of cards onto the top of the dashboard. He glanced at his wrist watch for the third time in five minutes. Seven eighteen. Tension tightened his face as he stared out again through the thickening snow towards the entrance to the flats.

'If Robson doesn't stop fornicating soon and get up he'll miss the plane.'

'Why did Comrade Radovanovic and our "friends" in Whitehall choose Robson?'

The swarthy man picked up the full-face polaroid again and stared at it hard before replying. His glance flicked anxiously from the photograph to the entrance to the flats then back again, as though willing the man to appear.

'I'm not sure they really did choose him. Robson, although he doesn't know it, chose himself.'

'How?'

'He happens to be the ideal cat's-paw. He knows Eastern Europe well. He also has an almost psychotic hatred of everything communist. That is very important . . . He is not beyond foolhardy actions, even though they may endanger himself, and he has shown himself to have a very low resistance threshold to attractive women.'

'Haven't we all, Comrade!'

'Shut up! This might be him now.'

Through the grey murk they watched a hunched figure carrying two shiny black plastic bags down the steps from the entrance to the flats. The driver reached quickly for the ignition key.

'Wait you fool!' The swarthy man's face twisted with contempt. 'Unless Robson is leaving for Sofia disguised as the hall porter and carrying two sacks of household refuse, that's not him.'

The driver sat back, coughing to hide his embarrassment.

'Perhaps I should go up and knock on his door to remind him of the time.'

The driver's attempt at humour jarred the taut nerves of the man beside him. 'Shut up! Foolhardy Robson may be, but a fool he is not. If he gets even slightly suspicious he's being used at this stage, the whole operation could fail.' The swarthy man's face bulged with anger. 'Do you want to play right into the hands of the Kremlin and Bodinski? They won't be as lenient as they were with Dubček! Failure will mean certain death for the First Secretary!'

The driver shrank in his seat under the unjustified outburst of his companion, and said nothing.

Less than a hundred yards away another pair of eyes watched impassively from behind the grimy windows of a red, mud-spattered Volkswagen. But the porter carrying out the rubbish caused no flicker of interest in them. The Volkswagen had been there much longer than the Mercedes. It had, in fact, taken up its position overnight in the unbroken line of residents' vehicles that are always stationed along the park side of Prince of Wales Drive. Streaked with the same uniform of London winter dirt as the Minis, Peugeots, MGBs and Renaults in front and behind, the Volkswagen sat anonymously in its place, far enough away along the kerb for its solitary Chinese driver to watch, without moving his head more than an inch or two, both the entrance to Robson's flat and the car from the Bulgarian Embassy.

The lashless eyelids narrowed slightly with satisfaction when the driver noticed that the side and rear windows of the Mercedes had at last become completely fogged with the condensed breath of the two men inside. There was no longer any likelihood of them noticing that the windscreen wipers of his stationary Volkswagen were in motion too.

The Chinese sat without moving, without looking at his watch. A copy of the *Daily Telegraph* lay folded on the empty passenger seat beside him ready to hide his face from any early passer-by, should the need arise.

His photograph of Robson, a dreary black and white mug-shot supplied by Robson himself four years ago when applying unsuccessfully for a journalist's visa for Peking, was not in the car. It remained locked away in a filing cabinet in the central strong-room registry of the Chinese Embassy in Portland Place. The single sheet of paper accompanying it in the transparent plastic folder carried a bald recitation of Robson's vital statistics from that same visa application. The patient Chinese had not brought the file with him because he had committed the image and the words and figures to memory the night before.

As he waited, his hand strayed to one bulging pocket of his high-collared tunic to reassure himself that the silenced Tsunyi automatic buttoned inside was ready to hand.

*

'Sod it, I'm not going!'

'But won't you lose your job?' She unhooked her leg from him, realizing it had become a restraining influence.

'BAPPA won't fall apart without me.'

'But mightn't you fall apart without BAPPA?'

'I'm more likely to fall apart without that leg round me. Come on.' He moved to replace it but she was quicker. She slid away and swung both bare legs on to the floor. She sucked air fiercely between her chattering teeth with the shock of the cold. Even when she'd buttoned the long white négligé right up to her chin the chattering didn't stop.

'Get up Jonathan. I've bought a present for you to take with you.'

He rolled over to watch her as she went through the door to the kitchen. Practically everything she wore was white. And even in that grey light she looked smoky purple through the thin cotton.

Why was she so keen for him to go to Sofia? During the three weeks he'd known her, he'd left her asleep whenever he went out in the morning. Why was she clattering crockery in the kitchen and humming like a piccaninny at quarter past seven today? It was only four hours since she'd finished her closing number at the club.

He heard a cup smash on the kitchen floor. The mild cursing that followed was near-perfect English.

All right! If that's how she wanted it! He'd go to bloody Sofia and cover the damned Party Congress.

He rolled out of bed and spent two shivering minutes crawling around on the floor looking for the belt to his dressing-gown. Then he realized he'd got it on inside out. In the bathroom the batteries in his shaver threshed briefly in their death throes before passing away for ever. Because he was still shivering he cut himself under the right ear with an injector razor blade that was bedded into a black plastic lozenge specifically to make self-inflicted wounds impossible.

In the kitchen she'd poured steaming hot tea into the two psychedelic gift mugs the garage at the corner had given them in exchange for seven Heron stamps. Beside it was a little bundle wrapped in several pink Kleenex tissues.

16

'It's your present.'

'Gift wrapped by Harrods, I see.'

'It's to help you through Bulgaria.'

She was fully dressed now in a white roll-neck sweater and tight trousers, and she'd tied a brightly coloured scarf round her black hair.

'Open it, Jonathan.'

'My hands are shaking with excitement. Do it for me.'

She unfolded the tissues and held it up by its chain.

'The chain's a real luxury.'

'Don't you like it?'

He couldn't decide whether the wide smile she was giving him was stage version or genuine.

'I've always wanted a take-along bath plug of my own.'

Something in the hardness of his voice made her smile falter. 'But didn't you tell me that baths in communist hotels never have any plugs?'

'Used not to have. You find the odd one nowadays.'

'I thought it would make you think of me whenever you took a bath.'

Sensing what was coming now, he drained the tea from the mug too quickly, burning his throat. 'I'd better get to the airport. I'm late.' He kept his eyes away from the white sweater and her face. Even at seven thirty in the morning she looked ready to pose for the cover of *Cosmopolitan*.

'Jonathan, I'm going too.'

The wind flung a fistful of snow angrily against the window in the silence.

'Not to Sofia.' It was a statement, not a question.

'No. My husband is coming back from Barbados today.'

'I thought you said it was all over with him.'

'It was. Maybe it still is. I don't know. But when you told me last week you were going to Bulgaria today, I thought it would be a good time for me to go, too.'

'After only three weeks.'

'We're from different worlds Jonathan.'

'What bloody difference does that make?'

'I wouldn't be right for you in Vienna. We should stick to our own.'

'I haven't been given Vienna yet! There's no guarantee that I will be. And anyway you're right for me here, there or anywhere. Don't knock yourself.'

She said nothing. He looked up at her quickly but the purple lids of her eyes were lowered determinedly against him. She pressed the tip of her index finger against grains of spilled sugar on the table top and stared abstractedly at the patterns they made against the pale skin. 'Beryl.' Although he spoke quietly his voice seemed to startle her. She turned her palm suddenly and flattened it against the table again as though to hide it. 'I would very much like you to be around when I get back from Bulgaria. It'll only be a few days.'

Another flurry of snow died noisily against the window panes.

'I thought for one horrible moment, Jonathan, that you were going to start talking there about being in love for the very first time.' She was looking at him directly now. Her black liquid eyes were wide and bright, starting to smile. 'I'm glad you didn't.'

She got up, pressed the bath plug into his hand and went quickly into the bedroom. He heard her sweeping the clutter of cosmetics and aerosol hairsprays from the dressing table into her giant shoulder bag. When she came back she had her coat and knee-length boots on.

'Goodbye, Jonathan.'

She leaned very hard into him. His hold was harsh and rough in return. They chewed hungrily at each other's mouths for half a minute before she broke and ran to the door. As she came down the steps to the pavement in the snow the driver of the Mercedes nudged the swarthy man. 'So that's the colour of the stuff he likes.'

They both stopped watching the entrance to follow her with their eyes. She came directly across the street towards them. The contoured knee-length boots made her long legs look longer than they really were. Even on a wet, slush-covered road in driving snow she moved with a teasing, easy-limbed grace.

'Calypso dancer at the Ocho Rios,' grunted the swarthy man with a trace of contempt in his voice.

She didn't give a second glance to the *Daily Telegraph* plastered inside the windscreen of the dirty red Volkswagen. Without pausing she stepped past it on to the pavement, pulled her collar high around

18

her ears and ran on beside the park fence, passing within twenty yards of where the Mercedes was parked. Seconds later she had disappeared into the grey, snowy murk.

'This looks like him now.'

The driver recognized the man coming out of the entrance to the flats from his photograph. Tall, dark-haired, hatless, wearing the kind of shabby, heavy-duty sheepskin coat favoured by early television reporters, he carried a small overnight bag in one hand and a portable typewriter in a worn-looking case in the other.

'Yes, that's Robson. Half past bloody seven, too. Get going.' The swarthy man's relief flooded from him like air escaping from a punctured balloon. The driver switched on the ignition and started the engine.

Robson moved quickly along the line of parked cars to his battered TR6 hardtop. He'd left the driver's window open two inches and snow had blown through the gap. A small puddle now covered the driving seat. Too angry to curse, he flung his holdall and typewriter furiously into the space behind the seats and began mopping up with his handkerchief.

At that moment the Mercedes moved off on the other side of the park fence to take up station at the gates opening onto Queenstown Road. Simultaneously the *Daily Telegraph* disappeared from the windows of the Volkswagen and its engine fired too, at first time of asking, like the adverts always promised it would in snow.

The TR had once been white beneath its six months' cover of dirt. The original body design, too, had been modified by Robson in a dozen different places during three years of boring and bumping through London's constipated traffic gut. Now his anger at the loss of Beryl, the wet seat, the cold and the snow all combined to catapult the battered car too fast away from the kerb.

He was into the Queenstown Road roundabout doing forty-five and sliding on the slush towards the central refuge before he let his foot up. Fortunately, the roundabout was clear of traffic.

He spun the wheel the other way and kicked the accelerator sharply again. The back end whiplashed against the roundabout's exit bollard, shattering the glass of a rear indicator and destroying the offside tail light completely. He slid for thirty yards along the wrong side of the long, broad approach to Chelsea Bridge, straightened and got up to eighty in overdrive before he had to throttle back for the Embankment lights on the other side of the Thames.

The debris of red and yellow glass from the TR was crunched into the slush first by the wheels of the Mercedes as it accelerated smoothly out of the park in pursuit. Twenty seconds later the Chinese picked up its fragments in his treads as he drove the Volkswagen cautiously through the roundabout taking care not to let the weight of the rear-mounted engine push him into a slide.

The Volkswagen's onward progress towards the bridge was equally unhurried. They knew Robson's destination was Heathrow. They had already decided on the spot along the airport road where they would hit him. As he slowed for the Embankment lights the Chinese driver took a walkie-talkie handset from the glove compartment and repeated a single Chinese codeword, twice over, to another Volkswagen, a blue one, parked three miles away to the West in the shadow of the high concrete stilts propping up the entry ramp to the Chiswick flyover.

Two

Robson lost a fierce battle for possession of the inside track round Sloane Square to the uncompromising driver of a yellow *Daily Mail* delivery van. He refused to admit defeat by touching his brake, however, until the last moment, and then was a fraction late with the clutch. So the TR stalled and the Mercedes came close to ramming him from the rear. Because the windows were tightly closed, the stream of curses Robson yelled at the van driver at the top of his voice didn't penetrate outside the car.

As Robson restarted his engine, three miles away to the East in Fleet Street, on the third floor of the British Amalgamated Press and Picture Agency building, Jock Baird, the World Desk day editor, was already committing to paper the hazardous assumption of his safe arrival in Bulgaria. Baird, in fact, was typing the last line in a schedule of news stories that he was promising to supply to foreign editors in newspaper offices and broadcasting stations around the world in the next few hours.

'Sofia:' he tapped with one finger; 'Soviet leaders expected for tomorrow's Bulgarian Communist Party Congress. Curtain-raiser by Jonathan Robson.' With a confidence he would have had difficulty sustaining if he had been standing in Sloane Square, he added, 'Robson will provide updating material from Sofia later in the day.' Then he hauled the schedule and its four carbons from the typewriter and, standing up, floated one copy over a bank of chattering teleprinters to land squarely in a wire basket on the desk of day copytaster, Gordon Miller.

Miller, who prided himself on his youthful efficiency, picked the sheet out of the tray immediately. He ran his eye quickly down the menu of news and names, and winced. It was heavily larded as usual with old-fashioned esoteric journalese. Baird had been with BAPPA more years than most people remembered. Unlike Miller, who'd joined the agency only a few years ago straight out of Cambridge, Baird had come up to Fleet Street through the ranks of the provincial press. He and the other old hands invariably overdid the jargon, sometimes to such an extent that Miller wondered how anyone understood it at all, outside the office.

In addition to Robson's 'Curtain-raiser' it promised an 'Up-dater' from BAPPA's correspondent in Geneva on the SALT negotiations with 'Dayleads', 'Interpretives', 'Sidebars', and 'Brighteners' if the story became 'transcendant'. There'd be a 'Backgrounder' on the OPEC oil talks in Algiers, a 'Situationer' from Bangkok on Thailand's new 'strongman' and an 'Up-summer' from Cairo on Dr Kissinger's latest Middle East negotiations. 'Dayside Wordage' on the EEC summit in Brussels was expected to be light during what Baird loved to call 'the evening paper trick'.

Still, he'd be retiring in a year's time. Good thing too. An old man who still wore a broad leather belt *and* braces on his trousers was, in his view, painfully out of place around the recently installed computerized equipment that could flash major news simultaneously to the furthest corners of the world in a matter of seconds.

One detail on the schedule aroused Miller's curiosity. All the correspondents getting star billing today were familiar to him except the last one.

'Who's this chappie Robson who's going into Bulgaria for us, Jock?'

'You might well ask, Dusty.'

21

Gordon Miller hated people calling him 'Dusty'. It offended the image of himself that Cambridge had given him. Only older people did it nowadays. Baird knew this and he'd be glad to see him go. But he'd pick his brains clean before he went, to give himself a leg up for the vacant job.

'How do you mean, Jock? No good?'

After years of experience Baird could tear incoming stories from the teleprinters all round him, read them and distribute them unerringly without pausing in his conversation. He was doing it now. 'I wouldn't say "no good" exactly. In fact, he's a first class newsman when he wants to be.'

'Drinker?'

'No, not more than most.'

'What then?'

'Bit unpredictable, I suppose. Not unreliable *exactly*. Can be brilliant. But he wouldn't be my choice for a sensitive beat like Eastern Europe – although he's had a fair bit of experience out there.'

Baird called over a long-haired, pimply-faced messenger boy and handed him a United Nations speech by Uganda's delegate. With a wink he instructed the lad to take it to the Africa Desk for special distribution to 'the media of the Dark Continent'.

'Whose choice is Robson then? Where has he sprung from?'

'He's a Barnes man.'

'I see.' Miller's voice went satirically sing-song. 'Old chum of the chairman, eh? Always helps.'

'More of a friend of the chairman's wife, I think, if we're going to be precise.'

Gordon Miller's ears pricked up. Baird's tone seemed deliberately malicious. He waited, but nothing else came.

'Come on, Jock, you old rogue. You can't spill me a titillating piece of political gossip like that, then withhold the punchline.'

Baird paused, remaining unnecessarily silent while he read a short piece from BAPPA's Peking correspondent knocking down the latest rumours about Mao's health that had emanated from Hong Kong. 'Robson was a bit like you, one of the BAPPA whiz kids a few years ago. Except he came to us via the north somewhere. *Telegraph and Argus*, I think. He's a smooth Yorkshireman, if that's not a contradiction in terms.

22

He had a brilliant spell of about four or five years with us. Got himself expelled from Africa and Moscow – when it was still considered a mark of prowess. He did spells in Budapest and Bucharest, then got the idea he was a genius with too much temperament and talent for a plodding day-to-day agency man.'

'What did he do?'

'Upped and went freelance.'

The skeleton staff of the night was gradually being augmented and replaced by day-shift journalists. Empty chairs at the World Desk and the satellite regional desks were filling up and the hundred or so teleprinters spread across the open editorial floor were beginning to rev up their background clatter to a higher pitch.

'But now he's back,' said Miller. 'I thought, like punch-drunk heavyweight champs, old BAPPA men never came back.'

'I think Robson's fallen on hard times. Got into a run of bad luck apparently. He made a lot of money from some mysterious deal a few years ago then disappeared for a while. He only emerged again after he'd lost most of it in the Poseidon fiasco. He's probably grasping at straws now.'

'When is he supposed to have done his grasping at the comely Lady Barnes?'

'In Moscow, strangely enough. Our master took his wife along during Robson's time there when he went to negotiate some new exchange contracts with Tass. The bargaining was unexpectedly tough and he spent three whole days closeted with the Russians. Robson was left to look after Lady B.' Baird paused and chuckled evilly. 'Did it much to her delight and approval, apparently. Least that was the story that got about.'

'Sounds a smooth operator.'

'Aye, he's a charming sort of bugger. Kind of bloke who's difficult to dislike. The Americans in Moscow used to call him "the dapper Bappaman". I forget why exactly. Something to do with his first assignment in Skopje.'

'And this trip to Bulgaria, it's his first comeback assignment?'

'Aye, he's on trial in a way, I suppose, despite his experience. He's probably after the Vienna office. The chief correspondent's job there is coming on the market next month.'

Miller grinned wickedly. 'Well, I'm sure that's not beyond Lady Barnes's generosity . . . if Robson rubs her up the right way. She may be getting on a bit now but she's only got to threaten to leave the old man again hasn't she, to get her way?'

The bell on one of the teleprinters clamoured repeatedly as a dispatch slugged 'urgent' began running in from the BAPPA office in Beirut. Baird and Miller walked quickly over to the machine and watched it print out the first few lines of a new hijack serial starring Palestinian guerrillas.

Miller bristled as Baird snatched up a yellow retrieval slip and jotted the code number of the Beirut story on it. He handed it quickly to the controller seated at the computer console who punched the details onto his keyboard. Within thirty seconds the computer would retrieve the Beirut 'urgent' from its memory store of the entire day's news input and retransmit it immediately without any editing to all BAPPA subscribers around the world. This might help the story land a minute or so before the competing agencies got it out and this kind of superior service could usefully be recalled when BAPPA broke the news to subscribers that contract rates were going up again next year.

Miller stepped back ostentatiously. He was put out. This was the copytaster's job. But he could hardly prevent his superior taking a hand if he happened to be about. Baird watched the type-heads of the outgoing teleprinters begin to drum rhythmically. Only when he was thoroughly satisfied that the item was running out smoothly did he turn sharply on Miller.

'Don't get too cocky, young Dusty. Take it from me, you don't know it all.' His voice dropped to a half whisper and he brought his lined, aging face close to the younger man's. 'Her Ladyship won't be running rings round BAPPA much longer. There's a battle of wills going on upstairs in our own executive corridors of power right now that could match anything the Kremlin has seen for ferocity . . . And Sir Someone Barnes himself might even be for the chop, if you ask me.'

Miller's mocking expression didn't slip. 'Oh dear, what will happen to poor old Robson's comeback then?'

The grizzled Scot stared hard at him for a moment. Then his normally gentle voice became really angry for the first time. 'It won't just affect Robson. Everybody here is a friend of somebody whether they like it or not, remember that. Somebody recruited you. Somebody recommended you for promotion. Nobody will be safe until it's over. Even your bloody degree won't give you immunity. So watch out for your own tender neck, Dusty Miller!'

Another 'urgent' bell began ringing somewhere and Baird swung round and strode away quickly through the banks of clattering machines. As he went he hooked his thumbs inside the waistband of his trousers and gave them a quick hoist as if he was emphasizing to the milk-sop Cambridge graduate watching him that even in the simple conflict between trousers and gravity, his canny Scottish nature didn't put too much trust in the seemingly foolproof double insurance of belt and braces.

Three

As Robson swung up the curving entry ramp to the Chiswick flyover, he noticed the chimney pots. He'd driven along the elevated airport road at rooftop level hundreds of times before without noticing them. But now, through the mist of flying snow, he suddenly saw them for the first time as a 'forest of upside down brick udders'. Saw them the way they had appeared to a bewildered, awestruck West Indian girl setting foot in England for the first time after five short years of life in the chimneyless tropics.

The Mercedes crept near enough to appear full-clear in Robson's driving mirror, but he failed to notice it.

Beryl's earliest and most startling impression of England had forced itself into his mind, he knew, because he had been replaying his own first vivid memories of her. And they were only three weeks old, not twenty years. But was it solely her powerful physical impact that he'd miss? Was it just that chocolate-purple body, that novel, startling difference that created the excitement between them? Too early yet to say whether he cared for any other reason that she'd gone.

Her restless, laughing vitality, that open physicalness, her unselfconscious delight too, in their difference, might they not all have worn thin soon? Maybe. Everything passes. Hadn't it started to do just that at breakfast? Shit, think about something else!

A blue Volkswagen, travelling unexpectedly fast, shot out round the Mercedes and tucked itself in behind the TR as Robson reached across the passenger seat and clipped an Alan Price cassette into the dashboard stereo player.

The plaintive, shouting voice of the Newcastle singer-composer suddenly blasted round the car full volume because the tuner had been left at full pitch.

'If you have a friend on whom you think you can rely, you are a Lucky Man,' screamed Price, as a grinning Chinese face in high-buttoned blue tunic and Mao cap appeared suddenly beside Robson, two feet away.

Robson didn't see the face because he was leaning to his left trying to turn the stereo down. But he clutched frantically at the wheel with both hands again as the blue left-hand drive Volkswagen accelerated and veered across his track, forcing him towards the railings that separated the fast road from a sheer drop to factory forecourts flashing by thirty feet below.

'If you've found the reason to live on and not to die, you are a Lucky Man,' yelled Price. Robson dragged the wheel over to the right and practically stood up on the brake in a fear reflex. The car went into a skid immediately, lurching on the slush. Robson's run of early morning ill luck, if that's what it had been, ended at that moment. The unthinking skid he'd started thumped him first into the kerb below the railings. Then, against all the odds, it swung him away and out past the Volkswagen which had shuddered to a standstill. He had a fleeting impression of the startled face of the driver turning to watch over his shoulder as the TR slid slowly past, striking the front wing a glancing blow, then straightening in the outside lane.

'If you've found the secret, well try not to blow it, stay a Lucky Man!' Price and his throbbing band became practically deafening, on the crescendo to the verse.

What happened next was over in a flash and Robson only had the vaguest impression of it from his driving mirror. The Mercedes behind had fallen back far enough to steer out round the Volkswagen, which was now jammed fast against the rails. But the Dutch refrigerated juggernaut pounding along close behind the

Mercedes had no chance of stopping or swerving round the blue car. It caught the Volkswagen on its high steel fenders and swept it up and over the railing like the cowcatcher of an old Western steam locomotive tossing tumbleweed from its track. Then the truck and its trailer jack-knifed across the two-lane flyover and overturned, blocking it from edge to edge.

Robson's first reaction was to stop. His hands were shaking, his heart was pounding and his mouth was dry. But then he remembered where he was going and how late he was and he put his foot down again towards Heathrow. If he stopped, the delay, he knew, would be endless. For what? He had no idea how or why the crazy bastard in the Volkswagen had lost control and cut him up. Perhaps he'd contact the police when he got back from Sofia.

He noticed the Mercedes behind wasn't stopping either and that reassured him of the good sense of his decision. When his hands stopped shaking he switched off the booming cassette player and drove on for a while in silence. By the time he reached the flat runways of the M4 motorway and turned on the radio, the road report on the BBC's 'Today' programme was warning motorists that the airport road out of London had been blocked by a collision.

When he reached Heathrow eighteen minutes later, he drove straight into the expensive short term car park because it was near the departure lounge. He had to run all the way to the Balkanair Tupolev 134 for Sofia which was parked at one of the furthest gates. He arrived breathless and sweating just as the flight list was being closed.

The swarthy man from the Mercedes watched him walk aboard with his portable typewriter from the observation roof on top of the Queen's Building. Then he ran quickly downstairs and from a public telephone he put in a call to the Bulgarian Embassy. He spoke very briefly and with obvious relief into the receiver. When he came out of the booth, a Chinese who'd just climbed out of a red mud-spattered Volkswagen carrying a copy of the *Daily Telegraph*, was waiting outside to use the phone. He stepped politely aside and the Bulgarian hurried past him without a second glance.

A few minutes after the Tupolev with its distinctive orange and green markings had climbed steeply off the runway into the low-banked snow clouds, a telex message prefixed 'Cranbourne' began ticking out from a cramped room in the airport security offices situated in the basement of Terminal Three. It read: 'Confirm as requested, J. Robson, news correspondent of BAPPA departed on Balkanair flight IZ 1404 to Bulgaria. Estimated arrival time in Sofia via Vienna 1230 GMT. End of message.'

A bored clerk in the Communications Room in the basement of the Foreign Office in Whitehall tore off the incoming message without reading it. But when he caught sight of its time and letter code, he sealed it quickly in a bright yellow envelope and dropped it into the messengers' tray marked 'For Immediate Delivery'.

Less than a minute later it was on its way to its destination – an office in a part of the building that even the most senior diplomats are wary of discussing in anything but the most circumlocutive and evasive terms.

Four

The bedside telephone chirruped briefly in the darkened third floor bedroom of the Hotel Lido in Bucharest. Georgina Morakova reached out and fumbled the receiver down on to the pillow so that she could answer it without putting on the light, without opening her eyes and without sitting up in the cold.

'*Da?*'

A succession of unexplained crackling noises threatened to become interminable. Because she knew they were caused by the Romanian State Security's listening devices and because she had long become accustomed to the fact that Communists didn't even trust each other, she waited patiently without wasting her breath. When the interference ceased, the voice of the swarthy man from the Mercedes came on the line from London.

'Comrade Morakova?'

'*Da.*'

'*Dobro Outro!* I thought you should know that there will be an unscheduled Balkanair flight to Sofia that might suit you later this morning.'

'At what time?'

'It's not possible to say precisely. The flight from London to Sofia will be diverted to Otopini airport because of . . .' the voice paused to emphasize '. . . temporary landing difficulties in Sofia. These should, I think, be resolved by lunch time.'

'What time should I get to the airport?' There was just a hint of nervous strain in her voice.

'Be there about twelve thirty. I hope you might find the aisle seat, 10f, a comfortable one. The cabin staff will have reserved it for you.'

'*Blagodarya*, Comrade.'

'I trust you will have a safe and profitable journey home.'

'Is there anybody from the embassy on the flight?' She spoke the sentence with slow deliberation.

'No. Nobody at all. But you will possibly find other new friends on board.' Even the distortion of the long distance line from London couldn't hide the extra heavy emphasis with which the swarthy man, too, was now speaking. 'I know that somebody as lovely as you, Comrade, is never wanting when it comes to making new friends. *Dovizhdane!*'

'*Dovizhdane.*' She reached out, replaced the receiver, switched on the shaded bedside light and, when her eyes had adjusted to it, picked up the two polaroid colour photographs of a dark-haired man that stood propped against the base of the lamp. One was a full face shot, the other showed the man in profile. Both were taken against an archway of red brick and sandstone.

As she sat on the bed studying the pictures she absently caught up her tousled red-brown hair in one hand and piled it on top of her head. 'How will you like me best I wonder, Englishman', she said softly to herself. 'A sophisticated lady . . .' She lifted her chin exaggeratedly and turned sideways to study her reflection in the dressing table mirror across the room. Then she let the long hair tumble back round her face and shoulders '. . . or a simple Balkan peasant girl?'

She sat staring into the mirror for a moment – then suddenly shivered. She flung back the bedclothes and hurried into the bathroom to run a hot bath.

A few minutes later, fully dressed, she sat down at the dressing table and took up a brush. She propped the photographs up on either side of the mirror and studied them again as she drew the brush thoughtfully down either side of her broad, pale face. 'You have an English peasant's face yourself, Mr Robson,' she told the photographs quietly, 'so I think perhaps you'll prefer sophistication.'

From her handbag she shook out a collection of expensive French cosmetics and, tilting back her head, stared intently into the mirror. Working with the deft assurance of an artist selecting pigments from his palette, she first heightened the shadows of her high Slav cheekbones then dabbed colour faintly on her lips and eyelids.

When she'd finished she rose, half turned, and pulled her woollen jersey tightly down around her hips. She stood staring into the mirror at the profile of her tall, strong body, but suddenly as if losing her resolution her face clouded. She leaned forward shakily to support herself with her hands on the dressing table. Her eyes closed and her head sagged forward towards the mirror. She didn't look up again for fully a minute. When she did, her face was clenched in an expression that was a mixture of determination and desperation. 'For God's sake,' she told her reflection fiercely in Bulgarian, 'don't let the bastard be indifferent.'

She straightened up quickly, picked up the photographs and tore them across the middle. Then she took her cigarette lighter from her handbag and set fire to them.

While they burned in an ash-tray she picked up her lipstick and eye-shadow set and dropped them into her handbag beside a small automatic pistol. When the photographs had turned to black ash, she put on a long suede coat and a fur hat, picked up her suitcase and let herself quietly out of the room.

On board the Balkanair Tupolev, twenty-six thousand feet above the icy waters of the Danube, the pilot's public address system crackled and came to life. 'Ladies and gentlemen, I apologize once again for that delay caused by our unavoidable diversion to Bucharest.' He spoke English with a thick Slav accent. 'However I assure you that the runways at Sofia are now clear and we shall be expecting to land there in about half an hour from now. We are at present crossing the River Danube which forms the border between the Socialist Republic of Romania and the People's

Republic of Bulgaria. Please fasten your seat belts now as we expect to encounter some slight turbulence during our approach. Thank you.'

'Great.' Robson's voice quivered with exasperation. 'After hopping up and down on the snow-covered runways of Vienna and Bucharest all bloody morning, we're now going to be shaken out of our wits getting into Sofia.'

'Part of another communist plot, would you say, Jonathan?' The fresh-faced middle-aged American in the next seat stared intently at Robson over the top of his gold-rimmed spectacles and rolled the question mockingly off his tongue in a quiet Boston drawl.

'Look, Ben, it's your first trip behind the Iron Curtain and I'm trying to put you straight, right?' Robson clipped his seat belt round his waist. 'I've never trusted East European airlines since the day I walked up the steps behind a pilot in Warsaw staring at two bloody great holes in the heels of his socks.'

'Want me to go up front and check out the Bulgar's footwear for you? Maybe they've discovered darning since then.' He made as if to unbuckle his seat belt and get up.

Robson didn't smile. Instead he folded his arms and leaned back thoughtfully in his seat. When he spoke, he addressed the adjustable air jets in the panel above his head. 'I have a theory, Ben. Watergate must have been a bit like the Black Death for you Americans. But it hasn't killed – just addled the brains of one in three of the population of the United States. Now even the *American Herald* is sending jokey political innocents from its London bureau to cover deadly serious Party Congresses in Eastern Europe.

'Jokey political innocents like Ben Bradley, what's more, who've gone soft on the Comms, the same way Ford has.' He continued to stare intently up at the air jets as if they might issue a confirmation of his theory.

'If we're going to be honest, we have to admit that the paper doesn't have anybody around like Jonathan Robson of BAPPA to send. Hasn't had since Senator McCarthy's heyday, I guess.' The American correspondent grinned this time and patted Robson's elbow as he spoke, to take the sting out of the remark.

Robson stopped examining the air conditioning and turned his attention to the muscular thigh movements of the tall, heavily built Bulgarian air stewardess coming slowly towards him along the aisle checking seat belts and offering boiled sweets. 'You know Ben,' he said at last averting his gaze, 'seriously now, it has been really very frightening to watch you Americans change so fast. The way you backed up the theory with deeds in Vietnam should have been a great lesson for the whole Western world. "The Communists aim to take us over so we all gotta fight 'em now, everywhere." It was the right attitude. Devastatingly simple but necessary and right.'

'Yeah, so long as the Americans took all the punishment and no damned Brits got shot.'

'I know, Ben. It was perhaps too simplistic. But now your pendulum's swung too far the other way. Now you're being blinded, because you want to be, by that magic new word in the mouths of men who, since Lenin, have been dedicated to destroying us — "détente". Suddenly in your book all the Comms, Russians, Chinese, what-have-you, are nice decent guys who've seen the error of their ways and only want the opportunity to admire and buy all our capitalist goods and know-how.' He shook his head in resignation.

'You won't even notice until you've sold them the last nut and bolt of Western freedom along with another half dozen nuclear power plants. Then we'll all wake up one morning ten years from now to find that what we've bought for ourselves in return is a nice, all-inclusive closely-supervised communist package tour from the cradle to the grave . . .' Robson stopped speaking suddenly and turned his head.

He had sensed that the girl with prominent cheekbones who'd boarded the flight during the diversionary stop-over in Bucharest was listening. Taken by surprise she stared straight back at him from her seat across the aisle. Their glances locked but she didn't look away. Instead she held his gaze steadily with wide unblinking eyes.

'Look,' Bradley was saying, 'Brezhnev needs the West now, don't you see? Unless he can pull the Soviet economy round he'll be put out on his ear.'

Robson turned back. 'Ben, it's not enough just to listen to the kind of public relations speeches Brezhnev makes at European Security Conferences in Helsinki and will no doubt make at this Congress in Sofia. If you're going to cover the East Europe beat, read the translated summaries of monitored domestic radio broadcasts. Get 'em from the BBC or Radio Free Europe. Get a good digest of what the communist theoreticians are writing in the party journals for the education of the *apparatchiks*. "Détente", "peaceful co-existence" are just cover terms. The new Brezhnev doctrine, if you read between the lines, is to build up Moscow's military and economic strength over the next ten years with the unashamed aim that in the mid or late 1980s when the balance of power has swung overwhelmingly in their favour – Bingo, one push and over we go!'

Screams rang through the cabin of the aircraft as the Tupolev dropped suddenly with the speed of an express elevator. Glasses and cutlery smashed and clattered in the galley. The engines roared erratically and the plane swung violently from side to side.

'Jesus, Jonathan,' shouted Bradley, 'you're right, the goddammed pilot has got holes in his socks.' He stared round-eyed at the English journalist. His face was the colour of chalk.

Five

'Relax, Ben, I told you East Europe would be a new experience for you.'

Bradley breathed deeply and leaned back into his seat. The colour began returning to his cheeks. 'Jesus, if that's what they call "slight turbulence" I hope I never fly into a storm with a communist pilot. I'm beginning to wonder whether it was worth coming all this way to Sofia for that dreary little junket tomorrow.' Robson screwed up his eyes thoughtfully. 'Don't be too sure it will be dreary, Ben. Moscow's loyal little ally might, if you ask me, have some surprise in store for us.'

Bradley snorted. 'Loyal ally? You can say that again. I hear they even carry open umbrellas on a sunny day in Sofia – in case it's raining in Moscow.'

Robson grinned. 'Whatever else is true Ben, Bulgaria's the most under-reported, unnoticed East European country of 'em all. That should put you on your journalist's mettle, for a start. Admittedly its history since the war has been pretty uneventful. No uprising like Hungary, no riots like Poland, no Russian tanks putting down revolts like they did in Prague and East Berlin . . .'

'Sounds to me as if it thoroughly deserves its total obscurity,' interrupted Bradley drily.

Robson was distracted briefly by the stewardess's brown legs as she moved past him again towards the front of the plane. The backs of her long strong calf muscles flexed and knotted like whipcord with every step. 'They're over-training the Olympic Squad,' he mused half to himself.

Robson shut his eyes to blot out the sight. 'Ben, what I was going to say was, that Bulgaria may not be as dreary as you expect . . . I believe it could even be on its way to becoming another powder keg for Moscow.'

'How's that?'

'Well, the country has an ageing leadership on the one hand, and on the other a growing younger generation of bright *apparatchiki*, who are not only better educated but who resent more and more the domination of the Kremlin. They're developing a growing sense of nationalism at last – which isn't surprising in a country which has been kicked around by outsiders since for ever.'

'Hell, Jonathan, even a simpleton journalist like me knows that Bulgaria's never shown any signs of biting the hand that feeds it. The Russians did liberate 'em from five hundred years of serfdom under the Turks y'know. They love 'em for that don't they?'

Robson nodded. 'It's precisely because the Bulgarians have been such close and loyal children in the past that any attempt to leave home now would be a body blow to Mother Russia. And apart from the ideological seizure their Kremlin parents would suffer, they would probably get even more upset because of Bulgaria's strategic importance in the Balkan peninsular. NATO's got Greece and Turkey here – at least that was the theory – China's got Albania, nobody at present has got the communist renegades in Yugoslavia, and the Romanians by clever intrigue are practically a law unto themselves. The Bulgarians could be itching to follow

34

Romania's suit. And if they did, it would put dynamite under the corridors of the Kremlin.'

'My dear chap', said Bradley, doing his best to ape an exaggerated upper-class English accent, 'you may not believe this but I did do some homework before leaving London. Bulgaria's foreign policy is more Soviet than the Soviet Union's. And there aren't any Russian divisions in Bulgaria now. But only because they're not necessary, right?'

'Well done Benjamin! You'll be telling me next that you know that the Bulgarians shake their heads when they mean "yes" and nod them when they mean "no".'

'Is that right?' queried Bradley in amazement.

Robson grinned and shook his head exaggeratedly. 'Yes, Ben, that's right.' He turned suddenly to the Slav girl across the aisle. 'Would you confirm what I've just told my friend?' She ignored him pointedly and stared straight in front of her. Bradley laughed uproariously. Robson turned back grinning. 'I was covering a Kruschev visit to Bulgaria a few years back, Ben, and in one speech he was ranting and raving against you Americans as usual. The *New York Times* man stood taking the speech down in his notebook and shaking his head in disbelief. Khruschev looked up, pointed at him, and said to the crowd: "You see, even our distinguished capitalist Comrade from the *New York Times*, agrees with every word I'm saying."'

Bradley smiled. Now he wanted to try it on the air hostess. When he called her and asked if there were two more whiskies on board they could have, she shook her head, said '*Da*' and went to fetch them.

'Okay, Jonathan, I concede defeat,' said Bradley raising his glass to Robson. 'You do know something about this neck of the woods. If you reckon the Bulgars down there are revolting, I'm prepared to believe it . . . Hey! What goes on?'

The airliner dropped again suddenly. But this time it righted itself quickly, although not quickly enough to help those passengers who had begun to vomit quietly into their little paper bags.

Robson turned in his seat to face Bradley. 'Look Ben, in the last thirty years since the "Comms" took over in Bulgaria — while nobody's been bothering to notice very much — they've pretty efficiently changed their little nation of eight million people from an agricultural country to a predominantly industrial one. This means the bulk of the population have changed radically from rural peasants to urban workers. To carry through this massive industrialization programme they've had to concentrate hard on education, especially science and technology. Per head of population they've now got about the fifth highest ratio of university students of any country in the world. Which means a lot more people better able to think for themselves, right?'

'Right, with you so far, Jon.' Bradley was concentrating hard on what Robson was saying to keep his mind and eyes away from the people around them using their paper bags. Bradley would probably have listened to Robson reciting nursery rhymes with equal intensity at that moment.

'These giant economic and social changes have been accompanied by no political changes whatsoever. The Bulgarian Communist Party has always been orthodox, rigid, conservative, utterly pro-Soviet. It takes no risks and keeps the economy and all these newly educated, newly sophisticated young Bulgars under tight uncompromising central control.'

'And the Party's run by a bunch of really old Comrades you say?'

'Geriatrics. The average age of the Politburo is sixty-five. One is eighty-four, three are seventy-five. The oldest leadership in the communist world outside of China – with the exception of Nikolai Radovanovic, who took over six months ago from the old man who'd run Bulgaria for twenty years before that. He's only middle-aged.'

'But he hasn't shown any very obvious signs so far of throwing out the rest of the old leadership and overturning their policies, has he?'

'Depends what you mean by obvious, Ben. To the outside world he's been feeling his way, establishing himself, if you like. But read between the lines of the party paper, *Rabotnicheske Delo*, and you'll see that the generation gap is beginning to cause the greatest strain where it hurts most: between the unimaginative old guard who still dominate the Politburo and the younger, better educated *apparatchiki* who are in the key organization and ideological jobs on the Central Committee secretariat. That's Bulgaria's nerve centre.'

Bradley nodded slowly and took another sip at his drink. 'So the new man, Radovanovic, is caught between the two, undecided which way to go?'

Robson glanced quickly round at the girl opposite as he spoke but she was staring out of the window on her side. 'Yes, and this is the problem, Ben, that all the party leaderships in Eastern Europe are having to face up to in one form or another. But Bulgaria's problem, in my view, is more acute.'

'Why Bulgaria, particularly?'

'Because she started from a cruder economic base. That explains the thirty uneventful years. This is partly a hunch but I believe it's about to surface now. And the long build-up could make the eventual explosion even bigger.'

Robson turned his head again quickly, certain now that he was being overheard. Sure enough she was staring at him. But this time her expression was startled. 'Okay Bappaman,' Bradley was saying. 'So that's the powder keg. But to make an explosion you need a spark. Where's that coming from?'

Robson dragged his gaze reluctantly back to Bradley. Through the window by the American's shoulder he noticed that heavy swirling snow was now blotting out the frozen landscape of Bulgaria far below. 'I'm not sure what it might be.' He glanced back quickly at the girl. She had turned away.

'But the political temperature is rising. Only last week one of the geriatric Comrades openly complained in a public speech that "nationalism in its most reactionary form – anti-Sovietism – is now marking up some success in the country".'

'It takes a bit more evidence than that to turn me on, Jon, with respect. Doesn't exactly make my pulse race.'

'It should do Ben, because in the evasive, guarded currency of East European public politics, that is a very open statement indeed of fear and-stroke-or threat. It's possibly the most significant political speech to come out of Communist Bulgaria since . . .'

The Tupolev tilted forward suddenly, shuddered and went into a fast dive. Bradley and Robson were pressed back in their seats and the remains of Bradley's drink shot up in the air. When the airliner levelled out Robson turned his head to see Bradley clutching an empty glass and gazing at the huge dark stain on his jacket and trousers. He let out a long breath and unfastened his seat belt.

'Out of the way Bappaman. I've got to go to the john to clean up. Got that drink clean down the outside of my neck.'

Robson grinned. 'Go carefully, Ben. It wouldn't surprise me if East European airlines were still using outside lavatories.'

Bradley moved off unsteadily towards the rear of the plane.

Outside the windows the blizzard raged silently and the falling snow led Robson's thoughts away from Bulgaria and back to Battersea and Beryl. Was she greeting her husband now at the airport? Or rehearsing a new number at the Ocho Rios? Because he was deep in thought the woman's voice speaking quietly close to his ear startled him. 'Mr Robson, if you'll excuse me, I wonder if a dreary little Bulgarian citizen might offer a piece of advice.'

He turned. She was leaning across the aisle towards him. She had taken off her fur hat now and shaken out her hair. He stared at her, momentarily at a loss for words. She continued in the same low confidential tone. 'If you know so much about the Socialist countries of Eastern Europe, I'd have thought you might have learned not to talk so loudly. Walls have ears in Bulgaria, you know.' She dragged her lips expressively downwards to lend ironic emphasis to her final statement. Her English was good with only the faintest trace of an accent.

'Forgive me for staring.' Robson smiled. 'But you're the least dreary Bulgarian citizen I've ever laid eyes on.' She returned his look steadily, but not the smile. 'Do you work for the Government?'

'I'm not intending to report you to Bulgarian State Security, if that's what's worrying you.' The corners of her mouth turned downwards again in the self-deprecating expression. 'But I do work for the government, the Foreign Trade Ministry – in the Engineering export department.'

'Yes, I could tell just by looking.'

'What?'

'That you were an engineer.'

At that moment there was a commotion in the gangway towards the rear of the plane. Bradley's embarrassed voice rose blurting out an apology.

'Hell, Miss, I really am awfully sorry.'

'Blast you, damn you, blast you! You Americans are too dreadful. Why didn't you stay in your seat during this turbulence?'

The other voice was upper-class English, petulant, spoiled. Robson turned to see an English girl with long dark hair who'd got on at Vienna thrashing herself into a lather over a drink Bradley had apparently knocked over from the table in front of her. Bradley was blushing and trying to make amends.

'Oh, do for goodness sake go away,' shouted the girl. Her ill-tempered tantrum left her white and speechless and Bradley was guided firmly back towards his seat by the strapping Bulgarian hostess.

'Mr Bradley, you seem to have a talent for spilling drinks.' The American journalist's eyes moved quickly from Robson's face to the girl's, then back again.

'Hey, what is this, Jonathan? No sooner is my back turned than you start working on this beautiful exclusive. C'mon, introduce me.'

Robson looked at her for a moment. 'Well, Ben Bradley, this is . . .'

'Georgina Morakova.'

'Glad to know you, Ma'am.'

'Miss.'

'Miss Morakova works for the government in Sofia, Ben. And listens to conversations in aeroplanes in her spare time. She wonders whether we don't talk too loudly.'

'I'm sure she's right, Jonathan, it's a bad habit the Americans and the English have. Take your young countrywoman sitting back there . . .'

Bradley pitched forward abruptly along the gangway. Robson grabbed his arm, dragging him back and bundling him into the seat beside him as the Tupolev dropped again. It rolled around the sky with engines roaring; more glasses broke noisily in the galley. Bradley clawed his way into the seat and got quickly into his belt. This time the rest of the passengers didn't scream but endured the jolting in silence.

When the plane was righted the public address system came to life and the pilot made an announcement first in Bulgarian, then in English.

39

He regretted that due to the effects of the turbulence, the undercarriage had jammed and they would therefore be attempting immediately an emergency landing at a military airfield outside Sofia. Everybody was to remain calm.

Robson leaned towards Bradley. 'You know, Ben,' he whispered fiercely, 'they didn't feel like turbulence bumps to me. There's no reason that I know of why snow should cause air pockets.'

'My God, Jonathan, don't you ever stop seeing Commie plots?' Bradley rolled his eyes. Then he suddenly turned away and reached for the paper bag jammed into the net attached to the seat in front of him. The airliner dipped its nose and began to lose height rapidly in the snow storm.

Six

In his office in the Chinese Embassy, a drab sandstone building standing at a junction on Boulevard Vitosha in the centre of Sofia, third secretary Wang Chieh-ping was at that moment carefully re-reading the telegram from Peking that he had just decoded. A few seconds later the door opened and his wife, Tsai Mei-li, entered. They exchanged no greeting. She simply moved forward and stood dutifully in front of his desk, waiting for him to raise his eyes to her from the telegram.

When at last he did look up, he motioned her into the chair facing him. Neither displayed the slightest familiarity with each other. She granted him the same kind of formality and respect she showed to all other third secretaries in the embassy. Perhaps even a shade more. Because she knew better than anyone that despite the lowly diplomatic status of his official cover job as the embassy translator for Bulgarian and English, in real power Wang outranked even the ambassador himself. She knew what at least half the embassy staff only suspected – that he was the Head of Operations in Sofia for the Central External Liaison Department – or CELD – the little known foreign intelligence service of Communist China, which maintains highly-trained agents in every one of its foreign embassies and many offices of the New China News Agency around the world.

The senior diplomats, including the ambassador, knew that through the CELD he reported direct to the most secret and most powerful intelligence organ of all in Peking, the Investigation Bureau of the Party Central Committee. And although they couldn't be sure, they suspected that he received his routine orders from the Bureau in specially-marked diplomatic pouches, delivered direct to him through the Vienna Embassy which, aided by Tirana, supervises the surreptitious and highly efficient Chinese espionage network in communist Eastern Europe.

In his office Wang treated his wife to precisely the same kind of stiff formality that she accorded him. She sat quietly while he gave the telegram a final scrutiny. For six years before being assigned abroad he had been an agent in the Cheng Pao Ko, the Political Security Section of the Chinese intelligence service which deals with counter-espionage at home. The meticulous training which had helped him destroy a creditable proportion of the few enemy agents who managed to penetrate into China during that time had made him hyper-cautious. He was neither going to chance misunderstanding the important cable, nor risk jeopardizing his position in the Sofia embassy by behaving indiscreetly with his wife.

They worked now as a team and they knew they were extraordinarily lucky to be together. Most married diplomats posted abroad from Peking had to resign themselves to four years apart from their wives.

Wang raised his eyes finally from the telegram, and held it towards his wife. 'You will note that this communication originated in the Wai Chia Pou.' He raised an eyebrow slightly to emphasize his reference to the Peking Foreign Ministry. 'But you will notice it also bears the insignia of the Premier's office, which indicates its contents have been seen and acknowledged by the Premier himself before being despatched with the authority of the CELD and the Investigation Bureau of the Central Committee.'

She nodded meekly.

'Read it please!'

She bent her head intently over the decoded cable. Her short dark hair was parted on the left and held out of her eyes by a single clip like a little girl's. Her features were small and regular. She wore the same grey tunic as her husband, buttoned high to her throat. She wore, too, the same shiny badge that he wore, showing a profile

41

of Chairman Mao Tse-tung in gold against a red background, just above her left breast. But the suit was cut in such a way that it revealed no hint of breasts, nor anything else about the real shape of the rest of her slight body underneath.

But Wang did not even let his eyes stray to the concealed outline of his wife's body. For despite the power deriving from his intelligence rank, this did not place him, or her, entirely beyond criticism in the weekly ideological meetings at which the embassy staff reviewed their work. At these meetings all criticized themselves and each other in accordance with the harsh proletarian standards of class discipline inherent in every line of the writings of Chairman Mao Tse-tung.

To have reached the powerful position of being a senior agent — or the wife of one — in the CELD was such a rare privilege that he insisted they both observe the strictest possible rules of conduct so as not to betray the slightest sign of a lapse from total dedication. And this self-discipline, he further insisted, should even extend to situations in which nobody else was present. Instead of looking at his wife now, he made quick neat notes on a pad in Chinese characters, setting out his plan of action.

His wife frowned in concentration at the paper as she read it through a second time. *'The intervention which we attempted in London on your strong recommendation concerning the British journalist Robson did not, because of an unavoidable accident, meet with success. Third Secretary Wu Fu-chieh was inadvertently killed in a road crash and Robson, we confirm, is now due to arrive in Sofia today on flight IZ1404 from London Heathrow.'* The cable continued:

Further, the highest responsible authorities in Peking reaffirm in answer to your query, that it is their determined objective to hinder and if possible undermine both the Geneva conference on Strategic Arms Limitation and the Multilateral Balanced Force Reduction talks in Vienna. If they are successfully concluded, Western Europe, having been tricked by the Soviet Union into signing the Helsinki declaration on European Security, will be further lulled into relaxing its vigilance vis-à-vis the Soviet Union and this will leave the socialist-imperialists free to further concentrate their strength around China's borders.

Therefore, your report suggesting that a plot to undermine the two conferences has already been laid by Kremlin extremists has been read with utmost care by comrades at the highest levels. Even though such a revisionist faction is composed of China's fiercest ideological enemies, our objectives for different reasons are similar.

Since you believe that Robson is attempting in some way to foil that plot, you are accordingly authorized by the highest organs of the Party to continue your investigation and take the necessary steps to see that Robson fails in his mission.

'Hsieh hsieh ni.' Tsai Mei-li finished reading and returned the paper to him with a little nod of thanks.

Wang's features were sharp and fine. His quick, alert eyes gave his face a brittle handsomeness. He looked at her speculatively for a moment and when she returned his gaze she saw a shadow of doubt in his expression. This turned to embarrassment as he spoke and he looked away from her. 'It is due to your sacrifices of the past two months in the cause of the international class struggle that we have this knowledge.' He hesitated then looked back at her reluctantly. 'Do you think the Jymeson woman might have lied about the plot, and about Robson, or even fabricated these stories – just to . . . win your affection?'

His wife looked back at him mutely, trusting utterly in his judgement, waiting for him to develop the thoughts he was expressing aloud.

'You have seen the policy laid down by the leading Comrades in that cable. We must be sure.' His eyes glittered with a new intensity. 'We must interrogate under duress. Telephone Jymeson and make an appointment at the special apartment for ten o'clock.'

She nodded obediently without looking at him.

'I shall need your help. So take the needles.'

He opened a drawer and took out a copy of Robson's visa application photograph. 'This is the man.' He handed it to her. Then with a curt upward motion of his chin, he signalled her to leave. She went out with the photograph, closing the door quietly behind her.

'Please remove all sharp objects from your persons. Lean forward as indicated in the safety brochure and cover your heads with your arms. Thank you.'

The Amazonian air stewardess, having made her final announcement, moved confidently along the gangway, reassuring the nervous passengers. Then she strapped herself into a backward facing seat by the galley.

The Tupolev roared lower. There was a loud 'crump' from beneath the plane. Then all the interior lights went out.

Against the muffled roar of the engines from outside, silence reigned inside the long fuselage. The snow was easing off but an early dusk was closing in as the aircraft swooped low over the perimeter of the military airfield.

It floated gently and evenly downwards. Robson saw through the window that a thick carpet of foam had been laid on the runway in preparation for the crash landing. He closed his eyes and braced himself for the impact and the roar of the plane sliding along the ice-covered concrete on its belly.

But no impact came. The Tupolev settle gently on to the runway in the regulation landing attitude and ran on fast, its wheels sending foaming spray splashing across the fuselage windows. It braked, slowed and finally came to rest in a complete silence.

Without a word the stewardess rose from her seat and moved quickly to the emergency exits, lifting the catches and knocking them clear. Canvas landing chutes tumbled outwards. Flurries of fine snow blew in with cold blasts of air through the open ports. The faint trumpeting of rescue trucks and fire engines became audible as they raced from their sheds on the far side of the airfield.

'The pilot very resourcefully managed to free the undercarriage shortly before landing,' the stewardess announced to the cabin over her shoulder as she peered out into the snow. 'But please use the emergency chutes to leave the aircraft.'

'Well, what do the two white-faced Western journalists think of that competent emergency landing?' Georgina Morakova's voice was soft and mocking. 'Are they satisfied, or are they still worried about the holes in our socks?'

The fire engines and military support trucks arrived around the plane, with sirens blaring deafeningly. Their whirling blue and orange lights flung erratic moving shadows into the darkened plane. One by one the passengers slipped from the warm, familiar belly of the cabin and out into the snowy wastes of a military airfield somewhere in Bulgaria.

Seven

'Jesus God, do I need this drink!'

Ben Bradley shovelled ice-cubes into a squat toothbrush tumbler, sloshed three inches of Queen Anne over them from the bottle Robson had produced from his case, and rushed into the bathroom to run some water on top of it all. He came back gulping voraciously at the glass.

'You know, I thought for a time there this afternoon I was never going to see the inside of a hotel room ever again.' He took another long pull at the whisky and stared round at the Balkan Hotel's unspectacular furnishings.

'Yeah and room service even managed to find some ice for us. Bulgaria is overcoming five hundred years of Turkish oppression at last.' Robson was lying back on his bed sipping a clinking glass of the same mixture.

'Jonathan, you know what? I think you knock them too much.'

'That's not a joke Ben, believe me. You'll get it everywhere you go here when anything goes wrong. It's not due to Communism — the Turks are to blame.'

'Okay, but I was really impressed by the way they swung into action after that emergency landing. No customs, practically. And they laid on that bus into town from the middle of nowhere in less time than it takes to say Vladimir Ilyich Lenin.'

'Almost as if they were prepared for an unexpected crashlanding there well beforehand.' Robson's voice was heavy with sarcasm.

'Jonathan, you're crazy. You're not trying to say that emergency landing was faked, are you?'

'I don't know. But I do have an uneasy feeling that they got the undercarriage out without any trouble well before we touched down.'

Bradley's face contracted in puzzlement. 'Why in hell's name would they want to do a crazy thing like that?'

'Let's discuss it some other time, Ben. We don't want the boys on the other end of the bugs in this room getting too excited.'

Bradley emptied his glass and set it aside. 'You think all the rooms are probably bugged, huh?'

'Not "probably", Ben. It's standard practice here and in any other hostelry frequented by foreigners. Visiting journalists are always allocated the same set of rooms on the fourth floor. No, don't bother scratching around. They're small enough and sophisticated enough these days to keep a team of specialists with all their gadgets fumbling around a single room in our embassy for a week.'

Bradley let the mattress fall back on its frame and straightened the covers. 'But why should they want to listen to our boring conversations. They can read what we write in our newspapers, can't they?'

Robson nodded. 'Of course they can. But you've got to remember that to people running a so-called dictatorship of the proletariat, every visiting foreigner, be he diplomat, businessman or journalist, is a potential spy for the class enemy, working to overthrow them. The distinctions between diplomacy, journalism and espionage are practically non-existent in their narrow "Comm" minds.'

Captain Uyri Zhermatov grunted contemptuously. 'The saviour of Western society is back!' It had taken him only fifteen seconds to get the tuning right on Room 409 of the Balkan Hotel because Section S. 14 (Monitoring) of the Comitet za Darzhaven Sigurnost – or 'D.S.' as the Bulgarian State Security organ is popularly known – was only three quarters of a mile away in a short cul-de-sac off the Boulevard Georgi Dimitrov.

'Pardon Comrade?'

'I recognize that voice!' Zhermatov was talking over his shoulder to his assistant. 'Jonathan Robson of the British news agency, BAPPA. A loud-mouthed capitalist braggart. I'll bet you fifty *stotinki* that he'll start telling us anti-communist jokes before very long.'

Zhermatov's assistant, a young Bulgarian named Trichkov who had joined the service from the modern languages faculty of Sofia

University two years before, tried, for his own immediate political safety, to look disinterested while listening intently to Robson's voice. 'Who is the American?'

'I don't know. He is new to me. But don't worry. His name will arrive with Robson's on the list from the airport visa desk first thing in the morning. Leave the identity space on the report sheet blank and I will fill it in for you tomorrow.'

Robson was still holding forth, slightly distorted, but coming through loudly. 'They fondly imagine, you see, Ben, that if we'd come here to assassinate their Party Leader we'd shout about our plans in our hotel bedrooms.'

'Do they censor our news stories too?' Bradley's slightly higher-pitched voice carried more clearly through the recording equipment.

'Not exactly. In Moscow and Eastern Europe generally, they simply record them, whether you telex or telephone them out, and if they don't like what you write, don't consider you "objective" – that is to say if you don't stay close enough to their own biased communist point of view – they'll probably expel you. That's standard, too, invisible censorship by threat!'

Bradley grunted. 'So if you want to come back next time, don't file critical stories now, huh?'

'Correct, Benjamin, you're catching on fast.'

Bradley grunted again. Then his voice brightened. 'I do hear that a certain callow reporter now known widely as the "dapper Bappaman" set out on his first foreign assignment to cover the Skopje earthquake toting a dinner jacket and black tie in his overnight bag. Because, they say, he'd heard foreign correspondents should be prepared at all times to respond to formal invitations.' Laughter and the sound of Bradley slapping his knee came over clearly. 'Did the earthquake victims enjoy you interviewing them in their soup kitchens in your DJ, Jonathan?'

A silence followed. Trichkov looked questioningly at Zhermatov, thinking the microphone might have gone down. He didn't know that Robson was ignoring the question. Didn't know that he'd long since concluded there was no successful counter to the 'he-took-a-dinner-jacket-to-Skopje' story. Trichkov didn't relax until Robson's voice began again.

'What I normally do', he said airily, 'is to try to brighten the lives of the poor "Comm" souls assigned to monitor our poisonous conversations by retailing them the latest jokes about themselves from the fraternal Socialist countries.'

'Do they have something to joke about out here?'

'Eastern Europe is the home of the desperate political joke, Ben. When there's nothing left to do, laugh! That's the theory.'

Zhermatov grunted and half turned to speak over his shoulder to his assistant, screwing up his eyes against the smoke of the thin Bulgarian cheroot hanging from his lip. 'What did I tell you, Comrade? The capitalist world's predictable court jester is about to perform for us.'

Trichkov ostentatiously laid down the pen with which he'd been making notes of the conversation. '. . . one they're telling in Budapest right now. The question goes: "What good news will Comrade First Secretary Radovanovic have for the Bulgarian people at the Party Congress?" "Well, Comrades," he will say, "I'm sorry 1975 was such a bad year – it's been much worse, hasn't it, than 1974. But the picture's not entirely black . . . it's much better than 1976 will be." End of joke.' Robson paused then raised his voice. 'Get all that up there in "Monitoring" did you, Comrades?'

Zhermatov stared expressionlessly at the amplifier. When he looked round at him, Trichkov, unsure of how to respond, avoided his eyes.

Through the microphones Bradley's chuckle sounded dutiful. 'The trouble with that story, Jon,' he was saying, 'is that you could tell it about the whole godammed world this year. Could be the State of the Union or the Queen's Speech . . .'

The bedside telephone began ringing.

'Ben, that's my call to London. I'm going to put a couple of paragraphs over about the so-called crash landing, and update my curtain-raiser on the Congress. Why don't you nip back to your room and change and I'll see you in the lobby. We'll go to the reception together in a taxi . . .' There was the sound of the telephone receiver being lifted. 'Hello, is that BAPPA, London . . . ? Give me a copy taker, please . . .'

When Robson had hung up and only tuneless whistling came from the receivers in room 409, Captain Zhermatov reached out and stopped the voice-activated reel manually. 'Okay, Comrade,' he said, brusquely, 'transcribe it! Leave out Robson's so-called joke. Comrade Radovanovic's department will be interested in the stuff about the crash landing.'

Trichkov took the tape to a transcribing machine beside his typewriter. He put on his headphones, pressed the pedal to start the player and began to type. His wife had studied English too and the only pleasure he would get from the job would come from the odd phrase or two of new idiosyncratic English that he would carefully commit to memory to delight her when he got home.

A puzzled frown creased his forehead as he transcribed the text of the jibe about the dinner jacket that went to Skopje. He stopped and looked up. 'Why are we recording and transcribing all this talk, Captain Zhermatov, rather than audio-sampling as we normally do on the foreign journalists?'

As soon as he'd asked the question he wished he hadn't. Zhermatov turned his squat, bulky body in his chair to glare at him, pulling fiercely at one side of his long drooping moustache. 'One of the things you must learn, Comrade Trichkov, if you are going to get on or even survive in this department is not to ask unnecessary questions.'

Zhermatov turned back to his desk and the translator sat looking nervously at his massive, bull-like shoulders and neck, trying to gauge how much disfavour he'd incurred. He already held Zhermatov in considerable awe because of his legendary wartime record with Radovanovic's partisans. Most of it was hearsay, admittedly, but the accounts of his exploits that were bandied about in the Security Committee canteen told of his savage and ruthless courage against the Germans and, more ominously, against anybody he came to regard as an enemy.

Zhermatov turned round again suddenly and caught Trichkov staring at him. His eyes glittered. 'Comrade Trichkov, I may as well tell you this now.'

The translator swallowed hard, frightened of what might be coming.

'Keep this to yourself. Tell nobody. Not even your wife . . . I have selected you to carry out a special assignment.'

Trichkov started. He was just a translator, English-to-Bulgarian.

'The assignment is of such importance that you must remain uninterruptedly with me in this room over the next two days.

You will take no breaks, and you will eat and sleep here until it is finished. You must do everything I tell you without hesitation. And above all, as I have pointed out to you already, you must ask no superfluous question.'

Trichkov, realizing he had no choice, nodded his assent dumbly.

Zhermatov, got up from his chair and walked over to where the translator sat. He let his hand rest on his shoulder as he stood behind him, apparently reading the text of his transcript. 'It will be safer from your own point of view', he said softly still staring at the paper in the typewriter, 'if you don't know exactly what's going on.' He paused for emphasis. 'So don't even ask to know.'

Zhermatov started to walk away, then stopped and spoke over his shoulder. 'Telephone your family now. Tell them you'll be away for two days. But offer no explanation for your absence.'

Then he went out quickly, locking the door behind him. He hurried along a dimly-lit corridor, let himself through a series of three double-locked security gates with his own pass key and took a lift down to the basement. He stepped out into the chill cold of the maximum security underground garage and returned the salutes of the two armed guards patrolling the specially-equipped surveillance fleet of Volgas, Tatras and Wartburgs. He moved quickly to a thick steel door below the exit ramp, looked round to make sure he was unobserved, then unlocked the door with his master key. He swung it open and stopped dead. He was staring at the squashed and distorted image of his own face six inches in front of him. His pouched cheeks had become narrow, pendulous jowls and his eyes were straight slits slashed across the width of his thin head. His Viva Zapata moustache crouched blackly round his bunched mouth like a predatory spider.

He stood staring for a moment at his reflection in the polished black surface of the massive Zil hearse, then turned and closed the door behind him. He had to edge sideways, nursing his bulky paunch carefully between the side of the hearse and the white-washed wall. With difficulty he rounded the long black and chrome bonnet and struggled free into the workbench area.

He slapped at his clothes, raising clouds of white dust as he walked over to the bench where a little dark-faced carpenter was busy marking up three long, rough-cut pine planks. He tucked his pencil behind his ear and stood back respectfully from his task as Captain Zhermatov approached.

'Carry on, Comrade, there's no time to stand about.'

The little carpenter nodded anxiously and got on with the marking as Zhermatov went to the adjoining bench and ran his hand over the smoothly planed sides of the pine coffin.

'That's the lid you're working on?'

Zhermatov spoke without turning round.

'The lid, yes, Captain Zhermatov.'

'But you haven't started the quilting inside yet?'

'I need to finish the lid and do a trial fitting first. Then I have to mark the breathing holes before I can finish padding and quilting, Captain.'

Zhermatov put one foot on the cross support of the bench and swung his heavy body up on to it with surprising agility. He stepped into the coffin and to the carpenter's amazement lay down, out of sight, breathing loudly with the exertion.

The carpenter waited a whole minute in silence. The breathing seemed to have stopped.

'Big enough for you, Captain, yes,' he called uneasily, when another minute had passed.

There was no reply. Then suddenly the head of the State Security officer appeared unsmiling over the rim of the coffin. 'Big enough for both of us, Comrade!'

The carpenter laughed nervously. He didn't know whether what the Captain had said was meant to be funny or not.

The two paragraphs that at that moment were ticking out from London on the general world news teleprinters of BAPPA were describing how a scheduled Balkanair flight from Heathrow to Sofia had made an emergency landing at a military airfield. The story would go straight on to the unused spike in most newspaper offices. Some chief sub-editors would fill two inches at the foot of a column with it when a major story fell typographically short. But because nobody was hurt or killed and the passengers had been mainly Bulgarians, it would excite little attention.

In the Foreign Office Communications basement, the duty clerk supervising the tape machines of Tass, the New China News

Agency, Reuters, the American and French agencies and BAPPA, read the story then ran his eye down his clipboard list of daily orders. Yes, he thought he'd remembered seeing it. '*Everything from Sofia by Bappa.*' He tore the item from the machine marked it 'Cranbourne', as instructed and sealed it in an 'Immediate Delivery' envelope of bright yellow. A messenger was just going out through the door so he called out to him and hurried over to slip it in his satchel.

Eight

The staircase of the Balkan Hotel looked as if it might be made of marble. It was covered, however, with an undistinguished carpet of a drab proletarian shade. Like the rest of the vast, dark, echoing building, it proclaimed its austere working-class grandeur from every flat, slab-like aspect. The builders of the hotel had been determined simultaneously both to glorify Stalin and also to demonstrate to the world that the Third Reich had not after all been the nadir in tasteless and soulless modern architecture.

As Robson descended the last flight to the lobby, a lanky, heavy-breasted woman fighting middle age every inch of the way, came up past him. She wore dark glasses, a bright green bandanna round her streak-blonde hair, too much lipstick, several jangling gold bangles on each arm and an expensive Italian suede coat slung round her shoulders. A king-sized cigarette with a gold band round it hung from her red mouth. Even when she was five steps past, her slipstream of expensive French perfume was still strung out behind her like a trawl net ready to ensnare any susceptible male fish that happened to be passing. Robson had reached the bottom stair without getting entangled and was starting across the lobby towards Ben Bradley, when he heard a loud scream above and behind him.

'Jonny! You sonofabitch! How dare you walk straight past me!'

Everybody in the lobby and on the stairs turned to look as she flung herself back down the staircase with what she clearly hoped would be seen as girlish exuberance.

She grabbed him by the shoulders and pulled herself against him in such a way that it appeared that *he* was embracing *her*. A lot of the excess lipstick transferred itself to his mouth and right ear.

'Gloria, so help me, I didn't recognize you.' He extricated himself breathless from her grasp. 'Although God knows I should have done. Nobody else but you would wear sunglasses at seven o'clock at night in Sofia in midwinter.'

'As damned rude as ever. Where the hell have you been for the last decade or so?' Her loud American voice echoed round the Balkan's cavernous precincts.

'I decided to go away and try to forget you, Gloria.' Robson was grinning broadly.

'Foreign Legion, Cowards' Detachment, huh?'

'Correct. How's your rich husband?'

'Richer and more tedious than ever, darling.'

'You still scribbling for that Los Angeles paper?'

'How else would I ever get away from him? I've fled to the People's Democracies today for a bit of freedom – and to do the Congress.' She laughed a practised, throaty laugh, then lowered her voice slightly so that only people within fifty feet could hear. 'I spotted your name on the register, Jon, when I signed in. What a surprise! Practically reached orgasm just standing there. I got them to give me the room next to yours.'

She pulled hard on her king-sized cigarette which had been slightly bent during their embrace, and gave him one of her best crinkle-eyed smiles through the smoke.

'Remind me to get the porter to padlock the connecting door.'

'Jonny, you won't escape me. I've become an aggressive, liberated woman since last time.' Robson let a little agonized animal moan escape his lips. Undeterred, she leaned towards him confidentially so he could feel the loose softness of her unsupported breasts against his arm. She spoke close to his ear, a real whisper this time. 'I saw you coming down the stairs you know, and went on by deliberately to test you. You're all right, aren't you? Haven't lost that hairy truck driver's zest have you? I've never forgotten that night in Budapest . . .' She laughed again, throatily.

Robson tried to remember how it had ever happened. Six, or was it eight years ago? He'd been drunk, perhaps. Depressed, lonely, at the end of his tether after a week behind the iron curtain. Foreigners got thrown together in self-defence. He couldn't remember. He looked desperately round for an escape route, saw Bradley and signalled him over.

'Do you two know each other? Ben Bradley, the *American Herald's* economics man, Gloria Zuckermann, Paris correspondent of the *Los Angeles* . . .'

'Hello, Ben, glad to know you.' She shook hands perfunctorily with Bradley and turned her whole attention back to Robson. 'You still freelancing, Jonathan, huh?'

'No, I'm here for BAPPA.'

'What!' Her shriek momentarily drowned out the din of the trams rattling by on the snow-covered cobbles outside. 'Why the hell have you gone back with them?' Then suddenly her lined face became earnestly serious and she reverted to her fifty-foot whisper again. 'Jon, if it's money trouble, I can talk to Harry, there'll be no problem, believe me.'

Robson, embarrassed, looked quickly at Bradley but he was staring hard in another direction.

'Look, Gloria, we're on our way to a reception, perhaps we'll see you there.'

She stared blankly at him for a moment. Then she looked down at the printed invitation card she'd been holding in her hand. 'You mean this thing from the Foreign Ministry Press Department that was waiting for me at reception. I haven't even looked at it.' She read off the card: 'Eve-of-Congress reception.'

'That's right. We've all got them. The Bulgarian first eleven will be mingling among us, apparently.'

'Hell I'd better hurry up and get changed.' She winked with exaggerated significance at Robson. 'See you later then, Jonny, huh? Don't forget what I said about Harry . . .' She squeezed his arm hard. 'Really glad you're here.'

The gold bangles on her arms jangled loudly as she skipped girlishly away up the staircase. After a few steps it became too much and she slowed to a walk. Once out of sight at the first landing she stopped, breathing hard, and pressed for a lift.

The interior of the run down Warszawa taxi reeked of a pungent mixture of vodka vapour and stomach fumes as if the driver now hunched sourly over the wheel had got thoroughly drunk last night then spent most of the day sleeping it off on the back seat with the windows closed. Robson and Bradley sat side by side holding their noses in silence as the vehicle shuddered and slid across the snow-covered stones between the tram lines.

Robson stared out at the dark-skinned crowds hurrying home-ward, their shoulders hunched against the cold. Lighted trams jammed to the doors with men in fur hats and women in bright scarves, screeched and lumbered by them in both directions. As the taxi swung across the bottom of Lenin Square he caught sight of the pencil slim tower of the Banya Bachi Mosque that rises above the city's rooftops as a symbolic reminder that five hundred years of Turkish rule has left modern Bulgaria, even today, teetering indecisively on the border-line between the cultures of Europe and the East.

The hung-over driver skidded wildly, took a wrong turning and they were going past the entrance to the Balkan Hotel for the second time when Bradley finally raised the subject of Gloria.

'She's an old friend of yours, huh, Jonathan?'

He didn't reply for a moment. He found himself not wanting to be disloyal. 'Gloria first snared me quite a few years ago, when I was new to the press corps that foregathers in these parts from Moscow, Vienna, and where-have-you, for these special "Comm" occasions. I think she used to make a speciality of preying on unsuspecting young men. But she's a good writer. Knows her stuff and can turn out a good analytical piece. And because she's a woman, she has some rather unusual long-standing contacts around these places.'

'A warm-hearted lady, if a little ageing now, huh?'

Robson paused, the sense of loyalty again censoring out any unkind comments he might be tempted to make. 'Yeah, Gloria's outrageous and can be embarrassingly direct in conveying the nature of her pressing needs. But I'm very fond of her – for her rarity value if nothing else.'

'Better lock your door tonight, Jon, I'd say, if you want to get some sleep.' Bradley was unaccountably still laughing at his own wit when they climbed out at the foot of the steps leading up to the square-columned Stalinist façade of the Bulgarian Communist Party Centre. Robson gulped gratefully at the cold air. He gazed up for a moment at the red illuminated star shining on its mast at the pinnacle of the building. He muttered an inaudible capitalist curse in its general direction and began walking on ahead leaving the fare to Bradley as the price for his immoderate enjoyment of his own humour.

Shiny Czech Tatras and Russian Zil limousines were parked in lines on either side of the building, their drivers sitting inside with heaters going full blast while they waited for the party and government leaders who were downing strong drinks and Black Sea *canapés* inside. As usual cars from the foreign diplomatic missions, both Communist and Western, were segregated in a rank on the other side of the street. The Austin Princess of the British ambassador with the Union Jack on its wing was parked, Robson noticed, at the front of the line.

He nodded towards it as Bradley caught him up. 'You might like to meet the British ambassador, Sir Charles Magnusson. He was in charge of the British Press office at the United Nations before he came here. So he's keener than most diplomats to see visiting journalists well briefed on the current vagaries of Bulgarian politics.'

'Lead me to him.'

'I met him first when he was ambassador in Prague before he went to New York. I sent him a telegram a couple of weeks or so ago to say I'd be arriving today.' They handed their invitations to a suspicious-eyed Bulgarian wearing a red armband, standing just inside the door. Satisfying him that they weren't assassins, they launched themselves into the crush of bodies that was putting up a loud roar of conversation right across the bright, plainly-decorated annexe to the Congress Hall.

'Will there be many other Western journalists here, Jon, for the Congress?'

'The usual crowd who like a swan round the Balkans. I'd guess the whole gang of East Europe watchers from Vienna will be in to get a look at Brezhnev.'

As if to confirm Robson's assessment, the correspondent of *The Times* at that moment tapped him on the shoulder as he pushed through the crush. 'Hello, Robbie, back on your old hunting grounds, I see. Like to meet Mr Wang from the Chinese

Embassy, who's positive the Russkies will attack us before they attack China?'

'Hello, Simon,' Robson glanced over the *Times* correspondent's shoulder at Wang Chieh-ping and his wife who were pointedly staring in a different direction. 'Later, Simon, thanks,' he said quietly and passed on closely followed by Bradley.

They reached a small clearing in the forest of bodies at the same time as a white-coated waiter. Robson reached out and grabbed two glasses of Bulgarian *slivova* from his tray. His eyes roamed quickly round the new face-scape as he sipped his drink. 'C'mon, Ben, there's Sir Charles over there . . . and talking to a real prize.' Robson's voice rose in admiration.

'Who's that?' Bradley was struggling again to keep up in Robson's wake through the crowd.

'That nasty-looking, bullet-headed Comrade in the tan-coloured suit with Sir Charles is Boris Bodinski, number two to Nikolai Radovanovic and, among other things, allegedly head of security both internal and external. So watch your step if you've got any CIA connections!'

Bradley grimaced and said nothing.

Sir Charles Magnusson and Bodinski were engaged in animated conversation and didn't notice the two journalists approach.

Robson cleared his throat loudly. 'Good evening, Sir Charles. Pardon my butting in but we Western correspondents get all too few opportunities of meeting such eminent Bulgarians as General Bodinski here close up . . . I wonder if he can give us any clue as to why a Balkanair flight from Heathrow nearly crashed and killed two famous Western journalists on landing here this evening.'

The tall, lean ambassador who had been a Marine Commando officer in the Second World War turned angrily on Robson. He didn't raise his voice but the note of censure in it turned it into a metaphorical shout. 'I don't know what you're talking about, Robson, and I doubt very much whether Mr. Bodinski does either.'

Robson hesitated, taken aback by the vehemence of the ambassador's response. 'Oh, in that case I beg your pardon, Sir Charles. May I introduce a colleague, Benjamin Bradley of the *American Herald*?'

The unsmiling ambassador inclined his head half an inch towards the American but did not offer his hand. Bodinski nodded briefly before speaking in halting but correct English.

'I'm glad you both survived whatever experience you're referring to, Mr Robson. May I wish you success in writing about the work of our Congress. We prefer, of course, objective reporting of the facts, not wild speculation or rumours. Good evening.' He moved away quickly through the throng before anyone could reply.

The ambassador, looking ill at ease, took a large gulp at his drink. Robson noticed that the hand he held it in was shaking. 'Look, if you don't mind, Robson, I've got more important business to attend to. . .' He planted his empty glass on the tray of a passing waiter and hurried away after Bodinski.

'*Very* helpful man, your ambassador, Jonathan. Got that unmistakable olde-worlde charm the British are famous for, hasn't he? Your telegram obviously did the trick.'

Robson shook his head. 'I don't understand it!'

'We'd do better tracking down some of the brash American members of the diplomatic fraternity, if you ask me.' Bradley scanned the throng trying to spot lightweight American suiting.

'Ben, this is very odd indeed, Sir Charles is normally the most courteous of men.'

Bradley interrupted him with an excited jab of his elbow. 'Hey, look. Over there. I may not be good at faces but that well-filled blouse is distinctly familiar.'

Robson tried to follow the American's gaze. 'Where?'

'Talking to none other than Comrade Bodinski, would you believe? Surely, Jonathan, you haven't forgotten that mane of red hair and those sucked-in Slav cheekbones.'

Robson stared over the heads of the crowd at Georgina Morakova's bare shoulders. She was wearing a lacy Bulgarian blouse and long traditional skirt, both embroidered with bright colours. Her hair hung in two thick plaits, decorated with broad white ribbons and she wore a matching white flowers in her hair, above her right ear.

'Well. We may not admire Comrade Bodinski's politics but his taste in traditional Bulgarian women is faultless.'

They both stood and stared. Her back was turned towards them but Bodinski's face, as he talked to her, was visibly cold and unfriendly.

'From here,' said Bradley, 'it looks to me more as if they're having a wrangle over engineering exports policy.'

Robson reached out, took Bradley by his right bicep and swung him a half turn to his left. 'If you look straight ahead, you'll see the Bulgarian big man himself, Nikolai Radovanovic.'

'The grey-haired Spencer Tracy character with the mournful face?'

'That's him, the Comrade First Secretary. The man in the joke!'

'That expression is pure condemned cell.'

'Probably just the outward manifestation of his bottomless Slav soul. Among East block leader's he's considered something of a glamour boy. He can turn on a dazzling smile under that grey quiff when he chooses.'

'What's his background, Jon?'

'He's the archetypal *apparatchik*. First Secretary of the Komsomol in his twenties, graduated with honours from the Lenin Machine Engineering Institute and after that he tore rapidly through the Foreign Trade Ministry, the Council of Ministers and the State Council in various administrative and organization posts, shining brightly at them all. He stepped up into the Central Committee secretariat in about '66 and that's when his career really took off.' Robson downed his glass of *slivova*, grimaced and lit a cigarette to deaden the taste.

'Within three years he'd become Secretary of the Central Committee and landed the plum job of chairman of the Party Ideological Commission. A year later he was in the Politburo.'

'That sounds a pretty impeccable commie *curriculum vitae*. How'd he finally get the top job? Marry the boss Commissar's daughter?'

'He's not married, as far as I know. But he was cute enough to keep his nose clean and sidestep the Old Man's last fling, the '74 purge, when he kicked out three of the leading contenders for his job among the new rising generation.'

'Yeah, I remember reading that. Wasn't there talk of corruption, illegal deals with Western business firms?'

'That was part of it. For me that shake-up was really conclusive evidence that Bulgaria was at last coming to the boil. Managers embezzling, presenting false accounts and the Party suddenly changing horses in mid-stream and switching a lot of resources away from heavy industry to make more consumer goods to placate the discontented population. All solid signs of what I was talking about on the plane.'

'But how did Radovanovic actually grab the reins? Why didn't one of the old guard take over?'

'The Old Man had been balancing the two factions for years – like a juggler keeping all his balls in the air at once. I guess when he went, he and Moscow both knew that to give the top job to one of his old Comrades would probably incense the new generation among the rank and file.'

'So Radovanovic was a compromise candidate?'

'Right. But now he's not toeing Moscow's line. The question, I think, is whether or when the Kremlin and Bodinski are going to jump on him – and how hard . . .'

Robson turned quickly as he felt a hand on his sleeve. The British ambassador had moved up quietly behind them again. 'Look, Robson, I'm sorry if I was a bit brusque just now.' The haughty, unbending man looked uncomfortable and embarrassed. 'In fact, I was probably downright rude. Truth is, I've got a lot on my mind. If you'd care to come to the residence after this, I'd rather like to have a quiet word with you.'

Robson looked sharply at him but the ambassador kept his eyes averted, fumbling in his pocket for his cigarette holder. 'I'd be glad to, Sir Charles.'

'Well, I'm blessed. If it isn't the dapper Bappaman.' Robson turned to look at the tall, weedy-looking Englishman who'd come up to the group and was standing beside him with hand outstretched.

'You know George Jymeson, my first secretary here?' asked the ambassador.

'Course he does, Sir! Jonathan and I were regular old drinking chums at the "Pipacs" in Budapest in '66. Remember, Jon-o?'

Robson shook the limp hand without smiling. 'Yes, vaguely. Weren't you Commercial second secretary. The one who always got sick after two Hungarian Babychams?'

'Steady on,' said Jymeson, 'don't exaggerate. Three!' He laughed uproariously at his refinement of Robson's joke, dislodging his thick hornrimmed spectacles in the process. 'Oops, Jymeson's drunk again,' he said and giggled.

He straightened the spectacles on the bridge of his thin nose and brushed his lank black hair from his forehead with quick nervous movements of a bony hand. 'Glad to see you've decided to grace those of us in the backwaters of Eastern Europe with your presence again, anyway. You must come round and have a slack handful of drinks with us while you're here. Meet my better half.'

'Love to,' said Robson, with obvious insincerity.

'Watch out, Jonathan, you're suddenly the most popular man in the room.' It was Bradley whispering in his ear. 'Here comes no lesser personage than Comrade Radovanovic himself. To give you an exclusive interview no doubt. Got your notebook ready?'

Radovanovic stopped beside Robson and held out a hand. 'Sir Charles, I'm very glad to have this opportunity of shaking the ambassador of Great Britain by the hand.'

Magnusson blinked rapidly, looking down at the Bulgarian's outstretched fingers, as if they concealed a booby trap. His own hands remained at his sides and he stood holding his head forward and his shoulders back in a peculiarly stiff position as if he were about to inspect a line of Marine recruits. The silence between the two men grew tense. 'Particularly this evening, you understand,' Radovanovic ducked his head in emphasis and lifted the offered hand slightly closer to the ambassador.

'I won't shake a hand that's intent on stabbing me in the back!' The British ambassador spat his words out in a sibilant torrent, barely audible even to Robson who was standing close beside him.

Radovanovic, undeterred, moved closer and lifted his unshaken hand to take the ambassador's elbow. They half turned, trying to isolate themselves from the press of bodies hemming them in.

'Sir Charles, I have always sought to foster friendly relations between Britain and Bulgaria. I believe our countries can together contribute much in consolidating world peace.' He paused and laid heavy stress on his words. 'Despite appearances to the contrary, and no matter what views Comrade Bodinski might have expressed to you, I have not changed that opinion.'

Magnusson detached the Bulgarian's hand from his elbow in a gesture of deliberate coolness. 'Nothing happens in this country without your approval, that I'm damned sure of . . .' He stopped short, biting back words he seemed to have suddenly thought better of.

George Jymeson was watching the exchange intently. All trace of gaucheness in the first secretary had disappeared.

Radovanovic's broad, heavy shoulders hunched and he leaned closer to the ambassador, his huge hands raised as though in supplication, on either side of his squarely-chiselled face. 'There are times, you will agree, when even the strongest swimmer gets caught up and carried along in currents more powerful than himself . . .'

The Bulgarian started to turn away, then paused. He leaned back towards Magnusson again, speaking softly. 'I trust your charming daughter will return from her skiing holiday in good health. Goodnight, Sir Charles.'

Because of his size, and his office, the crowd opened up rapidly in his path, then closed as quickly behind him. Nobody except the journalists and Jymeson seemed to have noticed the heat of the exchanges.

The ambassador turned suddenly on Robson. 'I'm going to start making my way now, Robson. If you leave within a couple of minutes I'll give you a lift to the residence in my official car.'

'Thank you, I'll see you outside, Sir Charles.'

When he'd gone, Bradley raised a quizzical eyebrow. 'I didn't catch all of that but it sounded like a fairly undiplomatic exchange to me.'

'Likewise.' Robson scanned the crowd quickly. 'Look, there's the American ambassador over there – Gloria's got him backed up against that potted plant. Go and rescue him.'

'Jesus, dare I?' Bradley stared aghast. Although she still wore her dark glasses to cover the wrinkles round her eyes, the front of her black, high-necked dress had been slashed open by Yves St Laurent or someone like him in a series of expensive peek-a-boo slits that revealed chain links of brown flesh down to an astonishing low point just below her navel. 'That's not a godammed journalist, that's a one-woman advertisement for Western bourgeois debauchery!'

'Weekend returns from Paris to Acapulco for that all-over sun tan cost Harry Zuckermann a lot of the money he makes merchandising diamonds, Ben. Have some sympathy. She's got to show it off to somebody, somewhere.'

Robson left Bradley staring dubiously towards his ambassador and began to push his way out through the crowd. He passed a plinth bearing larger-than-life busts of Karl Marx and Lenin behind which Captain Zhermatov was deep in a discussion with the head of the Foreign Ministry Press Department. Without interrupting his flow of conversation Zhermatov followed Robson's progress towards the door with his eyes. He allowed himself a little nod of satisfaction when he saw Georgina Morakova begin to follow, towards the door, a line, that would converge with Robson's track before he reached it. He failed to see Wang Chieh-ping put down his glass and move purposefully through the crowd towards them from another direction.

Nine

'Mr Robson, we met on the plane, remember?'

Robson turned in mid-stride. 'Is that Comrade Morakova beneath the fetching flora and those becoming peasant braids?' He smiled at her then noticed her face was tight and drawn. 'Why didn't you tell me that General Boris Bodinski was a good friend and-stroke-or enemy of yours?'

Her face stayed tense. 'Mr Robson, I am sorry, I am not in the mood for banter.'

'My apologies. But I couldn't help noticing that you were having a few not over-friendly words with the Deputy Leader of the Party just now.'

She seemed to ignore him. She was staring down into the glass clutched in both hands in front of her. Her face suddenly contorted. 'My God, why do you men fill this world with hatred and violence for your own mean and selfish ends . . .'

The vehemence of her words made her tremble. She kept her

head down and he thought for a moment she was crying. Neither of them noticed that Wang Chieh-ping had taken up a position behind a nearby column. He had his back to them but he listened intently while pretending to sip a fresh drink.

'Steady on,' said Robson gently. 'I plead not guilty to your sweeping charges against the male sex in general. I just report the hatred and violence, I don't start it.'

He'd hoped the lightness of the remark might provoke a smile, but she continued to stare into her drink avoiding his eyes. 'I'm sorry, I'm very on edge . . .'

'About that fake crash landing? Is that what's upsetting you – and the British ambassador?'

Her head came up suddenly and her eyes were wide with astonishment. 'How did you know?'

'I put two and two together. That's my job.'

She stared over his shoulder as though keeping watch. When her eyes came back to his face she spoke softly, so softly that he had to lean towards her to hear. 'I have just found out myself why it was arranged.' She paused and shook her head angrily. 'I'm so sick of this belief that the end justifies any means! No matter how many people suffer!'

He noticed that the bridge of her nose was slightly misshapen as if it had been broken. It gave her face a fierce, proud almost piratical quality. 'What do you mean exactly?' he asked.

She looked steadily into his eyes as though deliberating whether to speak or stay silent. 'What's happening here in Bulgaria . . .' She paused and looked quickly round. 'What's happening here now could have a devastating effect on all Europe. And beyond. And do you know what for? For an impossible political dream. And for that they're prepared to disrupt millions of peaceful lives.'

Wang moved half a pace backward around the pillar, his eyes narrowing as he strained to pick up every word of their conversation.

'Who do you mean by "they"?'

She didn't reply. She was staring nervously over his shoulder again.

'Who do you mean by "they"?' he repeated. 'Perhaps I can help.'

'Wild men in the Kremlin!' She paused and her hand flew to her mouth.

'No! I'm sorry, I've been very foolish! I shouldn't be talking to you like this.'

Robson felt suddenly angered by her tantalizing manner. He couldn't decide whether it was calculated or whether she was really frightened. He was intrigued nevertheless by the prospect of exclusive information. 'In the past, in the West, many evil men have been prevented from carrying out their plans by newspaper exposure . . .', he began.

Her eyes widened suddenly and she clutched briefly at his arm. 'It is very dangerous here,' she whispered. 'Would you meet me somewhere where we can talk?'

'Of course. Where, when?'

'Be at the little Lebed restaurant on the Pancharevo Lake . . . at mid-day tomorrow. I must go now.'

He reached out a restraining hand to her elbow. 'One thing before you go. I sense a strained atmosphere here tonight. Are Bodinski and Radovanovic at each other's throats?'

She stared at him in alarm and tried to pull free.

'Are they?'

She looked round wildly. He retained his grip on her elbow. She turned to him beseechingly. 'I must go. Much of what you were saying in the plane was right.'

She tugged free and disappeared quickly into the crowd. Robson watched her go. By the time he turned round Wang Chieh-ping had disappeared too, taking with him in his head the carefully-remembered details of their entire conversation and the time and place set for their meeting the next day.

Ten

The silence lengthened in the rear compartment of the ambassador's official car. A wordless gap of several feet of expensive leather seating separated the two men occupying it. Sir Charles Magnusson sat hunched in thought in one corner and Robson, having decided it was not his place to initiate anything, refolded the sheet of paper the ambassador had given him to read and relaxed into the seat cushions in the other. The uniformed chauffeur drove carefully over the rutted snow and ice so that the springs of the Princess smoothed the rough cobblestones to runaway flatness.

The message on the paper was short, simple and enigmatic: 'Yours daughter's safety will depend on your absolute co-operation.' There was no signature.

Two frozen-looking soldiers with fixed bayonets stamped their feet in open defiance of guard regulations outside the Georgi Dimitrov Mausoleum on the south side of Deveti Septemvri Square as the limousine passed through. There was not the remotest sign of anything 'devastating for all Europe' happening in the streets of the Bulgarian capital at that moment.

The British Embassy residence stood in a quiet, tree-lined street in a suburban corner of Sofia. During the entire ride there Sir Charles Magnusson said nothing. He had taken the typewritten note from Robson's hands without a word. He didn't speak until they were standing in the darkened street outside the walled compound of the residence. Then it was only to tell the chauffeur to wait to take Mr Robson back to his hotel.

When he'd given his instructions, he led the way briskly through the open gates towards the front porch. An official uniformed Bulgarian security policeman watched impassively from outside his little wooden guard hut on the opposite pavement.

The night inside the high walls of the residence compound was separate and silent. Robson looked up as he walked. The snow clouds had cleared and a multitude of sharply-focused stars were suspended in a bright breathless stillness as though waiting for events of significance to begin below.

The ambassador stopped without warning at the foot of the porch steps. Because of the dark, Robson stumbled into him. They both apologized simultaneously but the ambassador's voice was puzzled. 'This is a bit strange. I could have sworn I left all the lights on when I came out.'

'Lady Magnusson not at home.'

'No, she's in Athens — on a family errand!'

Robson remembered then that during his time as a second secretary in Paris, Sir Charles had married an imposing Greek woman, taller and haughtier than himself. She had vague connections with the Greek royal family. She had been the cultural attaché at the Greek Embassy when they met.

'. . . I left the lights on really to give myself a bit of cheer to come home to. All the staff have gone.' The ambassador was half talking to himself. 'Perhaps one of the fools turned 'em out before they left.'

'Possibly your main fuse has . . .' Robson didn't complete his conjecture. The ambassador stumbled, uttered a muffled curse and was gone. For a moment Robson stood stock still. Then through the gloom he saw a head emerge from the doorway.

'Blasted door was open too', said the ambassador. 'Just gave way as I went to put my key in the lock. Come on in.'

Robson stepped carefully across the threshold.

The footsteps of the ambassador started off down the hall. Robson hesitated. 'Sir Charles, do you think I should just nip out and ask that policeman on guard outside if he's seen anything suspicious?'

Robson stopped in the doorway staring at the guard hut on the other side of the road. The man had disappeared and the little lamp that had been shining above the hut when they arrived had gone out. He turned and hurried down the hall straight into something tall and heavy, that fell to the floor with him with a loud crash. He lay there for a moment, winded.

'You all right?' The ambassador was coming back carefully towards him in the darkness.

'Yes, I think so.' Robson struggled to his feet. 'Whether the same can be said for whatever I collided with, I'm not sure. It seems to have got horns. But I think it's dead now.'

'It'll be that blasted Athenian hat stand, one of Greta's family heirlooms. Quite worthless. Got pegs like spreading stag antlers. Shove it against the wall.'

The ambassador's footsteps marched away again and Robson followed them, more carefully this time. At the end of the hall they halted. As the ambassador fumbled with a door handle there was a loud bang from behind them.

'What was that?'

'I left the front door open, Sir Charles – to give us whatever light there was from outside.'

'Wind must have blown it closed.'

Robson was about to point out that there was no wind but the ambassador had finally opened the door he was fumbling with.

'Come on, this is my study. I always keep some candles in my desk for this kind of emergency. And some Scotch.'

The footsteps in front of him became muffled and Robson reached out to feel for the doorway into a carpeted room. He touched woodwork, edged forward and stopped. The sound of drawers being opened and closed confirmed he'd found the study.

'Where the devil did I put those candles? Ah, here's one.'

Robson heard the scratch of a match and waited for the flare of light.

But instead he heard the sound of a blow, followed by a grunt of pain. Matchbox and candles clattered noisily across the desk top.

'No lights. And no movement.' The orders came disembodied from the darkness. 'Both, please be sensible.'

'Who the blazes is that?' The ambassador's question was a shout of angry astonishment.

The door of the room closed suddenly and there was a sound of the key turned in the lock.

'You can't see it in the dark but I have a gun.' The voice spoke English with a heavy Russian accent.

'Don't make any false moves, Robson,' said the ambassador hurriedly.

'Attacking gunmen in darkened rooms isn't one of my party tricks, Sir Charles!'

'Shut up! Shooting diplomats is not one of my tricks. But I will do it if necessary.'

'For the Party, no doubt,' added Robson heavily.

In the silence that followed there was a faint click and Robson wondered whether a safety catch being removed sounded like that.

'I will come straight to the point, Sir Charles,' said the voice, ignoring Robson. 'I wish you to grant me political asylum.'

'Who are you?'

'I am a Soviet intelligence officer. A colonel in the KGB. I know much that would be of interest to your people in London and Washington. I wish to defect to Great Britain.'

'We don't make a practice of accepting defectors under duress, at gun point!'

Robson recognized that the ambassador had now recovered his composure and was employing his best *Honi soit qui mal y pense* voice.

'I apologize, Sir Charles, for the methods I am forced to employ. The fact is my circumstances leave me no choice. The time element is vital. I cannot risk your government's refusal.'

'How do I know this isn't some kind of trick?'

'You will have to trust me, Sir Charles. You have no alternative. Perhaps if I tell you that it was I who planned and carried out the kidnapping of your daughter today during her return from her skiing holiday, it will give you some idea of my rank and seniority.'

'You swine!' The ambassador's voice began moving, then stopped as if he'd caught himself suddenly. 'So you fixed the crash-landing!'

'Yes, Sir Charles. But your daughter is safe and she will remain safe as long as you co-operate. Regard it as simply an extended part of her Austrian holiday. Do as I say and she will return sunburned and healthy. Fail to co-operate and . . .' the voice stopped as if its owner were thinking hard, '. . . her body will perhaps be found in a crevasse below the ski slopes at Innsbruck!'

There was a long silence before the British diplomat spoke again. When he did, his voice was quietly under control. 'What do you want of me?'

'I simply require you to make certain arrangements . . . First, you must announce immediately the sudden death of your daughter here in your home. Then you must make provision for her body to be driven immediately to Greece for burial in the family cemetery of your wife.'

'What are you going to do?'

'A hearse containing a coffin will arrive at this house shortly after dusk tomorrow. If you do exactly as I say, your daughter will be inside, under sedation, but otherwise unharmed. The coffin will be brought into the house and without anybody except ourselves seeing the miracle', he paused and cleared his throat for effect, '. . . she will rise from the dead.'

The defector's voice was flat and unemotional as though, Robson thought, he had practised the speech over and over.

'I shall take her place in the specially ventilated casket. Your chauffeur will then drive the hearse across the border into Greece and on through to Athens.'

Another long silence. A car rattled down the long cobbled avenue outside and passed by without stopping. The defector cleared his throat loudly from the darkness. 'Well, Sir Charles?'

'You won't get away with this blackmail.'

The anonymous voice sighed loudly. 'Sir Charles, once I am in the West, once I begin to reveal what I know, I think tonight and your daughter's temporary absence will be seen as minor discomforts – and quickly forgotten.'

Captain Zhermatov looked across at young Trichkov on the other side of the recording machine. 'Reception from the residence is very clear tonight,' he said softly. The boy nodded.

They both bent their heads towards the amplifier as the ambassador came in fiercely again. 'Where is my daughter? What have you done with her?'

Zhermatov cocked his head listening intently for the answer.

'She is not far away and we are keeping her safe and well. In case I have not made it clear, I should perhaps emphasize this measure is to ensure that you are not tempted to communicate anything of this to your Foreign Office superiors in London – even by your most secret cyphers. They might advise you to refuse co-operation. Your daughter is my insurance policy. Rest assured, Sir Charles, if you send any radio traffic at all, even though we are unable to decode it . . . she will die.'

The narrow brown tape on the recording machine spun on over a silence that lasted half a minute.

'Doesn't look as if you have much choice, Sir Charles.'

'You keep out of this, Robson,' the ambassador snapped. 'It's none of your damned business.'

'Who is this man with you, Sir Charles?' The voice of the defector sounded irritated. 'One of your political secretaries?'

'He is a British journalist.'

'A journalist? I trust you realize the importance of persuading him to keep his mouth and his typewriter case shut . . . for your daughter's sake . . .'

The two men listening in the monitoring room of S.14 clearly heard the long agitated breath that the ambassador drew before he spoke again. 'You leave me no choice but to co-operate with you, damn you . . . I shall make the arrangements you have requested.'

'Good, Sir Charles, you are very wise. I shall return here through the garden at dusk tomorrow.' The defector's voice began to grow fainter. 'I will leave you the fuse plugs here on this windowsill. But don't switch the lights on for five minutes after I have gone . . .'

The French windows slammed.

Zhermatov reached out and switched off the machine. Trichkov watched in puzzlement as his burly superior took a box of matches from his pocket. 'Don't you wish to record the rest of the conversation, Captain? Surely they will discuss their reaction now.'

Zhermatov lifted the spool of tape from the machine and handed it wordlessly to Trichkov.

'Transcribe it?' He stared at the older man's expressionless face trying to read its meaning.

Zhermatov nodded slowly and handed him the matches. 'No! Burn it, Comrade.'

'Burn it?' Trichkov's face had turned pale. 'But that requires the written authorization of three signatories, including General Bodinski. Have you got his authorization?'

'Do as I say. Burn it . . .' Zhermatov stood up and reached inside his tunic. He seemed to loosen the pistol in the holster beneath his armpit.

When the young man had begun tugging the tape off the reel into a tangled pile on his desk, Zhermatov turned back to the amplifier, adjusted the fine tuner by a millimetre or so and increased the volume. He jammed his hands into his trouser pockets and stood listening carefully.

Robson sat for at least half the stipulated five minute period in the dark without saying anything. The ambassador hadn't moved either or uttered a word.

'Will you inform London, Sir Charles?'

For a while Robson wondered whether the diplomat had heard his question. Then the desk creaked as he stood up.

'Robson I deeply regret the coincidence which caused you to be present during that . . . confrontation. I had intended to tell you in complete confidence of my daughter's disappearance since you clearly flew in on that same plane from which she was taken. I'm not thinking too clearly tonight, I suppose, and perhaps I thought you might be able to throw some light on the affair.' The ambassador snorted angrily in the darkness. But I'm damned if I wanted you present during . . .'

His voice died away again and there was another long silence. Robson shifted uneasily, at a loss for words. 'But I *was* here, Sir Charles,' he said at last. 'And maybe I can help. Will you tell London?'

'No, of course not. I can't possibly take that risk.'

Robson heard him move across the room. There was the clink of glass and a moment later the ambassador was standing beside him. 'Here's one to keep you going until we get the lights on.'

Robson groped for the tumbler of whisky in the dark and they both drank. 'Sir Charles, is your daughter tall, rather pretty, with very long black hair?'

'Yes, that sounds like Angela. Why?'

'She was on our flight, I think. Seemed perfectly well then, although that's perhaps not much comfort. I didn't see her at all, unfortunately, after we slid out of the plane.'

There was another long interval of silence. But the journalist didn't attempt to break it this time.

'I must of course demand, Robson, that you treat everything you've seen and heard here tonight in the strictest confidence.' The ambassador paused, as though hoping he wouldn't have to say more.

Robson sensed he was putting his official hat firmly back on after the brief departure into the personal realm.

'There can be no question of your writing anything of this for BAPPA, of it getting into the newspapers or on to the BBC . . .'

It was Robson's turn to take a deep breath. 'It goes without saying, Sir Charles, that I have enormous sympathy for your predicament. But I'm not sure you can "demand" that I do or don't do anything. I work for my news agency, not the Government.'

The ambassador moved suddenly nearer in the darkness. 'Perhaps you've forgotten you were present, Robson, by dint of my personal invitation, at what amounted to highly confidential, although unorthodox . . .' He broke off, searching for a suitably intimidating formulation of bureaucratic language, '. . . unorthodox, er, government negotiations. Your presence was admittedly accidental, but nevertheless, you were my guest and therefore I can demand that you respect these governmental confidences.'

'I think, with respect, you're getting your lines somewhat crossed, Sir Charles.' Although the room was still pitch black, Robson felt the ambassador bristle.

'You are British, Robson,' he snapped, 'or had you forgotten? Do you imagine that being a journalist absolves you from your responsibilities as a citizen? Your first loyalty is or should be to the Government that protects your interests.'

'Sir Charles, you're perhaps not clearly aware of it, but you're asking me to respect confidences on the basis of my personal sympathy for the unfortunate predicament you and your daughter find yourselves in. There's nothing official about it. As far as I can see you're doing your duty as a father by complying with that defector's demands while failing to do your duty as an ambassador to the British Government.'

'What exactly do you mean?'

'The Government would very likely reject the demands. That's the way government policy has been developing towards hostage-takers, as you well know.' Robson paused to drink some more whisky. 'I might argue that it's my duty as a British reporter to reveal how my country is being held to ransom and laid open to a possible communist plot on account, if one puts it in its baldest terms, of the personal self-interest of one of Her Majesty's ambassadors.'

There was a sound of movement across the room and Robson guessed the ambassador was groping for the fuses by the French window. A moment later he heard what sounded like a cupboard door swing open. Then the lights came on and the ambassador was standing blinking by the open fuse box. When Robson's eyes became accustomed to the light, he noticed that the diplomat's face was pale and the muscles of his jaw were clenched tight.

'If you write this for tomorrow's papers or it gets on the BBC tonight, Robson, you could in effect be murdering my daughter.'

Robson bit his lip thoughtfully. 'How do you know this is not a trick, Sir Charles? How can you be sure this man is simply a defector? Couldn't he be a fake, or a plant?' Robson could see that the ambassador had already thought of that possibility — and decided he still had no choice. 'How do you know that in putting your daughter first you're not jeopardizing Britain's security yourself, in some way that will only become clear later?'

'The one fact that guides my actions, Robson,' said the ambassador quietly, 'is that my daughter disappeared from an airliner that was diverted to a military airfield seemingly for the express purpose of kidnapping her. Have you no sympathy for her plight?'

He moved back to the bottle of whisky on the sideboard and refilled his glass.

'I have every sympathy — with you and your daughter. But you can't be sure they won't murder her anyway, then say she fell to her death in the Austrian Alps.'

The ambassador put his glass down suddenly. He turned his back on Robson, rested both hands on the sideboard and lowered his head as though suddenly weary.

'I'm sorry if this sounds brutal, Sir Charles, but revealing the plot in the papers or on the radio might even save her. It might tempt them to produce her live and well and scotch what they can then call another "diabolical Western press slander". It could provide them with a way out.'

'Robson, you must know that I can't risk that. Put yourself in my position.' His voice was muffled, because his chin was sunk on his chest.

Robson took a deep breath. 'What you've discovered painfully for yourself tonight, Sir Charles,' he said gently, 'is how the interest of one individual can often conflict directly with that national interest which you, from professional training and by second nature, normally put above all else . . .'

The ambassador turned and looked up suddenly, his eyes blazing with anger. 'Robson, I'm not prepared to stand here in the British residence being lectured by a bloody news agency reporter on how I should perform my official duties!'

'Just let me finish, Sir Charles,' said Robson quietly, 'then I'll leave and walk back to town if necessary . . . Presented with the necessity to choose between those two loyalties, personal and national, you've risked ignoring the impersonal British national interest for the here-and-now, flesh-and-blood interests of yourself and your daughter . . . and on those grounds you can't demand of me that I respect your confidences on account of the Official Secrets Act.'

The ambassador stood glaring into his face for a moment then turned away again.

Robson drained his glass, set it down on the tray beside the bottle and walked towards the door of the study.

'Robson!'

The journalist turned in the doorway.

'Are you, or are you not going to file something that might cause the death of my daughter?' The ambassador was standing bolt upright again, against the sideboard, with his shoulders thrown back.

'I long ago decided that I would write nothing unless you desperately wanted me to, Sir Charles', said Robson evenly. 'I just wanted to make it clear to you that it was a voluntary and personal decision based on human sympathy . . . and nothing to do with governmental coercion.'

The ambassador's shoulders relaxed and sagged. His face was suddenly void of all expression, as if his mind were already elsewhere.

Robson stared thoughtfully at him for a moment. He was remembering Georgina Morakova's warning. 'Sir Charles, do you really accept that man's story at face value? Is he a genuine defector, do you think? Or could there be something else, something bigger, behind all this?'

The ambassador screwed up his face and rubbed the palm of his hand agitatedly against his forehead. 'I don't know, I just don't know.'

Robson turned to go. 'I'll be on my way now. Don't hesitate to ring me at the hotel if you feel there's anything I can do. Goodnight.' Robson walked out into the hall.

'Take the car, Robson,' the ambassador called after him. 'It would be foolish to walk all that way.'

Outside, the light over the security policeman's hut was on again. The guard stood beneath it staring out impassively from under his cap as Robson climbed into the back of the ambassador's car.

As the sound of the Princess's engine died into the distance, the guard opened the door of the hut, went inside, and picked up the telephone.

Eleven

Phyllis Jymeson stood staring at the fine wisps of dark hair curling on the nape of Angela Magnusson's neck. Young, slender, curved like a swan's, she thought.

She glanced in the mirror at her own hair. When she bent forward she could see the roots beginning to show grey again against the darker tint of the rest. She cursed silently to herself. The next damned visit to London from god-forsaken Sofia was still a month away!

In the mirror she watched the ambassador's daughter bending intently over the playing cards on the coffee table. She had scraped her long hair back, tied it with a ribbon and piled it up on her head because of the heat in the room.

'Damn! Damn! Damnation! This silly game of patience just won't come out, Mrs Jymeson.' The girl slapped the cards exasperatedly on the polished top of the table. She looked up to find the older woman smiling to herself as she patted her hair into place before the mirror. 'I'm so bored here. When am I going to be able to go home and see my father?'

Phyllis Jymeson didn't reply. Instead she turned away and stooped to open the metal door of the tiled central heating kiln in the corner of the room. With slow deliberation she shook coal onto the already blazing fire from a copper bucket.

'Oh, not more coal, surely, Mrs J', said the younger girl, pouting. 'I'm roasting already.'

'I like it as hot as I can bear in the snowy time.' The woman spoke softly and smiled directly into the girl's eyes. 'Take your cardigan off if you're too warm.'

Phyllis Jymeson unbuttoned her own cardigan and shrugged it off. She watched the girl remove hers and turn back to the cards on the table. She let a minute pass then unfastened the top two buttons of her blouse and walked slowly across to look down over her shoulder.

'That red ten will go on the black Jack, you silly old sausage.'

Angela Magnusson giggled. 'Yes, of course, how stupid of me!' She picked up the cards behind the ten and moved them across.

'And the seven will go on the eight, look.' The older woman pointed, then let her hand drop casually on the girl's shoulder. 'You're as blind as a banana.'

Angela Magnusson laughed again. 'Yes, I am being dim, aren't I?' She began turning over the cards in her hands again, banging them down on the table in fours. Phyllis Jymeson moved closer to the sofa so that her thigh brushed against the girl's shoulder. As she watched the cards, she moved her hand and began very gently twisting a wisp of stray hair on the nape of the girl's neck, winding it into a ringlet around her finger.

'You have a very pretty neck, Angela,' she said softly, and bent her head towards her.

'Please don't touch me.' The girl stood up suddenly and backed away, spilling the cards in a gaudy puddle on the carpet.

At that moment George Jymeson opened the door. He'd just come in from the snow and the tabs of his fur hat hung down either side of his thin face like a spaniel's ears. He stopped brushing the snow from the shoulders of his overcoat and his eyes narrowed suddenly behind the thick black hornrims. He looked from his wife's flushed face to the sulky-looking girl and back again.

The three of them stood for a moment frozen in a triangular tableau, saying nothing. Then Jymeson quickly removed his hat and overcoat and hung them up in the hall before coming back into the room and closing the door behind him.

'Well, how are we all getting on here at home?' His joviality was obviously forced. 'Looks like somebody's dropped a slack handful of cards on the floor, eh?'

He moved across the room and bent to pick them up. 'Like to make me a cup of good old English char, would you, dear, to take the taste of that foul Bulgarian *slivova* away?'

His wife glanced down at her watch then hurried from the room without speaking.

'How were we faring with the patience? Getting it out, were we?' Jymeson straightened up and put the pile of cards on the table beside the half-finished columns.

'Mr Jymeson, I'm not good at patience. In fact,' she turned to face him, 'I'm really a very impatient person. I wonder if you'd be kind enough to explain to me what's going on.' Angela Magnusson's tone was petulant. She had the manner of a child who had rarely been denied anything she asked. 'I get a telegram calling me back from my skiing holiday today, we practically crash-land at some dreadful airport in the wilds and you and Mrs Jymeson are waiting there for me but there's no sign of my father. What's happening?'

Jymeson pushed his spectacles an imperceptible distance up the bridge of his nose with one long, bony middle finger. 'Angela, I've told you already that your father's express instructions are for you to wait here until he calls for you. In the meantime, do as I say. Believe me, there are good reasons for these instructions. You must be patient.' He put all his charm into a face-creasing smile. 'Here, have another shot at finishing the jolly old patience while I go and have a word with my wife in the kitchen.'

As he left the room she flung herself furiously on to the sofa and dashed the jumbled heap of cards back onto the floor.

He shut the hall door and locked it soundlessly. He went into the kitchen, closing that door carefully behind him too. When he turned to his wife, his face was white. 'You flesh-obsessed bitch, can't you even keep your hands off the ambassador's daughter.' He was hissing the words between clenched teeth, trying not to let his anger get the better of him. 'Are you trying to ruin this whole bloody set-up? Send her screaming out of the house?'

She looked coldly up from the tea tray she was preparing and brushed a strand of hair from her face. Then she calmly refastened the top buttons of her blouse. 'Go to hell,' she said quietly. 'Go right to hell and screw yourself to the inside wall.' She stared at him with contempt disfiguring her face.

'God, if I'd only known when I married you what went on at your bloody convent school . . .'

'You bastard! You skinny impotent, emasculated bastard! I detest you . . .!' She picked up the steaming kettle of water and swung it towards him. He stepped forward and hit her hard on the side of the head with the flat of his hand. As she staggered back open-mouthed he plucked the kettle from her. She clutched at the sink to prevent herself falling and hung there watching him pour the boiling water calmly into the teapot.

Before he'd finished she struggled up and slipped past him. She wrenched open the door, picked up her coat and handbag in the hall and was out of the front door before he'd realized her intention. When he heard the sound of the car starting he cursed softly beneath his breath. He stood indecisively for a moment then picked up the tray and took it through to the girl in the next room.

Angela Magnusson's face turned expectantly towards the door as he entered with the tea. 'Was that somebody coming in the front door, Mr Jymeson?'

'No, Angela, that was just my wife slipping out for a bit.'

'Oh! I thought it might be my father arriving to get me.'

'Angela, I'm sorry I can't be more explicit but perhaps you ought to accustom yourself to the idea that you'll be spending tonight and possibly tomorrow night here with us. Two lumps?' He looked up at her solicitously.

'No sugar, thank you.'

He poured tea and handed it to her. 'Angela,' he asked casually, 'my wife didn't do anything to upset you, did she?'

The girl bit her lip and turned back to the cards on the table. She hesitated, flushing. 'I suppose I'm a bit irritable. I think she was just trying to be nice to me.'

'Did we know about Mrs Jymeson?' asked Trichkov quietly.

Zhermatov nodded. 'Yes Comrade.' He had taken off his hat and under the neon strip lighting his bald, gnome-like head gleamed as if it had been polished with beeswax. 'We have long known of her predilections – and her husband's special "status".'

The tape spun on recording nothing but silence for a long time. Then the girl began speaking again. 'Mr Jymeson, how did you know the plane wouldn't try to land at Sofia airport? How did you and your wife get to that military base so quickly to meet me?'

'Let's not worry about that now, my dear.' Jymeson spoke hurriedly. 'Tell me about Innsbruck. Slack handfuls of blond-haired ski-instructors like Adonis himself, hanging about the place all the time were there?'

*

The hall smelled faintly of a mixture of creosote, carbolic soap, disinfectant and dust. On a small notice board inside the unpainted door to the entry passage hung what she knew was a roster showing which tenants had to clean the stairs and passageways, which weeks. As usual she stopped by the notice board to comb her hair and touch up her lipstick. And she tried without success in the gloom to see whether there was a bruise turning out on her temple.

When she'd finished she put her mirror and lipstick away and glanced out into the snowy street to check that nobody had followed her. Then she moved into the darkness at the back of the hall. As her feet echoed on the first of the three flights of uncarpeted wooden stairs she was seized by a sudden apprehension, as she had been on all her previous visits. There was something repugnant in the drabness of the state-owned block, the strangely impersonal odour of basic cleaning materials, the shadowy darkness of the stairwell. They almost unnerved her this time. She stopped halfway up the second flight, listening. There was no sound except her own anxious breathing. She thought of the shy slender woman waiting nervously in the sparsely furnished flat at the top of the stairs – and moved on again.

The landing was in total darkness. She had to cross it with her arm held in front of her until she felt the chipped paintwork of the door. Then softly she knocked twice. The darkness remained complete even after she heard the sound of the door ease open. The lights inside the flat, as usual, had not been switched on.

'Mei-li?' she whispered.

The sibilant reply was unmistakable. Phyllis Jymeson stepped across the threshold and in the pitch darkness put her arms around the slender Chinese woman.

Although Tsai Mei-li accepted the embrace mutely and without resistance as always, Phyllis Jymeson was suddenly pleased. Despite the darkness she could feel that Mei-li had discarded the heavy shapeless tunic and trousers she wore in the embassy and had put on the traditional full-length *cheongsam* of soft Shanghai silk that she had brought back from the China Crafts Centre in Baker Street as a present for her.

She had always refused to wear it before. Such things, she'd explained shyly, were considered 'decadent' and 'bourgeois' in the People's Republic of China.

'Shall we put some lights on, Mei-li?'

'No light, no light!' The Chinese woman's voice was urgent but barely audible as she closed the door and moved off along the hall. Carefully shaded lamp-light fell faintly across the passage as she opened the door to the small bedroom.

'Mei-li, thank you,' she said breathlessly, when they were inside. 'You look truly beautiful in it.' The Chinese had unclipped her short hair and brushed it so that it fell softly around her cheeks.

She ran her hands lightly over the Chinese woman's shoulders and down her arms, pressing the smooth silk against her slender body. She could feel the sharp narrow hip bones of the Chinese as clearly as if the robe was another skin. The top of her dark head barely reached up to her chin. She looked down at her, her eyes bright, her breathing uneven.

The Chinese avoided her look and smiled faintly towards the floor. Her utter submissiveness aroused a new intensity in the English woman.

'You've got nothing on under there, Mei-li.' Her smile was lop-sided and she swallowed hard. 'You're ahead of me. We must be equal.'

She quickly unbuttoned her tailored Simpson's coat. While the Chinese folded it and placed it carefully on a chair by the bed, she removed her skirt and sweater, stepped out of her underclothes and hurried across to slip her arms around the slender figure from behind.

The wrap-over robe had no buttons. The Englishwoman brushed her lips against the crown of the dark head and slid both hands inside the robe, pressing the child-like body of the Chinese hard against her naked groin.

Mei-li responded to the embrace, tensing herself against the quickening movements of the taller woman and covering her hands with her own as they moved more urgently across the front of her body.

'Mei-li, lie down!' She gathered her up and lifted her bodily on to the bed. She tugged the silk robe open and removed it completely. She paused for a moment, staring down at the amber

81

body of the naked Chinese. Then she leaned forward and ran her hands lightly up and over her flanks. The Chinese shivered but her lowered lids kept her eyes meekly hidden from the other woman's gaze. She stopped suddenly and took her face gently in both hands. 'Mei-li, look at me,' she pleaded. 'You never look at me. Just this once, please.'

The Chinese looked up wide-eyed into her face for the first time as the dark figure of Wang Chieh-ping stepped soundlessly through the door behind them and grabbed the Englishwoman brutally by the hair. He clamped her mouth with his other hand, cutting off the scream that rose bubbling in her throat and dragged her free of his wife's body with such violence that thick hanks of her hair came out in his hand.

Mei-li rose swiftly from the bed and without looking round, took baggy grey denim trousers and a jacket from a cupboard. She put them on, tucked her hair inside a blue peaked worker's cap, then reached into the cupboard again. When she turned round, two slivers of bright metal glinted in her tiny fist.

Twelve

Phyllis Jymeson's legs threshed wildly as the Chinese woman moved across the room towards her clutching the needles. In desperation she reached up behind her to try to disentangle Wang's hands from her hair. She found his face with one hand and gouged her nails deep into his cheek. Three long gashes spurted blood and Wang let out a shout of pain.

In his fury, he swung the naked Englishwoman clear of the floor by her hair and flung her back onto the bed. She crashed screaming against the brass-railed bed-head. He sprang up beside her and knotted her long hair close at the roots around the rails, leaving her head, neck and upper body arched painfully backwards.

Phyllis Jymeson was too shocked to cry out now, even though he no longer covered her mouth. She tried to support the weight of her body with her hands. She couldn't move an inch without intensifying the excruciating pain in her scalp. Her chest heaved and she moaned continuously in her breathing. Her eyes, now sightless with pain, stared up towards the ceiling.

'Quick, the needles!'

Wang spoke deliberately in clear English and the English-woman's eyes widened in horror. He took two pairs of handcuffs from his jacket and quickly manacled each of her wrists to the base of the bedrail.

His wife stepped up to the bed holding two slender gold needles in her hand. Her face remained blank and immobile as she took a firm hold of Phyllis Jymeson's head from underneath. She opened her mouth to scream, but no sound came out. Her body had frozen now into a painful arc and she watched petrified as, in one quick movement, Tsai Mei-li leaned close over her face, picked her spot, then jabbed the point of the first needle deftly into her face at a point exactly equidistant between her two eyebrows. The needle went in at an acute downward angle. Without pausing, the Chinese woman looked again, picked her spot and thrust the second needle upwards through the soft flesh at the point of her nose. No blood appeared from either puncture of her flesh.

Phyllis Jymeson's face had frozen into a mask of terror from which the two golden spikes jutted incongruously. She remained absolutely motionless, hardly breathing. Even her moaning ceased. Tsai Mei-li turned quickly, and took a small black box from the cupboard. She opened it and attached two wired electrodes to the ends of the gold needles. She sat down on the bed with the box on her knee, flicked a switch and carefully watched a dial in the box as a quiet steady hum indicated that a low voltage current was passing into the needles. She adjusted the dial then looked questioningly towards her husband. 'It's at ten.'

He bent over the Englishwoman until his high-cheekboned face filled her vision.

'Increase the current five points,' he said softly over his shoulder.

Phyllis Jymeson's whole face began to lose its feeling as the numbness spread outwards from the vibrating needles. Her stiffly arched body, which the two Chinese made no move to cover, also seemed to be growing cold all over. But although her manacled arms were still supporting much of her weight, and her hair remained tied painfully close to the bedrail, she no longer felt any real pain. She was aware of the smallest sound and movement in the room but her consciousness seemed to be growing numb too. A feeling of pure, almost detached terror throbbed through her mind in rhythm with the slowly pulsating current in the needles. She waited and expected to die.

When Wang spoke again his voice seemed to her to echo as if it was coming through a public address system.

'Tell us why Robson is here.'

'I've told Mei-li already.' She gabbled the words in a quavering voice.

'Increase the current.' Wang moved his face to within six inches of hers.

'You told her only that Robson was being sent to foil a plan being mounted by Soviet revisionists to wreck the conferences on Strategic Arms and force reductions in Europe. What is this plan? Tell us more about Robson's intentions and his links with the Morakova woman. Is he an MI6 agent?'

The quiet electronic hum rose steadily in intensity in the silence that followed.

Phyllis Jymeson's mouth moved convulsively but nothing came out.

'Reduce the current twenty-five per cent,' he said quickly to his wife without looking round. He paused. 'We've reduced the current sufficiently for you to speak now.'

Some of the muscles in the Englishwoman's face had begun twitching fast under the stimulus of the needles and she had to make an effort to control her trembling jaw. 'My husband doesn't tell me all his business,' she gasped at last.

Wang, studiously avoiding her nakedness, stared up without expression at the blank wall. 'You have told my wife that you hate your husband. You have also said that you have read his secret papers and passed some information to her already, to spite him and to encourage her to see you again.' His cold face betrayed nothing of his emotions. 'Before you leave here tonight you will tell us all you know – or neither your mind nor your body will ever be of any use to you again.'

Phyllis Jymeson's whole head had begun shaking now; sweat coursed down her face and dripped on to the cheap bed cover.

'With one further twist of that dial, you can be made into a living vegetable — with only dry beds where the rivers of your nervous system should be.' He made a sudden hand signal towards his wife. 'You have two minutes to choose.'

The silence that fell abruptly in the room as the current was switched off lasted for almost a minute. Phyllis Jymeson's face collapsed in relief. Tsai Mei-li reached forward as if to remove the wires from the needles but her husband waved her away.

'You have two minutes in which to tell us everything. After that, if you remain silent, we shall start the current again — at double intensity! Only fifteen seconds of that will be required to remove the faculty of speech from you for the rest of your life . . .'

The Englishwoman's face worked convulsively for a moment. Then words burst from her in a fast gabble. 'There is no plot to wreck the conferences . . . it's a trick, a trick . . .'

Wang leaned over her again. 'You're lying! I heard the Morakova woman telling Robson at the reception tonight there was a plot by Kremlin extremists!'

'Yes, yes yes, that's right; it's a plan to confuse him. There is no plot . . . no plot . . .' Phyllis Jymeson broke off moaning and gasping. 'What I told you before was wrong. I saw part of my husband's papers, only the part concerning the "information" for Robson. I didn't know then. He is . . . to *think* there is a plot . . .'

'Why? Tell us why.'

She began moaning again. 'Untie me first, please untie me!'

'After you have told us why.'

Her eyes rolled wildly as though she was close to hysteria.

'Robson is just a stooge, he's not an agent, just a . . . journalist. He's being used for something else . . . he doesn't know anything . . .' She broke off suddenly. A strange gurgling sound came from her throat and she began to cough.

'What is he being used for? Who is using him?'

'The ambassador's daughter has been kidnapped . . . a crash landing . . . but really she hasn't been kidnapped at all, although her father thinks she has . . .' She went into another coughing fit and Wang waited impassively for her to recover. 'A false defector went to the embassy, he's a fake too . . . all part of the Bulgarian

plan . . . the Cranbourne plan, yes, Cranbourne . . . Cranbourne
. . .'

The terrorized woman's words suddenly tailed off into an agonized moan. She began shuddering convulsively along the length of her whole body. Uncontrollable spasms wrenched her head from side to side. She screamed loudly with the pain from her tethered hair and Wang fell forward to cover her mouth. He motioned his wife to untie her and unfasten the handcuffs. While she was doing this Phyllis Jymeson suddenly went limp.

They lowered her quickly onto the bed and Mei-li flung the silk robe over her. The Englishwoman lay still without moving. She was barely breathing. Mei-li ran to the cupboard for extra blankets and covered her quickly. She poured some hot water from a giant thermos flask by the bed into a cup and forced it between her lips.

Wang stared at his wife with a growing fury contorting his face. 'Too much current!'

She stared meekly at the floor. 'Not too much,' she said quietly. 'Her reaction was unpredictable. Everybody responds differently . . . But she will regain consciousness in a few minutes.'

'She has not told us everything!' Wang's eyes were dilated with anxiety.

'Do not worry she will recover soon. We shall be able to resume interrogation then.'

Wang stared wildly at his wife. 'But we have misinformed the top leadership in Peking.' His voice dropped to a whisper. 'Do you realize what this means?'

'She says there is something else, another purpose for which Robson is being used.' Tsai Mei-li looked apprehensively at her husband as she spoke.

'It doesn't matter what else he is doing. We must kill him now anyway! Otherwise our mistakes will be discovered and we will be recalled.' His voice rose almost to a shout. 'Do you want to undergo "reform-through-labour" and spend the rest of your life in the fields?'

Tsai Mei-li went to the thermos again and poured another cup of steaming water. She held it wordlessly towards her husband.

'Yes, that is what we must do', said Wang smashing his fist agitatedly into the palm of his other hand. 'Even after his death we can report that the plot has failed for other reasons!'

His wife motioned to him to take the cup of hot water and her placid meek behaviour suddenly seemed to calm him. He sipped thoughtfully at the scalding water, looking down at the inert, unconscious figure of Phyllis Jymeson. Her breathing had become more regular and from time to time her eyelids flickered.

Wang looked round at his wife. She was quietly replacing the acupuncture needles in their felt-lined box and packing them with the electrode equipment into her canvas shoulder bag.

Thirteen

Jonathan Robson hacked away at his ageing Imperial Good Companion portable, using the two-finger 'pick-and-peck' method of the unprofessional Fleet Street typist. He sat sideways to the dressing table in his Balkan Hotel bedroom because it was too low to get his knees underneath. The portable typewriter skidded slowly across the glass-covered surface under his hammering fingers and he had to drag it back to the centre after every second paragraph.

But even though he picked and pecked, and even though the smoke from the cigarette in his mouth was curling up into his eyes, the carriage scudded back and forth in rapid bursts of up to fifty words a minute.

He was hauling the last yellowish square of newsprint copy paper from the machine and separating the carbons when the telephone rang. He carried the sheaf of papers across the room, sat down on the bed and began correcting his story with a ball-point pen as he picked up the telephone.

'Your call to London, Mr Robson.' The hotel operator's English was thickly accented.

She'd got his call quickly ahead of all the other journalists waiting impatiently in their rooms because he'd dropped in at the switchboard earlier on the way to the bar and slipped a couple of old copies of *Harpers & Queen* and *Vogue* that he'd brought specially for the purpose to the switchboard girl. Her eyes lit up and she hid them quickly under the cushion she sat on. He'd promised he'd bring James Bond novels next time. He was moving to Vienna soon, he said. She smiled again. Decadent western literature, that was the way to get your calls to London quickly. The old tricks still worked!

'BAPPA, London.'

'It's Robson, Sofia, here, who's on the desk tonight?'

'It's Gordon Miller tonight, Jon.'

'Put him on for a second, interrupt if necessary, will you, Harriette. Then I'll want copy.' The grey-haired old biddy who'd run the evening switchboard shift for the last twenty years probably hadn't realized he'd not filed a story since 1965. Didn't even realize he'd been away.

'Miller here.' The night duty editor's voice was crisply self-important.

'It's Robson in Bulgaria. I'm just going to put a piece on about a power struggle developing here among the Bulgarian leadership on the eve of the Congress . . . Just wanted to tell you that it's going to be pretty strong stuff but I can't source it too hard. We'll probably be on our own with it too. Don't want you ringing me back at three in the morning asking "who says?"'

'An exclusive, eh? A real live scoop.' Miller's banter was half jocular, half offensive. 'All right, I'll ask you that question now, then. "Who says?"'

The night editor's tone, the hint of deliberate aggression raised Robson's hackles.

'I say!'

'Really? Surely I don't have to tell an old BAPPA hand like you, Mr Robson, that we need firm quotable sources for stories we're going to put our seal of approval on for distribution to the responsible media around the world?'

'I don't think we've met, Mr Miller, you must be fairly new.' Robson laboured the insult. 'I know Eastern Europe well, I've read some unmistakable signs with my own eyes here tonight. I've based my story on that. It's not possible to spell them out in detail.' He was angry with himself for having stated the obvious about his past to the young night editor. 'But you can trust the story, that's all I wanted to assure you.'

'I know the Vienna job's coming vacant soon but don't strain too hard for it, old boy.'

The crassness of Miller's remark shocked Robson into silence for a moment.

For several seconds the rhythmic clatter of dozens of teleprinter machines was the only sound coming down the line from the factory floor of the London newsroom.

'And by the way,' Miller went on blithely, fully aware he'd scored, 'if you specialize in writing about power struggles, you should be here tonight.'

'Really?' said Robson, in a tight voice. 'Why's that?'

'Oh, the lights are burning bright tonight in the BAPPA corridors of power. Extraordinary board meeting been going on since ten this morning. The "profits-first" mafia of the organization are ganging up on the old school of working journalists. Trying to ease the chairman himself out, no less, they are. They want more American business methods ... streamline, rationalize, more computers, you know the sort of thing.'

'Fascinating,' said Robson in a bored voice.

'I hear you're a good chum of our Sir Someone Barnes, Robson, is that right . . .? Or was it his good lady wife?'

Robson took a long deep breath. 'Miller, I've got a story to dictate. If you've got anything really important to say, call me back after I've finished with copy. Meanwhile perhaps you'd be good enough to transfer me.'

'Surely, old boy. I'll be looking forward avidly to reading this great Bulgarian exclusive.'

The line clicked several times and the drum of teleprinters disappeared abruptly. Banging and clattering indicated that the typist in the soundproof booth in the corner of the newsroom was putting on her headphones.

Miller's hostile manner had rankled Robson and he was unnecessarily short with the copytaker when she asked him to spell his name.

'All right,' he said sourly when she'd got it, 'if you're really ready now, I'll spell everything longer than four-letter words ... Sofia, February nineteenth, colon. *Bulgaria's party leadership is tonight locked in a fierce struggle for power which could rock the communist world to its foundations in the same way the Prague Spring did in 1968. New paragraph.*' As he waited for the typist to catch up Robson cradled the telephone receiver between ear and shoulder and lit a fresh cigarette. 'Get that? Okay . . . *On the eve of the eleventh Bulgarian Communist Party Congress which will be attended by the top Soviet leaders, hints of growing hostility emerged here tonight between Party First Secretary Nikolai Radovanovic and his deputy, Boris Bodinski.*' Robson drew rapidly and repeatedly on his cigarette as he listened to the drum of the typewriter keys from the other end of the line. 'Okay? *Radovanovic, it is now believed, has recently been trying to turn previously loyal Bulgaria on to a Romanian-style course, independent of Moscow. He also seems to want to bolster up Bulgaria's lagging economy by encouraging more direct trading with the West, full stop. It's now clear that Bodinski is staunchly opposed to this policy, and is taking an increasingly aggressive and open pro-Soviet stance, full stop. The dramatic collision of these two men and their factions in the presence of the Russian leadership at tomorrow's conference could have far reaching effects on the unity of the Warsaw Pact bloc, full stop* . . . better get that to Miller now before we go any further.'

Robson ran his pen quickly through the rest of the story, correcting and amending while the typist took the first page over to the night editor. He didn't notice the bedroom door opening quietly. 'Okay, ready for some more?'

'Guess who, Jonathan.'

The high American trill and the overpowering assault of expensive French perfume thrown on by the bucketful didn't leave him much room for error. 'Gloria, sweetheart, do you mind pissing off for a bit. I'm trying to dictate an extraordinarily exclusive story to London.'

'Charming!'

She took her hands from his eyes and came round in front of him. Without her dark glasses the pouches around her eyes looked like scar tissue. She still wore the open slit dress and was reminding him of it by holding her half-length mink coat carefully open with both hands. She leaned towards him until her breasts practically fell out of the front of the dress. 'Are we allowed to ask what this marvellous story is about, you ill-mannered, oafish Brit?'

The London copytaker was saying hello, hello, was he still there.

'Go away, Gloria, I'll tell you later.'

She swayed huffily towards the door. Then she stopped and turned on her impish, little girl face. 'Oh, Jonathan, I got this from that nice desk clerk. Look.' She took a key from her handbag and held it up. 'For the connecting door. See you later, huh?' She drew her mink tight around her, glowered at him theatrically from under her lowered false eye-lashes then turned and swept out, leaving the door open. Robson rolled his eyes desperately towards the ceiling and got up to close it behind her.

He put the rest of his story over quickly, hinting at the tension he'd sensed at the reception, detailing the personal background of the two Bulgarian leaders, their past relationships with Moscow and what steps the Kremlin might take to try and whip Radovanovic, the country and its Party back into line.

He put the telephone down, placed another cigarette between his lips and reached into his trouser pocket for his lighter. As he did so his hand closed round an unfamiliar package.

He drew out the little bundle of pink tissue and unwrapped the bath plug Beryl had given him that morning. He held it up by the chain and stared at it thoughtfully.

He got up and went through to the bathroom. The big old-fashioned bath had large iron faucets – and its own plug on its own chain. Times had really changed. Robson tried Beryl's plug in the hole anyway and turned on the hot tap. The water ran quickly out round the edges of the plug. It was too small. He removed it and dropped it into the wastebin beside the lavatory. The end of Beryl, the end of her bath plug.

He suddenly felt weary and wrung out. It seemed several days since he'd left London – left her. The delayed flight, the 'crash' landing, the reception, the defector at the residence. Had all that happened within just a few hours?

He pulled off all his clothes, remembered Gloria in the next room and locked the bathroom door. He checked it again before he stepped into the steaming bath.

With only his head above water he began going back over the events of the day.

Had he really been right to harden up what he'd seen and heard pass between the ambassador and the two Bulgarian leaders into an outright 'power struggle' story? Radovanovic's reference to Bodinski might have been ambiguous but he wouldn't have written the story if Georgina Morakova hadn't confirmed the impression that something very big was afoot in Sofia . . . Christ, of course he was right! Don't start doubting your professional instincts now. There were enough bloody imponderables.

But why had that sniffy bastard, Miller, whom he'd never met or heard of, had it in for him? The world seemed full of people these days who hated and intrigued for no reason at all. Forget him. Miller wasn't important. Clearly something very strange indeed was going on in Sofia. And one thing was sure. Crack it ahead of the opposition and there would be no problem about landing the Vienna bureau. It would re-establish his reputation quickly in his area of specialization. On the other hand if his power struggle story turned out badly he might be expelled from Bulgaria . . .

He woke up shivering and coughing. The freezing cold bath water had begun seeping into his mouth.

As he stood up spluttering he saw the handle of the bathroom door turning silently. He stepped out of the bath and grabbed a towel. His teeth were chattering with cold. He began towelling himself vigorously.

'It's locked, Gloria, for God's sake. I'm having a bath!' He yelled loudly through the door and went on working with the towel to restore warmth to his chilled body. 'I'll see you down in the bar in ten minutes. Buy me a double Scotch!'

No wisecrack came in reply. The handle was still now and there was only silence from the bedroom. He held the towel around himself with one hand, opened the door and looked out.

The bedroom was empty. He padded barefoot over to the connecting door to Gloria's room. It was still locked. He ran to the bedroom door and wrenched it open.

The wide corridor outside was quiet and deserted.

Fourteen

Zhermatov belched loudly, wiped the last traces of Bulgarian goat's cheese from his moustache and handed the sheaf of papers back to his assistant. He waved his hand dismissively. 'Drunken ravings. Western hacks always invent power struggle stories when they can't find out anything else.'

His young assistant didn't reply. He had transcribed and translated Robson's dispatch with a growing sense of apprehension. He had also transcribed the exchanges between Robson and Miller in London and the female who had interrupted, but without making much sense of them, or learning any new words – except 'pissing off'.

'Shall I photocopy these for usual distribution, Captain?' His voice was wary after the unauthorized instruction to burn the residence tape. A nagging worry was growing in the back of his mind that the secrecy which Zhermatov had sworn him to might be connected with the power struggle Robson had written about. And if it was, he was afraid that he might already be getting involved against his will on one side or the other.

'Yes, usual full distribution. If that story has gone to London it will be disseminated all over the world in half an hour – it will be on the BBC World Service, the Voice of America, Radio Free Europe and all the other capitalist propaganda outlets by midnight. There's no reason why we should try to keep it from anybody here.'

The younger man hesitated, remembering Zhermatov's earlier warning. 'Do you ... do you think any of it's true, Captain Zhermatov?'

The fat man's face clouded with anger. 'I said it before, I say it again for the last time. Don't ask to know, just do as you are told.'

Zhermatov pushed his plate away among the debris on his cluttered desk, brushed the remaining crumbs of the bread and cheese from the front of his double-breasted jacket and reached for the telephone. He dialled a number and the thin nervous voice of the carpenter in the basement came on the line.

'How is your work going, Comrade?'

'I shall finish the lid within the hour, Comrade Captain. Then it will only be a matter of the quilting, padding and ventilating to make it comfortable . . .'

'Yes, yes. What time do you think it will be finished?'

'By three o'clock in the morning, I should say, Comrade Captain. Is that soon enough?' He still sounded worried about becoming the occupant of his finished product.

'Just complete it as fast as you can,' said Zhermatov brusquely and hung up.

As he rose from his chair, one of the bank of voice-activated recording spools monitoring the Hotel Balkan began to spin. The young Trichkov ran over to it and turned up the voice of Ben Bradley dictating his news copy to the *American Herald* in Paris. As he was adjusting the distort-control, the fat fist of Zhermatov reached across the machine and punched down on the cut-off switch. 'We don't need to bother with Bradley any more.' He turned and walked towards the door. 'I'm going out for an hour or so,' he said without looking back.

The young man listened apprehensively as Zhermatov double-locked the door from the outside. His elephantine footsteps echoed for a long while along the corridor before they finally died away.

Robson slipped quietly into the crowded bar of the Hotel Balkan and took a seat at the shadowy end of the counter. He was concentrating on avoiding the boisterous group of correspondents that had congregated at the far end of the long room.

He'd decided to try and stay out of their way because some of them would soon be getting urgent calls from their foreign editors in London asking them to check out the exclusive power struggle story that they were getting in Fleet Street on their BAPPA new service teleprinters.

Fleet Street papers hated using agency copy if they had their own men on the story. And, if asked to do a follow-up, their men on the spot would first make a bee-line for the agency man who'd filed the original, to try to find out what it was all about. If they couldn't find him, their editors might use his story with his BAPPA by-line on it – which was bad for them but good for him. So Robson had made up his mind: a quick placatory drink with Gloria, a snatched meal in the restaurant, if it was still open, then back to bed with the telephone off the hook and a 'Do Not Disturb' sign on his door.

He ordered a large Scotch and, without much hope, some hot water with it because he was still shivering from waking up in the freezing bath.

The barman nodded his head apologetically.

'Never heard of hot water in whisky on a cold night, Comrade?' asked Robson with mock incredulity.

The barman nodded his head again sadly. 'For five hundred years . . .' he began.

'Yes, I know', said Robson, patting his hand. 'Those damned Turks have got a lot to answer for . . .' He handed over a small fortune in *leva* and *stotinki* for the Scotch and, still trying to remain inconspicuous, sipped it without looking round. It wasn't difficult because, in addition to the group of journalists, there were in the bar the usual sprinkling of Western businessmen, mainly Germans, and a large Russian package tour group. The Russians were responsible for most of the noise that was being made. There was no sign of Gloria.

He was wondering idly where she was when out of the side of his eye he saw a pair of sturdy bovine ankles arrive at the foot of the next stool but one. He recognized them immediately. The last time he'd seen them they had been walking along the aisle of the Balkanair Tupolev, supporting the heavily-muscled body of the Amazon air stewardess.

Now they were easing their owner up onto the stool and her skirt was rucking up sufficiently in the process to make him more certain than ever that his guess on the plane about those heavy rippling thigh muscles and whipcord calves had been correct. 'Legs like that could only have been built for the 1976 Bulgarian Olympic Squad,' said Robson brightly. 'But don't tell me! It's a field event . . . er . . . shot or discus, yes?'

She gave him a hostile stare as if she hadn't heard, then looked away over his shoulder. When the barman came over, she ordered a soft drink and paid for it.

'Trainer's orders, eh?' said Robson and clucked his tongue sympathetically. But still she ignored him and after taking a sip from the drink she climbed down from the stool and strode away in the direction of the juke box that stood in a shadowy corner of the bar. She was fully six feet tall in her flat-heeled shoes.

Robson turned and watched her bend over to peer at the song titles. Her muscular backside jutted towards a fat Bulgar sitting beside the juke box in the gloomy corner. Grinning lasciviously, he reached out, patted it and uttered a low inaudible remark. The air hostess turned and gave him a furious scowl before moving out of range and turning back to the task of selecting the record she was looking for. Although Robson was watching closely it was too dark for him to see that a card had changed hands.

As the stewardess returned to her stool the scratchy strains of the Beatles yelling 'She's Got a Ticket to Ride' followed her across the bar.

'You'd lose marks too for your out-of-date records on the juke box,' said Robson.

The barman shrugged. 'At least they're British, not Turkish!'

'Or Russian,' said Robson.

'Old songs are often the best songs,' said the hostess defiantly from her stool. The big girl tossed her head and Robson winked at the barman for want of something better to do. As he did so he picked up his drink and moved to the stool next to her, smiling broadly. 'So you spy on foreign visitors to Bulgaria in your spare time under the direction of your secret police coach in the corner, do you?' asked Robson loudly.

'I don't know what you talk about.' She continued to allow him only the benefit of her glowering profile.

'Ordinary Bulgarians aren't allowed in these big hotel bars. Only selected "glamour" girls who can suss out the visiting firemen.'

'I must go now.' The big Bulgarian stewardess climbed awkwardly down from the bar. She almost overbalanced and reached out to steady herself with one hand on Robson's stool.

'Watch out for another crash landing,' said Robson cheerfully.

She pressed her clenched fist hard against his knee. 'I'm sorry,' she said shortly. Still without looking at him she picked up her handbag and hurried out. Robson left the card that she'd slipped under his thigh where it was until he'd finished his drink. When he picked up his change from the bar he pushed the card in among the notes and put them into his wallet together. Then he climbed down from the stool and headed for the dining room. He stared into the shadows by the juke box as he went by. But Zhermatov had already gone.

The dining room was on the point of closing and the surly waiter looked at his watch pointedly as he showed Robson to a corner table. As he chose his meal he held the card the girl had given him carefully inside the menu with his thumb. The words on it were handwritten in red ballpoint. 'I will come to your room at midnight.' Robson put it back in his pocket, ordered *Kebapcheta*, pickled vegetables and a glass of Mavroud and decided that whatever the Amazon had in mind for tonight could go on without him. All he wanted was to eat, get back to his room and hang up that 'Do Not Disturb' sign.

He finished his meal quickly without being discovered by the rest of the press corps, took the lift to the floor above his own and walked quietly down the stairs. He peered round the corner of the corridor to satisfy himself that Gloria wasn't hanging about waiting to pounce, then tiptoed swiftly to his door.

The bathroom light was on. He didn't remember leaving it on. But then he didn't remember switching it off, either. He pressed the switch of the main bedroom — but it remained in darkness. So, Turkish influence was still strong in the light bulb factories!

He shrugged and undressed in the faint light from the bathroom, flinging his clothes on to a chair in the gloom. It was cold enough in the room to make him shiver again. He returned quickly to the bathroom to clean his teeth, rinse his face and comb his hair. Then he hung the sign outside the door, locked it, switched out the light, and fumbled his way carefully across the darkened bedroom. He removed the telephone receiver and got into bed.

It was a double bed and he pounded the pillows into a shape he liked before settling down with the covers pulled high round his ears. As he relaxed his memory immediately produced a spontaneous and vivid flashback of Beryl in bed with him eighteen hours before. He dismissed the image before it could take too strong a hold. He pulled the covers tighter around his shoulders and shifted to a new position, determined to sleep quickly. But something pressing between his shoulder blades abruptly drove all thoughts of sleep from his mind.

Fifteen

He didn't move for fully thirty seconds. His body was held rigid by the shock. But the room remained still and quiet. He realized suddenly, he was holding his breath. Then he remembered the connecting door and relaxed.

'Gloria!'

He half shouted her name in a mixture of exasperation and relief. He turned over quickly, flung back the covers and reached out in the darkness.

His hand encountered the slack flesh of one of her breasts. But she didn't move or respond. He touched her neck, her face, her hair, then withdrew his hand. She was utterly still and her body was neither warm nor cold.

He pressed the switch of the bedside lamp but no light came on. He rushed to the bathroom, turned on the light there and ran back. Gloria was sprawled half on her back, half on her side in the bed. She wasn't wearing a stitch of clothing. Even in the half darkness he could sense she was dead.

He checked for pulse, heartbeat and breathing, knowing it was futile, then stood back staring down at her. Reluctantly he reached for the bedside telephone. At first he couldn't understand why the receiver was missing. Then he remembered he'd removed it. He groped around, picked it up, raised it to his ear – then changed his mind and put it back again. He sat down on the bed staring. The bulb had been removed from the bedside light.

He ran into the bathroom again unscrewed the bowl of the second light over the mirror, removed the bulb and returned to the bedroom to fit it into the empty socket. He switched the lamp on and looked down at Gloria's lined, heavily made-up face. Her eyes were closed and her face was strangely composed.

He realized only slowly that he was shivering violently. He went to the wardrobe and got out his long, towelling dressing gown. He took the bottle of Queen Anne whisky into the bathroom and poured a measure into a toothbrush glass. He drank it down, standing by the washbasin. When he'd stopped shaking, he rinsed the glass distractedly and returned to the bed. He peered closely at the dead American woman. He could see no signs of violence about the head or neck. He pulled the cover right back from her.

Her long, heavily tanned body was unmarked too – except by time. Heavy dieting had left her lanky frame bony and wasted-looking around the paler area of her pelvis, and the blonde-streak dye she used on her hair needed attention. Her feet were, strangely, the youngest-looking part of her body, small, neat and smooth. The toe-nails were painted bright scarlet. But the fierce sun which she'd hoped would rejuvenate her had accelerated the wrinkling march of time across her face and her white lolling breasts were lined with age creases too. A sense of desolation engulfed him. Gloria Zuckermann looked like a crumpled puppet which had had its strings cut without warning.

Suddenly he could see the faces of the Bulgarian police as they peered, prodded and photographed her body, stripped not only of its life, but of all dignity too.

He turned and ran to check the connecting door. It was unfastened. In her room Gloria had spread out half an acre of creams and cosmetics across the dressing table. Her hairbrushes, mirrors and sprays were scattered on chairs and tables and a pair of expensive silk pyjamas were laid out on the bed beside a white, fur-trimmed négligé. It was as if she hadn't been able to decide how to dress for the wait in his bed – and then had decided on nothing at all.

He took the silk pyjamas back to his room, dressed her in them, then carried her back through the connecting door and put her in her own bed. The key for the connecting door was still in the lock on Gloria's side. He put his hand in his dressing-gown pocket before grasping it and locking the door. Finally he removed the key altogether and put it in her handbag.

He listened carefully at the door into the corridor for several minutes. When he was sure it was absolutely empty, he stepped out, leaving Gloria's door closed but unlocked, and returned to his own room. At least now she'd be found respectably clad in her own bed. He'd arranged her so she appeared to be sleeping.

There were other good reasons for making the switch, too, he'd told himself as he went about his grim task. However honest and straightforward he was with the Bulgarian police, he was bound to be deeply involved in the enquiries, almost certainly treated as a suspect if she was found in his room. Even if he weren't, there was the inevitable gossip and scandal. Harry Zuckermann wasn't going to be pleased with him and he had no desire to make an enemy of that very rich man. It wouldn't help him at home either. The BAPPA board wouldn't thank him for dragging the agency into that kind of story – and it would probably write *finis* as far as the Vienna job was concerned. He had suddenly realized, as he was humping Gloria's body through the connecting door, how much he wanted Vienna now. What else was there?

While he was arranging the corpse in the bed he was horrified afresh not only by her death but also by his own cold-blooded selfishness. At one point he found himself remembering that there would now be no prospect of an interest-free loan from Zuckermann Diamonds Inc. Almost immediately he genuinely turned full circle and regretted having been such a callous, unaccommodating bastard to Gloria since her arrival in Sofia. He blamed himself for lacking generosity of spirit, compassion. But hell! Hadn't she been a middle-aged nymphomaniac who made a bloody public nuisance of herself? Was this what psychologists called survival remorse?

He had made one final careful inspection of Gloria's neck and face in the brighter lights of her room. The thought had crossed his mind then that perhaps, incredible though it seemed, she had simply died of 'natural causes' while waiting in his bed for him to come upstairs. A simple heart attack. It was still an outside possibility; against it, Gloria had seemed full of her own particular brand of rude health earlier that night.

Even after a very close scrutiny he had not been able to see any sign of what might have caused her death. The only mark of any kind had been a slight reddening of the skin between her eyebrows. But that was so faint it might have been caused by her eyebrow tweezers.

Robson began dressing. Subconsciously he knew he couldn't get back into bed and sleep. He poured the remainder of the bottle of Queen Anne into the toothbrush glass and filled it to the brim with water. He drank it down, leaning on the washbasin staring at his white face in the bathroom mirror. It was while he was looking at himself that the obvious struck him for the first time. It began in his mind as a faint possibility, then hardened more rapidly into a seeming certainty.

Gloria had been killed in his bed. She had been mistaken for him.

He saw his face tauten in the mirror as the knocking on his door began. He stood frozen to the spot for a second, then moved quickly to turn out the bathroom light.

He waited quietly in the dark. After a break the knocking continued, insistently. When at last it stopped, Robson strained his ears for the sound of footsteps going away down the corridor. Instead came a heavily accented woman's voice – one that he knew.

'If you don't open the door, Mr Robson, I shall scream until the whole hotel comes running.'

He remembered the card she had slipped to him in the bar.

Noiselessly he walked to the door. He opened it. Wearing a long winter coat and boots, smiling triumphantly, she leant against the far wall of the corridor. The smile never left her as three men materialized from behind the door, grabbed Robson, and dragged him quickly towards the back stairs of the hotel.

In the office in Whitehall to which the bright yellow envelopes marked 'Cranbourne' had been delivered throughout the day, a night-duty man finished reading the BAPPA nightlead from Sofia. He pulled aside an expensive cuff to consult his gold watch. Nearly midnight. He sighed. The Old Man had said only that he'd call in to see how everything was going 'before he turned in'. Was he going to stay up all night? He yawned and at that moment the telephone rang and his superior came on the line.

'How's it going, Clarkson?'

'To plan, sir, it seems. Only one slight kink. Robson's broken out a pretty nifty power struggle story on his first night there which isn't far out at all . . .'

'I know, I heard it on the news,' said the voice irritably. 'What else?'

'Jymeson's report says it's working perfectly to plan, sir, no worries his end.'

'Hmph. I wonder. All right, goodnight.'

'Goodnight, sir.'

Clarkson stood up, yawned once more and took his coat from the peg behind the door. He checked his watch again. He'd just make the last underground to Cockfosters. He turned out the light and closed the door behind him. Outside in Whitehall, sleet was turning to a fine soaking drizzle as he hurried towards Westminster Tube Station.

Sixteen

The two Bulgarians in fur hats and greatcoats sitting on either side of Robson in the back seat of the Volga said nothing. They had spoken no word since seizing him outside his bedroom door. They had used a minimum of violence very effectively and Robson sat quietly between them, flexing his fingers and massaging his wrists. The third man drove.

They had made no attempt to manacle or silence him. Their behaviour and their expressions did both jobs effectively.

Robson looked out at the long, dark cobbled street along which they were driving about a mile north-east of the hotel. He recognized the Hristo Smyrnenski Museum which housed the works of Bulgaria's most vaunted working class poet. He had visited it once when the poet's name figured prominently in a cultural purge.

No lights shone in the windows of the dilapidated houses. If any of Sofia's workers were quartered in them, they were certainly all asleep, refreshing themselves for another day of building socialism. Halfway along the street a dozen houses had been pulled down and the gaunt shells of two unfinished high-rise apartment blocks were already growing to fill the toothless gap.

The car stopped by the building site. The street was both empty and silent; the cold seemed to have frozen all noise. The pavements were solid with hard-trodden snow and Robson slipped and slithered between his escorts as they pulled him from the car and across the open ground between the two half-finished buildings. High above, giant cranes on the twin blocks were just visible standing out like great irregular crucifixes against the freezing dark sky.

Robson shivered as he stumbled through the deep snow of the building site, propelled by the three men. He had had no time to grab his coat before they rushed him from the hotel. They were making for a small builder's hut in the corner of the site. Robson could see the red glow of a watchman's brazier flickering through the dirty window. A few steps short of the door the three men stopped and released his arms.

Puzzled, he looked round into their dark faces. One motioned him forward towards the door of the hut with a nod of his head. Robson stepped away from them and put his hand on the latch of the door. Then he stopped and looked round to make sure. The man gesticulated for him to open it.

He swung the door open and stepped inside, leaving the three men standing in an arc in the snow.

The only light in the shack came from the glowing coal brazier. Beside it stood a table cluttered with dirty coffee cans and papers. The rest of the shack was piled high with bags of cement and building tools.

Robson, still shivering, stepped quickly across to the fire, stretching out his hands towards the warmth. He recognized the pungent aroma of Bulgarian cheroot smoke a second before the rotund bulk of Captain Zhermatov emerged into the firelight from the shadows behind the cement bags. His gnome-like head looked even more enormous in a massive fur hat with ear muffs tied across the crown. He dropped the cheroot he was smoking on the floor and squashed it with his heel. He looked at Robson thoughtfully as he removed the heavy riding gauntlets he wore on his hands and unbuttoned the fur collar of his greatcoat. 'I'm glad you were able to come Mr Robson.'

His English was good despite his strong Slav accent. He reached inside his coat, withdrew a packet of cheroots and walked over to the brazier. He picked up a red coal with the stoking tongs and lit his cheroot with it. He continued staring at the journalist. 'Tanya persuaded you no doubt? A rare woman. Very strong. The strongest I have ever known.'

'She's not my type.' Robson chafed his bruised wrists vigorously over the fire. 'But from what I saw in the Balkan bar she clearly attracts anal fetishists like you and I'm prepared to believe she satisfies the sado-masochistic cravings of the entire Central Committee single-handed.'

Zhermatov puffed furiously on his cheroot without taking his eyes off Robson. Then he turned away to peer out through the grimy window. 'It's started snowing again,' he said softly. Robson stood looking at the back of his fat neck through the haze of smoke and waited.

'We understand you are keen to become head of the BAPPA office in Vienna, Mr Robson', said Zhermatov suddenly without turning round.

'How the hell do you know that?' Robson wasn't able to hide his astonishment.

'We have talked to Beryl.'

'Beryl! Where?'

'In London, in her dressing room at the Ocho Rios.'

'When?'

'A few hours ago. She was very helpful. A little puzzled, of course.' He still kept his back to Robson.

'You bastard . . . Who are you?'

'She is perfectly all right at present, I assure you. We took her flowers. She was most concerned to know if you were all right. We told her your health would remain good so long as she helped us with some information.'

'What do you want?'

'To help you get the Vienna job.'

'I don't need your help. What do you want in return?'

'To give you an exclusive story for your agency.'

'I'll try to manage without!'

Robson's Yorkshire accent, normally unrecognizable, was thickening noticeably now as his anger rose. Zhermatov took a large khaki handkerchief from his coat pocket and blew loudly into it. He patted and fussed his nose elaborately for a long time before putting it away. 'We have an old Bulgarian saying, Robson,' he said quietly 'You don't have to go to hell to light a cigarette.'

'Very pretty. We have an old English saying too.'

'Yes? What's that?' asked Zhermatov politely.

'Fuck off!'

Zhermatov walked over to the brazier and peered closely into the journalist's face. 'You are being very unwise, Robson.'

104

'Really?' Robson feigned astonishment but didn't move from the fire.

'Yes, really. Because if you don't accept my offer of exclusive information, we will not only not help you get Vienna . . .' He paused and leaned closer still. 'We will also make it impossible for you.'

'How do you propose to do that?'

Zhermatov stepped back and continued to study the correspondent's face in the light of the fire. 'With half a dozen telephone calls! To my colleagues in the Ministries of State Security in all the fraternal Socialist countries! Within twenty-four hours you will be *persona non grata* on a permanent basis throughout Eastern Europe. Would BAPPA want a man in Vienna who was banned from the area he's covering?'

'You bastard!'

There was another long silence. The wind was rising outside and the draught under the badly-fitting door made the fire glow suddenly brighter. 'You want to hear the story now? Rest assured you will make your name with headlines around the world with it.'

Robson took a deep breath. 'What sort of story?'

'A murder story.'

'Whose?'

Zhermatov's voice was flat, expressionless. 'One of our leading Comrades.'

Robson kept his eyes fixed on Zhermatov's face. 'Which one?'

The Bulgarian didn't answer.

'Whose team are you on? Bodinski's or Radovanovic's?'

The glowing coke shifted suddenly and let a shower of red ash fall noisily into the catch-pan underneath. Zhermatov stared down at it, wide eyed, deep in thought. When he raised his head again to look at Robson his lips retreated suddenly from his teeth as though he were in pain. 'That is the most dangerous question anyone can ask in Bulgaria tonight, Robson.'

'Did Gloria Zuckermann ask somebody that question – is that why you had her killed?'

The Bulgarian cocked his head on one side for a second like a puzzled dog. 'Gloria Zuckermann?'

105

'An American journalist. Dead in Room 410 in the Balkan Hotel.' Robson watched the swarthy face carefully but it betrayed nothing.

Zhermatov fumbled inside his coat, pulled out a ballpoint pen and a tiny note pad, wrote down the room number, and put them away again. Then he clasped his hands behind his back and walked over to the window again. Outside the snow-fall had become a blizzard.

'Where and when is this murder of a "leading comrade" to take place?'

'At the Party Congress in the morning.'

Robson stiffened. 'How will your official propaganda organs deal with the Comrade's disappearance?'

'A resignation on the grounds of ill-health will be officially announced afterwards,' said Zhermatov shortly. 'You will be the only one in a position to reveal the whole truth to the world. You will attribute your story simply to "well-informed sources".'

'When do I get the details?'

'In the morning. Half an hour after the Congress has gone into its closed session.'

'Where?'

'You will go to the Dimitrov Mausoleum at ten thirty to survey the embalmed remains. You will be contacted in the crowd there.'

A sudden thought struck Robson. 'Do *you* know *who* is to die? Does the victim himself know yet?'

Zhermatov said nothing. His head wagged slightly but Robson couldn't tell whether he was nodding 'No' or shaking 'Yes'.

'What do you get out of it?'

'The truth will be known,' said Zhermatov quietly. 'My motives are the same as yours in this respect, Robson.'

'Bullshit!' Robson's voice rose incredulously. 'Since when have you "Comms" given a damn for truth?'

Zhermatov turned fiercely on him. 'Don't forget, Robson, that in this country we are not only communists but we are Bulgarians too.' He stopped, breathing fast. 'And we are very intolerant of those who cross us.'

The two men stared steadily at each other in the flickering light. 'There is much truth in legend, Robson,' said the secret

106

policeman softly. 'Do you know the story of the ancient Bulgar leader?'

'No, but I'm sure you're going to tell me.'

'God offered to give him anything he wished – with the proviso that he would also do the same *doubly* for his neighbour. So he said, "Lord then take out one of my eyes".'

The dying fire crackled in the silence. Robson turned to the coke bucket and refuelled it noisily. 'Thank you for the warning,' he said gravely, when he had put the bucket back in its place. 'I'll make sure I never move in next to a Bulgarian.'

Zhermatov was looking at him speculatively. 'Do you see the sense now of accepting my generous offer?'

'What about if I don't want the Vienna job badly enough to get involved in your murderous games?'

'You will. You are a survivor, Robson. We have gone fully into your background. You foolishly lost your financial independence in the insane capitalist *débâcle* of Poseidon. You need a job. You need money badly. Your system in the West puts pressure on the individual to bite and claw to provide himself with a selfish living.' He sighed. 'But you will see the truth and sense of history in the end. You will all become communists one day, Robson . . .'

At that moment the door of the shack burst open and two uniformed soldiers armed with Kalashnikov automatic rifles burst in followed by a great flurry of snow. 'Quick, Captain Zhermatov! Come quickly,' the first one yelled.

The secret police chief swung furiously on the men, screaming at the top of his voice. 'Get out! Get out!'

'But Captain . . .' When they saw his furious face, his bulging neck, they went as fast as they'd come, slamming the door hurriedly behind them.

'Before you go, *Captain Zhermatov*,' said Robson heavily, 'why don't you tell me what's really going on? Why the fake crash landing, why does a KGB colonel want to defect to London?'

Zhermatov leaned forward suddenly across the brazier until his face was close enough to Robson's for the journalist to smell the rancid goat's cheese on his breath. 'At the end of it all, Robson, everything will become perfectly clear to you — if you are still alive.'

He pulled on his riding gauntlets and glared at the journalist. 'Ten thirty at the mausoleum,' he said and turned and rushed out of the shack into the snow, shouting furiously after the soldiers.

Robson heard the sound of a jeep start up and roar away along the street. The sound of its engine faded quickly into the distance, leaving the night even more emphatically silent than before.

Four miles away in an apartment block in the southern suburbs reserved for Bulgaria's top leadership, a uniformed general who commanded the First Bulgarian Army, and therefore the Sofia garrison, paced distractedly back and forth across his sitting room. Several times he stopped indecisively by the telephone, made as if to pick up the receiver and make a call, then changed his mind.

When the loud hammering on the door began he didn't even seem surprised. And when the knocking stopped and the door suddenly splintered and crashed inwards, the general found himself facing a resident KGB captain whom he knew quite well. Behind him five Bulgarian men and half a dozen armed soldiers crowded into the flat.

The Bulgarian general looked at them coolly for a moment. Then he sprang across the room. The Russian KGB man shouted an oath and rushed after him.

The general skidded through the hall, crashed against the side of the open door, recovered his balance, lurched into the bathroom and closed and locked the door behind him. The troops kicked and beat it down with their rifle butts in four seconds. But when they entered, the room was empty. The Russian KGB captain moved to the open window and looked out.

Seven stories below a dark twisted shape, blacker than the surrounding shadows, lay motionless on the snow.

Not far away in the most luxurious apartments of all, built exclusively for members of the Party Politburo, a telephone rang. The grim-faced middle-aged man who picked it up listened wordlessly to the excited voice on the other end. Then the line went dead. But he did not replace the telephone immediately. He stood holding the receiver to his ear for fully a minute longer, staring dully at the wall. Then he replaced it and crossed quickly to the bedroom where his wife was sleeping to close the door. He took a revolver from a drawer in the hall and checked that it was loaded. Then he walked into the bathroom, shut the door firmly behind him, and put the cold barrel of the gun into his mouth.

Twice as he trudged back to the hotel through the darkened side streets, with his jacket collar turned up around his ears, Robson caught sight of jeeps, filled to overflowing with armed security troops, flashing across lighted main road junctions ahead of him. Occasionally a shiny black Russian Zil limousine roared by with curtains drawn across its windows. He stopped several times to listen, half expecting to hear the sound of gunfire. But no other sound broke the still of Sofia's wintry darkness.

PART TWO

Congress

Seventeen

Pale winter sunshine glinted on the fresh morning snow and the dull blue barrels of the Kalashnikov automatic cradled in the arms of the security guards ringing the Bulgarian Communist Party Centre on the north side of Deveti Septemvri Square.

Most of the two thousand delegates to the opening of the Party's Eleventh Congress were already inside the hideous Stalinist structure that spans the space of several blocks in Sofia's city centre. The square on to which it faces commemorates the Russian-backed military take-over of the ninth of September 1944 which has since become transfigured in the official Bulgarian memory as a Socialist revolution.

The armed guards scrutinized the credentials of late-comers to the Congress with the same slow, double-check thoroughness which they'd inflicted on every single pass-bearer who had gone before. Two of them spent four minutes each going over Robson's Congress badge, his press accreditation and his passport before they reluctantly let him through. Even after they had cleared him, they continued to eye him with deep suspicion and watched him every inch of the way as he walked up the steps.

He was stopped seven times more in the corridors and on staircases for further checks before he arrived among the other dozen or so Western journalists on a balcony overlooking the main hall. As he took his seat he failed to notice that Tsai Mei-li was staring fixedly at him from her place in the adjoining gallery for diplomatic observers. Her face was drained of colour.

'Hi, Jon, thought you'd defected.' Ben Bradley slapped him on the shoulder in greeting.

'Not till next Wednesday.'

'Hey, you know something, Jon? They dragged one of the American staffers from UPI off half an hour ago for questioning. Know what for? They said, "Are you carrying a weapon?" and he, being a wise guy said, "No. Do I need one to cover this Congress?" and wouf! he's just got back this minute.'

Robson grunted and stared down at the sea of communist heads below. Over the platform hung three great red banners on which white lettered slogans ten feet high expressed the wishes that 'the Great and Glorious Bulgarian Communist Party', 'the Eternal Friendship with our Brothers of the Soviet Union', and 'Marxism-Leninism' would all enjoy great longevity. Giant portraits of Marx, Engels, Lenin and Georgi Dimitrov flanked the empty dais.

'Where's your beautiful friend, Gloria, this morning, Jon, huh?' Bradley leered and banged Robson heartily on the back again. 'Keep you up most of the night, did she, fellah?'

'I haven't seen her since last night, Ben.'

It was the truth. On arrival back in his room in the Balkan he'd written up his notes before falling into two hours of troubled sleep, fully dressed. He half woke when he thought he heard a quiet movement in the next room. But he'd dismissed it as a dream. At seven he woke properly and checked. Her room was empty. It had been cleaned, fresh towels had been laid out, and the bed was made up with fresh linen. There was no sign of Gloria Zuckermann's body or any of her belongings. He remembered then the careful note of the room number that Zhermatov had made in his book.

'Look here, Robbie old boy, this isn't good enough, you know.' The *Times* correspondent detached himself from a group of journalists from TASS and IZVESTIA and grabbed Robson's elbow. 'Had a bloody call back from London on your story in the middle of the night. Hitting this power struggle angle up pretty hard, aren't you?'

'I don't think so, Simon, maybe not hard enough.'

'Nobody else is saying it, you know. I had to bloody well tell them to run your BAPPA piece in today's paper if they really wanted the story. I wasn't going to start trying to match those insane ravings of yours in the middle of the night. Come on, what's it all about? Where's your evidence?'

At that moment the subdued roar of the delegates in the hall below quietened suddenly. All the journalists turned to crane forward over the balcony as the door at the side of the dais opened and a group of men in dark suits began filing out.

As one man, the two thousand delegates began to clap furiously, craning up in their seats to catch their first glimpse of the real, live walking body of the leader of one of the two most powerful

114

countries in the world, the First Secretary of the Communist Party of the Union of Soviet Socialist Republics.

The tall, bulky figure of Brezhnev marched sombrely beside Nikolai Radovanovic. The Russian's heavy jowled face bore its usual florid flush but his features were grimly set and unsmiling as he clapped his hands perfunctorily in response to the audience's applause. He didn't even glance at the more elegant figure of Radovanovic beside him. The Bulgarian leader walked with his handsome silver-quiffed head determinedly erect and he too clapped back at the Congress without a flicker of expression on his sternly set face.

'He looks more "condemned cell" than ever this morning,' whispered Bradley. 'Do you really think he's for the chop?'

Robson shrugged impatiently, giving all his attention to the line of men now mounting the steps to the rostrum.

The square, stocky figure of Boris Bodinski walked one pace behind the leading pair, his brown bald head weaving slightly from side to side as though trying to conduct a final and conclusive personal security screening on every last individual in the crowded hall. Beside him walked the quick, ferret-like figure of the bespectacled East German party leader, Erik Honecker. He was gazing at the back of Brezhnev's head with the same kind of rapt adoration he had always shown in the presence of Walter Ulbricht – until he finally overthrew him. The mournful face of Hungary's Janos Kadar pressed close behind. He marched in step with the tough little Romanian, Ceasescu, whose permanently quizzical, puzzled expression gave little outward hint of the iron political will that had made him all-powerful in Romania.

The Chinese and Albanian leaders were, as usual, conspicuous by their absence. The Bulgarian Politburo and leading officers of the Central Committee secretariat followed behind. The line of men filed to their seats on the platform under the banners and portraits, and turned to face the body of the hall. They stood unsmiling, clapping perfunctorily at the delegates who rose to their feet, applauding even harder in their turn. The Russian and East European journalists in the press gallery stood up and began clapping furiously too.

Robson, Bradley, the *Times* man and other Western correspondents kept their hands pointedly in their pockets or behind their backs. A few were taking photographs for their own private albums. Two photographers from *Time Magazine* and *Paris Match* had been allowed down in the hall with a handful of official communist cameramen and were snapping away furiously with their telephoto lenses from a roped-off square twenty yards from the platform. But after precisely four minutes, the two Western photographers and their communist colleagues were ushered unceremoniously from the hall. At the same time the groups of newsmen and diplomats on the observation balconies were approached by civilian ushers wearing red arm bands and bulky bulges under their left armpits. A few of the uncrowned communist heads of Eastern Europe glanced up incuriously to watch the journalists go.

Within two minutes the photographers and reporters were gathered neatly into a government bus outside ready to be driven back to the press centre. There they would have to sit and wait for the official announcements and whatever versions of the main speeches the authorities chose to grant them.

The heavy doors swung closed behind them and the Eleventh Congress of the Communist Party of the People's Republic of Bulgaria began its proceedings on behalf of its eight million inhabitants under the habitual communist cover of total and absolute secrecy.

'I can hardly bear to miss "The Report on the New Drive for High Social Labour Productivity",' said Bradley, glancing down the Congress agenda as the bus pulled away across the square. He grinned at Robson over his gold-rimmed glasses. 'Where do you think the real guts of this Congress will lie, Jon?'

Robson leaned over and pointed a finger at an item halfway down the paper. Bradley read it aloud: '"Report by the Central Control and Auditing Commission of the Central Committee on Party Discipline". Beneath such rigmarole do the seeds of high human drama lie, Jon, huh?' Bradley shook his head. 'You could have fooled me.'

Robson looked out of the bus towards the square-pillared Dimitrov Mausoleum, standing several hundred yards beyond the Party Centre. The squat, single-storey, modern building looked like the base and bottom tier of a grey-brown architectural wedding cake from which the upper tiers had been removed. The security cordon for the Congress stopped short of the Mausoleum and the regular contingent of soldiers in their comic-opera Balkan uniforms were on duty. A thin, straggling line of tourists and provincial Bulgarians queued outside as usual, waiting to file past the embalmed remains in the glass casket inside. Robson sat back in his seat and looked at his watch. He felt tense and on edge. It was ten fifteen.

As he climbed slowly up towards the balcony from which the newspapermen had watched the Congress assemble, Zhermatov nodded curtly to each of the tense-faced men who stood guard on either side of the staircase. He'd hand picked all of them carefully for their personal loyalty to himself. Their eyes watched his carefully for any inflection of expression that might tell them something of the tense inter-party conflict they knew was now near to a climax.

He occasionally addressed a word or two to a guard and got a quick and eager shake of the head in reply.

He still wore his fur-collared greatcoat and his over-large fur hat but only one of the heavy riding gauntlets. He carried the other one, leaving his right hand free. With his great head he motioned the three guards standing at the balcony above the podium to move back into the shadows of the staircase. They retreated and stood with the other guards at the top of the stairs watching silently as he put his ungloved hand inside his coat and moved closer to the rails. He looked down and for an instant his eyes met those of Boris Bodinski. Bodinski held his gaze, nodded once almost imperceptibly, then looked away. As he did so Radovanovic rose to his feet and placed a sheaf of papers on the wooden lectern from which all speakers would address the Congress. Suddenly he held both arms aloft in a dramatic gesture. 'Comrades,' he shouted, 'long live the great and glorious Communist Party of Bulgaria.'

An enthusiastic roar of approval rolled back at him from the auditorium. Still holding his arms aloft he leaned closer to the microphone to make his voice heard above the continuing cheering and applause.

'Long live Marxism-Leninism!'

The cheers rose to a new intensity again. On the platform Brezhnev glanced up at the banners and his face darkened. He turned and fixed his eyes on the back of Radovanovic's head and waited angrily for the next slogan.

'Long live the Fraternal Co-operation of all *independent* Communist Parties throughout the World!'

Brezhnev stiffened in his chair. His fists gripped the arm rests tightly. Even louder cheering and applause greeted the heretical slogan which for the first time in thirty years had stressed independence and failed to acknowledge the supreme and unshakeably close friendship between Bulgaria and the Soviet Union.

Up by the pillar of the balcony, Zhermatov loosened his hand inside his coat.

Radovanovic still stood with his arms raised – but now he was beginning to make flattening movements with his hands, asking for quiet. His eyes were bright, his body tense with excitement.

'Comrades, a new era in the history of our party is about to begin . . .'

The sharp explosive crack of three pistol shots rang out from the balcony where Zhermatov stood. The hands of one of the leaders flew to his chest. Red blood stains spread quickly out around his fingers as he slipped down on to the platform in a crumpled heap.

As if in response to an unseen signal, doctors and stretcher bearers ran forward quickly from the side of the hall to tend the fallen man.

Eighteen

It took Robson fifteen minutes to walk back from the press centre to the Dimitrov Mausoleum. The queue winding into the doorway had dwindled to fewer than a dozen when he joined it. Snow lay thickly on the ledge above the door. It was from this miniature podium that the Bulgarian leaders saluted the annual celebratory May Day parades as they marched across the brownstone cobbles of Deveti Septemvri – a tiny Toytown copy of Red Square and the

Lenin tomb.

His palms were sweating in his pockets by the time he turned into the gloomy entrance to the Mausoleum. Several men in fur hats and heavy mufflers joined the queue behind him as he waited. Their breath steamed in the cold, bright air and they stamped their feet and looked around at nothing, waiting.

The soldiers at the door clutched their rifles close to their legs and, without turning their heads, watched the crowd from the corners of their eyes.

Inside, the darkness was lit mostly by the illumination directed onto the remains of a man who'd died twenty-five years before. The crowd shifted forward under the eyes of black-coated mausoleum attendants, pausing without actually stopping. Most of those ahead of Robson passed in an awed, eerie silence.

The cold pickled flesh that the communist soul of Georgi Dimitrov had once inhabited lay on its back, dressed in a grey single-breasted suit, its hands folded across its chest. An embroidered coverlet came halfway up its middle.

Robson glanced around. Everybody in the line was still staring dully into the glass case. He turned back to look himself.

The eyes were closed in the sallow waxen face but one ear looked as if it had not been embalmed as well as the rest of him and the lobe was ragged as if a small part of it had rotted away. His moustache was black, streaked with grey, and like the hair of his head, looked to Robson as if it might have been dyed surreptitiously at regular intervals over the years.

The line shifted forward suddenly, closing up a gap. There were now about six men and women between Robson and the observation point nearest to Georgi Dimitrov's lifeless head. He glanced at his watch. Ten thirty. He had booked an urgent 'Blitz' call to London for ten forty-five from his room in the Balkan.

He looked over his shoulder. The queue had grown again and it stretched back through the door. He scanned the faces in the gloom. All men, all fur-hatted. All avoided his gaze.

Robson noticed that an unkempt figure with lank, shoulder-length hair behind him was, in defiance of a sign on the wall, smoking a cigarette. He drew on it furtively, keeping it cupped in his hands so that the attendants couldn't see it.

The line moved up a pace.

'Godammed hypocrites,' muttered the man as he moved forward. It was an American voice.

Robson wrinkled his nose. It was no ordinary cigarette the American was smoking.

'All the bastard ever did is out-talk Goering at the Reichstag Trial.' Robson glanced round but nobody else in the queue seemed to notice the drop-out tourist's mumbling. He moved another couple of paces nearer the glass-cased catafalque and stared ahead at the waxen face.

'Godammed Comintern intriguer . . . window dresser . . . that's all he was . . . godammed window dressing for the "'44 military coup".' The smoker took another drag on his cigarette. 'Why doesn't somebody tell the Bulgars that he was purged and yanked off to Moscow in '49 . . . tell 'em exactly how he died during the Stalinist terror?'

Robson shifted uneasily. The American's muttering was getting louder. 'Why don't they put Chervenkov in there too, eh? Poor bastard was disgraced for Dimitrov's crimes.'

'Shut up,' said Robson fiercely over his shoulder. 'Or they'll lock you up. This isn't bloody San Francisco.

The American scowled at him and took another surreptitious drag.

As Robson turned back, the short man in front of him suddenly grabbed the sleeve of his companion and pointed at Dimitrov. 'Look, his ear's rotten,' he exclaimed in a loud, surprised voice in Bulgarian. 'One ear's going!'

One of the black-coated attendants hurried forward, took the man by the arm and pulled him roughly out of the line. He propelled him rapidly towards the far door, speaking in a low insistent voice. At that moment another attendant spotted the American smoking the remains of his cigarette.

'No smoking in here!' he yelled suddenly. His voice echoed loudly in the sepulchral quiet of the Mausoleum. The smoker flinched and started backwards. The attendant lunged towards him, knocking into Robson and pushing him roughly against the glass side of the catafalque. As he stumbled back Robson felt a hand go into his overcoat pocket. Then the attendant recovered his balance, grabbed the American and started to frogmarch him away.

At that moment both entrance and exit doors of the Mausoleum slammed shut. All the lights except for a spotlight, shining directly on Dimitrov in the casket, went out. In the half darkness, the volley of shots exploded like a fast-cracking stockwhip. The attendant holding the American staggered and fell. The American, suddenly released, looked over his shoulder in surprise. Then he too flung back his head and sagged to the ground.

The orderly queue of people broke up into a confused, milling crowd in the semi-darkness. Some ran to the two fallen men, others stared apprehensively into the shadows by the doors. Robson put his hand into his overcoat pocket and felt a leather pouch that the attendant had slipped into it. Then a hand tugged at his sleeve and he spun round to see the man who'd shouted about Dimitrov's 'rotting ear' gesturing towards an area behind the glass catafalque. 'You must get away, quick, they've been shot,' he whispered. 'Bodinski's men are everywhere now.'

The little man scuttled off into the darkness and a moment later a small side door opened, letting in a shaft of daylight. Robson saw the man dash through, then the door slammed behind him.

Without looking round Robson himself made for the same door, and stepped out into the snow-covered gardens behind the Mausoleum. The little man had already disappeared among the sprinkling of mid-morning strollers in the small, tree-lined park.

Robson hurried down the length of one long avenue and came out on Gurko Street. He had planned to cut across the snow-covered flower beds to Sofijska Komuna but he didn't want to do anything to attract attention to himself now. He turned right along Gurko Street and made a detour to avoid turning in the direction of the Mausoleum. He hurried through Alabin Street, turned right along Car Kalojani and reached Alexander Stamolijski at the busy junction next to Lenin Square. He looked round then for the first time but could see nobody following him.

The blue-painted trams were rumbling and clanking through the cobbled streets packed with their human cargo. The stores were trading and housewives were humping their shopping bags homeward as though nothing could ever disturb the mundane rhythm of their lives.

Robson walked quickly up the steps to the front door of the Hotel Balkan and hurried through the empty lobby. Rather than wait for the lift, he ran up the stairs two at a time. In his room he flung off his coat and hat. He was sweating profusely. He took out the leather tobacco pouch and went into the bathroom. He closed the door and locked it, and opened the leather flap. Inside embedded in the dark Bulgarian tobacco was a single slip of lined paper.

On it were ten words written in ink in block capitals: 'RADO-VANOVIC SHOT DEAD ON PLATFORM TEN TWENTY-FIVE. UNKNOWN HAND.'

As he stared at it, the phone began ringing in the bedroom. He paused. All right, so he couldn't verify the story. Maybe they were using him, for what didn't matter. Old fashioned though the idea was, a scoop was a scoop. It could make Vienna a cert, couldn't it? He hesitated, then flushed the paper down the lavatory. When the London office of BAPPA came on the line he asked to be put straight through to the desk. Baird was duty editor.

'Listen Jock, don't ask any question, just write down what I say. This is a once-in-a-lifetime exclusive.'

'Okay, shoot,' said Baird, coolly.

'Sofia, Wednesday. *Nikolai Radovanovic, who has been trying to free Bulgaria from Moscow's heavy-handed rule, was today murdered on the platform of the Bulgarian Communist Party Congress.*'

'Christ almighty,' said Baird softly and wrote 'Flash' in large capitals above the story. He turned round quickly and handed the sheet of paper to the teleprinter operator sitting behind him. Before he had written the first word of Robson's next paragraph bells were ringing on teleprinters in the newsrooms of BAPPA's subscribers all round the world, drawing attention to the Sofia 'flash' that began running in immediately.

'*Highly placed East European intelligence sources told BAPPA's correspondent in Sofia that Radovanovic was shot dead by an unknown assassin as he addressed the opening session of the Congress at about ten thirty local time this morning.*'

Robson was drenched with sweat now. He half expected the line to go dead at any moment. Or for the door of his room to fly open to reveal men come to arrest him.

'Hold on, Jonathan', said Baird, and turned to give the second paragraph to the teleprinter operator. 'This sounds great, keep coming. I knew you'd do well out there.'

'The assassination must have happened minutes after correspondents left the Congress hall having watched the Soviet leader Leonid Brezhnev and Radovanovic take their seats with other East bloc leaders. Both Brezhnev and Radovanovic sat side by side looking grim and unsmiling as I left with the other correspondents.'

Baird again broke off briefly to give out the copy to the man on the teleprinter. 'Writing yourself a by-line into the story, eh Jon?'

'Look, Jock, this is a bloody exclusive I'm telling you!' shouted Robson anxiously. 'If we should get cut off now, just pick up background from my last night's story.'

'Sure Jon, sure.' The old man, from years of experience, was ice cool. 'Don't get prickly, it's a great story. Keep on giving us more, we're all having multiple orgasms on it, believe me.'

Baird heard Robson start to laugh despite the tension in himself. But the laughter cut abruptly when the line went dead. And it stayed dead despite all attempts by the BAPPA switchboard to reconnect with Sofia.

Nineteen

In the basement of Section S.14 (Monitoring) of the Bulgarian State Security Committee the little carpenter sat crouched on a stool by his bench, his wizened, nut-brown face screwed tight into concentric lines of anxiety. He chewed the skin inside his right cheek constantly and rubbed his hands rapidly together as if lathering them with invisible soap.

He kept his eyes carefully averted from the finished pine coffin that stood on the workbench above him. Its smooth surface shone dully from the impregnation of beeswax he had applied. The lid was in place and the ventilation holes he had made along the flanged lip of the lid were disguised with decorative studs.

He got up and hurried across the workshop for the twentieth time. He squeezed between the wall and the shiny black Zil hearse and tried the handle of the door in the wall. It was still locked, as he knew it would be.

He paced anxiously up and down the narrow cellar, still avoiding looking at the coffin which he had worked on through the night. Could he really be its intended occupant? There was no reason. He was too insignificant. He had never done anything wrong. Or had he unconsciously? Everybody did something wrong some time, didn't they? But he couldn't remember any single transgression. On the contrary, whenever he was called in to do work in the gloomy 'D.S.' building, he had always gone out of his way to ingratiate himself with everybody he encountered. His wife had urged him to do so for the family's sake. 'Do exactly as they say, Grisha,' she reminded him when she handed him his sandwich box at the door of their flat. 'Ask no questions, don't look left or right, do your best work and come straight home afterwards.' She said it every morning without fail.

For the hundredth time he thought back to the four-minute period when Zhermatov had come down to inspect the finished coffin at six o'clock that morning. He'd examined everything thoroughly but he had not spoken a word until he was going out of the door. Then he barked a simple order at him. 'For security reasons you will stay here until further notice, Comrade! Make yourself comfortable!'

The carpenter made another unsuccessful attempt to read his fate from those few words, then gave up and began biting the inside of his cheek again.

At eight o'clock some rancid goat's cheese and some stale bread had been brought in on a tray with a glass of natural yoghurt by a young man whom he'd not seen before. The bread and cheese still stood on the workbench by the coffin, because he had no appetite. He had gulped down the yoghurt eventually to quench his thirst. He was very tired, but he couldn't sleep. There was nowhere apart from the floor to lie down – unless he took the lid off the coffin and climbed into its quilted interior. And he recoiled in horror from the thought. He paused to pick up some shreds of the brown padding material from under the bench. He'd already swept up the wood shavings thoroughly. He shuddered. The cellar was cold now that he was no longer working.

He beat his arms against his sides to warm himself and wondered how much longer . . . His wife would be worried sick. He'd tried the telephone a dozen times but the line was always dead. He picked it up again. Silence. He looked at his watch. It was just coming up to eleven o'clock.

Upstairs, Trichkov sat rigid with tension, listening intently to the amplified sounds coming through his headphones from the hidden microphones in the telephone and walls of Robson's hotel bedroom. He checked his watch again. Yes, he'd given the English journalist exactly three minutes on the telephone to London before cutting him off, as Zhermatov had instructed.

What he'd heard Robson dictate had made his blood freeze. Even now he could still feel the dampness of the sweat that had broken out round his temples. He sat immobile listening to Robson bellowing into the receiver and banging loudly on the cradle of the telephone.

He was deeply afraid, although he didn't know of what. He couldn't get the frightened face of the little man locked in the basement out of his mind, for one thing. Why was he being kept prisoner with a coffin and a hearse? He'd seemed terrified when he took the food in at eight o'clock. He wished again he could telephone his wife and ask how she and their baby son were. To be out of contact when things like this were happening must be driving her to distraction. What would be happening in the streets? Fighting, arrests? It was terrible not knowing. She'd pleaded with him not to work at the Committee. He wished fervently he'd listened now.

Robson finally banged the phone down and for several seconds gave himself up to unbridled cursing. This was followed by the sound of him stamping around the room. Then a door banged very loudly. After that the microphones conveyed only complete silence from Room 409.

In Fleet Street the rain lashed down and, in accordance with a natural London law which has, as yet, not been defined, the traffic ground inevitably to a standstill. Bored, vacant-faced passengers on the top deck of a number 11 bus caught fast in the jam outside the offices of the British Amalgamated Press and Picture Agency passed the time staring into the first floor windows of the boardroom where a meeting that had begun early yesterday morning was continuing.

They could see that the man with his back to the window had taken his jacket off to reveal the expensive grey silk of the back of his waistcoat. They could see too he was speaking angrily because his neck was red. They didn't know that he was the man Gordon Miller referred to as Sir 'Someone' Barnes, that he was a CBE and chairman of BAPPA, but the more perceptive among the stranded bus passengers could see that most of the hard-faced men around the table were looking at him very sourly indeed and that each in his turn was replying sharply and unsympathetically to the points he was making.

The closed windows of the boardroom and the bus killed all sound of the heated argument that was raging inside about the relative profitability of concentrating on economic and stock market information as opposed to pure news which had traditionally been BAPPA's major saleable commodity. Because buses, taxis, lorries and private cars were jammed solid from St Paul's right through to Trafalgar Square by the mystical influence of the rain, the passengers on the number 11 were still gazing through the window two minutes later when the boardroom door flew open and Jock Baird burst in. He was in his shirt sleeves and they watched him wave a piece of paper in his hand then bang it on the table in front of the chairman.

They didn't know it contained Robson's 'flash' about the sensational Sofia murder of Radovanovic and neither they, nor the chairman himself, knew at that moment that this would prove to be the final straw that would break the back of his control of the agency. Baird's mouth moved rapidly, explaining how Robson had been cut off in mid-sentence, how this dramatic story was a world exclusive so far with no other agency at all running it yet, even some fifteen minutes after BAPPA had put it out. Baird retreated after getting the chairman's approval for despatching another correspondent immediately from London to Sofia to help Robson on what would clearly become a major running world news story of the next few days or even weeks.

In the Chinese Embassy in the centre of the Bulgarian capital Wang Chieh-ping was reading from his red-covered copy of

'Quotations from Chairman Mao Tse-tung'. He was conducting the closing stages of the weekly 'Fan Sheng' meeting. Everybody present had recited a detailed self-criticism of their work and political study during the past seven days and they now waited expectantly as Wang prepared his closing oration. He announced that he was going to quote finally from Mao's writings on the subject of 'Revolutionary Heroism' and they obediently turned to the relevant section in their books. Wang set his eyes ablaze with fierce dedication as he read. 'Thousands of martyrs have heroically laid down their lives for the people!' He stared round challengingly at the group seated in front of his desk. 'Let us hold their banner high and march ahead along the path crimson with their blood!'

The group matched his verbal zeal as they chanted the quotation rapidly back at him in unison.

'Be resolute, fear no sacrifice and surmount every difficulty to win victory!' he shouted and closed his book as the circle gave it back to him in their loudest voices.

Then they all stood and faced reverently towards the large framed portrait of Mao on the wall. Three times they chanted *Mao tzu chih wan sui!* – the ritualistic wish for the long life the Chinese have been accustomed to offer to their emperors and leaders down the centuries. Then they turned and filed towards the door. As they went, Wang signalled to his wife and one other cadre, a tall, burly Chinese with a scowling countenance, to stay behind.

When the three of them were alone, Wang switched on the portable radio on his desk, tuned in Radio Peking and turned up the volume far enough to make the discussion they were going to have about Robson unintelligible to any Bulgarian monitoring devices which might have remained undiscovered after the last meticulous search by the visiting team of electronic specialists from Peking.

Twenty

Outside the Balkan Hotel in Lenin Square, BAPPA correspondent, Jonathan Robson, stepped off the pavement into the traffic and waved down the first Warszawa taxi that came by. He opened the front passenger door and got in next to the driver. Those

Bulgarians who did take taxis, ever conscious of the class struggle, rode in the front to make things look more comradely. Riding in the back was only for corrupt Westerners living out their dying capitalist's delusions of grandeur. In the front he would look less conspicuous.

'Pancharevo Lake, please, Comrade.' Robson didn't look at the driver but stared out through his side window. Already he felt something of a marked man.

The long snow-covered hump of Mount Vitosha that dominates Sofia in the same way that Vesuvius dominates Naples glistened white in the bright sunlight away to the south. Robson stared at it, but didn't see it.

The taxi headed out of town on the main E 20 Sofia–Istanbul international highway and the mountain quickly disappeared behind high rise blocks of worker's apartments in the suburbs. Robson didn't see these either because his thoughts were already racing ahead to the Lebed restaurant at Pancharevo Lake, sixteen kilometres to the south-east of the capital on the Samokov road.

When the taxi turned south off the main highway just past the airport they found that the road hadn't been sanded and on the thin covering of snow the seemingly hyper-careful driver dropped his speed to around forty-five kilometres an hour. When they came to a downhill stretch he switched off the engine altogether and coasted in neutral. On a second gentle slope he switched off again and the speed of the taxi dropped somewhere near to walking pace.

'What the hell are you doing, Comrade?' shouted Robson in exasperation. He used a mixture of the Russian he'd half learned in Moscow and what little Bulgarian he'd picked up on trips to Sofia.

The driver turned and smiled broadly to show his one gold-filled incisor to its best advantage. But he said nothing.

'Does the Party tell you to switch off your damned motor to fulfil your norms?'

The driver nodded slowly. 'No. Each morning I get issued with enough petrol for one hundred kilometres.' He tapped the milometer on the dashboard by way of illustration. 'So I save by switching off the engine.' He drove in silence for a while, letting the sunlight dart in on the gold filling again in the course of a slow crafty smile.

'And what's in it for you?'

'When I've done a hundred kilometres I stop, siphon off what petrol's left and sell it on the black market for four *leva* a litre.'

'Switch the bloody engine back on quick', said Robson menacingly. 'I'm in a hurry – I'll pay you for your black market losses.'

He slapped a five-leva note on top of the dashboard and the driver accelerated away fast down the hill.

Even so the journey to the Lebed took forty-five minutes.

The restaurant, as its Bulgarian name suggests, sits right at the edge of the Pancharevo Lake, like a 'swan' about to launch itself across the flat expanse of water.

It was deserted except for three bored-looking waiters when the taxi pulled up outside. Robson asked the driver to wait but he stoutly refused for no reason that he would reveal, so he paid him off, plus his black market subsidy, and walked out onto the jetty where metal tables and chairs were set out for summer-time eating and drinking.

There was no sign of Georgina Morakova.

An obsequious, narrow-shouldered waiter in white jacket and black trousers came shivering out onto the terrace to ask him in passable English if he wanted something.

'I'd like a coffee and a large Bulgarian cognac, please, to warm me up,' said Robson, standing where he was and looking down at the frozen surface of the lake.

'Out here?' asked the waiter incredulously.

'*Da, da*, out here. I need fresh air.' He pointed to his chest and coughed exaggeratedly.

The waiter nodded sympathetically and hurried inside.

He sat down at one of the tables by the railings and looked out at the snow-covered hills that sloped down to the lakeside from the north. There was not a human soul in sight. He gulped the cold air into his lungs in deep draughts. Had too much happened since the reception last night for Georgina Morakova to keep her appointment?

The waiter brought thick sweet Turkish coffee in a tiny cup and a large cognac the colour of dark molasses in a balloon glass. He stood and watched Robson sip the coffee, grinning foolishly.

'Those Turks may have kept us down, but didn't they teach us how to make coffee?'

Robson nodded absently.

'Tourist? Here on holiday, Comrade?' The waiter had one hand on his mouth and Robson noticed all his finger-nails were bitten jaggedly down to the quicks.

'No.'

'On business?' He stood back biting simultaneously at what was left of the nails on the first two fingers of his right hand. Robson drank half the cognac at one go, then gasped as the acrid liquor hit the back of his throat. He sipped some more coffee quickly to take the taste away.

'Business, yes?' prompted the shivering waiter in case Robson had forgotten he was still there.

Robson stared out over the yellow-painted railings towards the frozen hills again. 'Piss off, Comrade,' he said quietly.

The waiter retreated, chewing even harder on his non-existent nails. Inside the glass door of the restaurant he picked up the telephone. When he got his connection he spoke quickly into the receiver, glancing furiously through the glass from time to time at the hunched, fur-hatted figure of Robson sitting out over the lake in the freezing cold.

Robson checked his watch. It was twelve fifteen. He looked back to the landward side of the restaurant. The path wound round the side of the lake in both directions. On the far side of the path for a couple of hundred yards were planted shrubberies, giving way further on to natural undergrowth and small trees. A quarter of a mile along the lake to the south was a small jetty where yachts and water-ski boats would be moored in the summer. A few ducks flapped and squawked plaintively on the ice around the end of the landing stage, but they were the only sign of life.

Robson lit a cigarette and glanced back at the restaurant. The waiter was standing inside the glass door staring out at him. He turned his back on him and scanned the lake and shore once more.

After five minutes of total inactivity he turned and waved to the waiter. He hurried out. Robson took a twenty-leva note from his wallet and folded it into a tiny square.

'Comrade, if you stop biting your finger-nails for five minutes, this is yours.'

130

'Eh?' said the waiter, squinting down his bony nose.

Robson took the waiter's hand turned it face upward, opened his fingers, put the little note-bundle in it and closed them round it. 'Five minutes, remember. Now bring me another cognac and coffee.'

'*Da.*'

Robson grabbed his sleeve and pulled him back. 'But before you go, Comrade, tell me, have you seen a lady out here this morning?'

The shifty little Bulgar screwed his brow into a contortion that he imagined mimed thought. 'A lady?'

'Yes.' Robson made the traditional two-handed curving motions in the air that men the world over employ symbolically to describe women to each other.

The waiter's face suddenly cleared. 'I don't know. But half an hour ago I see somebody down by the landing stage feeding the ducks. Whether that was a lady I couldn't tell from here.' Robson got to his feet and began moving off. 'Hey, what about the other coffee and cognac?'

'You drink it, Comrade,' called Robson over his shoulder. 'It will take your mind off your finger-nails.' He made a mental note to put twenty-leva down on his expenses sheet under 'Grats. for inf. and ass.' which the BAPPA news editor reluctantly accepted as gratuities for information and assistance, and moved off at a fast walk down the path alongside the shrubbery.

He slowed as he came abreast of the landing stage and peered into the trees. He could see nobody.

Turning, he walked out along the little jetty and looked down at the pitiful ducks. They had found, or made, a small hole in the ice and were sitting huddled together in it. But it wasn't big enough for them to swim in. They seemed totally baffled by the situation. 'Likewise,' he thought.

At that moment, he heard a woman's voice call his name, softly, from the trees behind him.

Twenty-One

When he turned round he could see nothing except the slender trunks of the young trees standing black against the snow. A path had been trodden into the wood from the end of the jetty by people coming, he presumed, to the lake to skate.

Robson waited but nobody appeared and there was no further sound. He walked quickly off the jetty and stepped on to the path. The trees grew close together in thicket clumps and the path snaked around them, sometimes doubling back on itself. As he walked his breath steamed in clouds in the cold air and he was glad of the coarse cognac inside his stomach. On an impulse he turned to look back along the path. But it was empty.

The sudden drum of horses hooves muffled by the snow startled him. He stepped off the path, held his breath and listened. The hooves were galloping, coming towards him. He slipped quickly through the trees and stepped out into a long clearing in the wood that was used as a camp site for tourists in summer.

The black horse passed within feet of him, going like an express train, its ears flattened along its head. Georgina Morakova, fur-headed and wearing a heavy leather riding coat, was crouched low over its mane. She turned towards him as she went by and with her face contorting against the rush of cold air, yelled loudly in his direction.

Robson stood staring after her. Her words had been totally unintelligible. He had no idea what her warning was, if indeed it was a warning. The flying hooves of the horse flung up a fine mist of snow in her wake as she thundered down the clearing. Without reining the horse back, she turned left at the bottom and plunged on through a gap among the trees, still going at full gallop.

Robson looked quickly around him. Still there was nobody in sight. The sound of the hooves died away and nothing else disturbed the silence of the woods and lake. To his left were a series of heavy rustic picnic tables and benches built of tree-trunks and planks. He walked over, brushed the snow from a bench and sat down. He pushed his hands deep into his overcoat pockets, hunched his shoulders round his ears and waited.

Two minutes later the horse and rider reappeared down at the end of the clearing, moving fast towards him again. He continued sitting on the bench even after she'd reined in the snorting animal beside him. She looked down, her face flushed and her eyes bright. 'I am sorry,' she gasped, fighting the head of the horse which was still shifting and stamping with the excitement of the gallop. 'I couldn't wait any longer . . . We'd waited half an hour already and he was very cold . . .'

Robson stood up to help her as she swung out of the saddle.

'Thank you.' She turned and looked anxiously into his face, still breathing fast. 'The little waiter at the Lebed is a known informer. I had to stay out of sight up here . . . and it was so cold for my horse . . . just standing.'

'It's damned cold for me too.' Robson gazed down the clearing. 'But Radovanovic will be feeling the cold more than either of us right now – he's been shot.'

Her expression didn't change. She nodded quickly. 'How did you find out?'

'A big fat secret policeman named Zhermatov told me. You know him?'

'Yes . . . But why should he tell *you*?' She was speaking half to herself.

'I've been wondering that too.'

She shrugged suddenly. 'Your analysis on the plane has come true, eh? Brilliant deduction, Mr Robson.' Her voice was bitter, sardonic.

'Is that what you were going to tell me – that the Russians and-stroke-or Bodinski – were going to have Radovanovic shot.'

She turned away, her face hardening around the mouth and eyes. 'He never had a chance!' She spoke viciously, without looking at him. 'It was inevitable. But it was only part of what I planned to tell you. And since last night two other men have died . . .'

'Who?'

She named the commander of the First Bulgarian Army and Radovanovic's closest supporter in the Politburo. 'Both killed themselves to avoid arrest by the KGB.' She paused. 'But they were really murdered . . . hounded to death. Zhermatov should have told you that too!'

Robson stared hard at her and whistled softly. 'So the army's still keeping up Bulgaria's old putschist tradition, eh?'

Georgina Morakova wasn't listening. Her forehead had creased in a puzzled frown. 'But I still don't understand why Zhermatov . . .' Then she swung suddenly to face him. 'Have you reported the story?'

'Yes. It will be all round the world by this time.'

'So that's the reason,' she said softly. She paused. Her eyes looked straight into his. 'That means you are in danger too now.'

'What do you mean by that? Is Zhermatov Radovanovic's man? Is he trying to pull the carpet out from under Bodinski?'

She nodded absently. 'But they will deny it!'

'How the hell can they?'

'They will announce only that Radovanovic resigned because of ill health. The Congress was in secret session. Security will be total. And everybody there will be very frightened too . . . They will try to arrest you for questioning . . .'

Robson studied her face carefully, wondering if she were genuine. She looked steadily back at him. 'Maybe you're right. We'll see. But what exactly were Radovanovic and his supporters trying to do?'

She shook her head quickly in a little gesture of hopelessness. Her tone was sarcastic. '"Clear out the Muscovite Old Guard", "assert Bulgaria's sense of nationalism", "take a leaf out of the Romanian book" . . .' Her eyes blazed with sudden anger. 'You're the uninvolved Western journalist who can come up with the well-turned phrases . . . put it into your kind of words, make it cold and clinical!'

She stopped, bent her head, kicked angrily at the snow with the toe of her riding boot. The black horse pulled back in alarm. She turned to quieten him and her anger subsided as quickly as it had come. 'Whatever words you use, it's failed,' she said quietly. 'As I suppose we all knew in our hearts it would.'

'Why were you so sure?'

'We're twenty-five years too late.' She closed her eyes for a moment and left the words hanging, unexplained.

'What do you mean?' asked Robson gently.

'The Yugoslavs broke with Stalin in 1948, didn't they? Albania defected to China in 1961. Over the last ten years the Romanians have managed a partial defection. Now the Russians only have helpless little Bulgaria left in their soft Balkan underbelly.' She opened her eyes and her voice rose angrily again. 'But it's not only that . . .'

A sudden sound in the wood behind them made them both turn. The horse shook his head and whinnied softly. The sun had disappeared and the high bright sky of half an hour before was now filling rapidly with lowering snow clouds. The light in the clearing had suddenly become dull and harsh. But there was no sign of anybody approaching.

Robson stared into her face. 'Look, let's be quick. It doesn't feel much safer here than it did at the reception. What did you mean last night when you said that what's happening here could have devastating effects outside Bulgaria? Why has the British ambassador's daughter been kidnapped? Why the faked crash landing? Why does a KGB colonel want to defect?'

She looked startled. 'How did you know that?'

'I was with the ambassador last night at his residence when the alleged defector put the screws on him!'

She considered his answer silently for a while before replying. 'Mr Robson, I hope I am not wrong in deciding to trust you.' She looked over his shoulder, down at the ground, then back to his face again. He suddenly recalled the feeling he'd had at the ambassador's residence. Was she, too, reciting carefully rehearsed lines? Or was the tension of the last thirty-six hours making him suspicious even of totally innocent actions.

'You must have made up your mind about that long before dragging me all the way out here. You said last night you were sick of the belief that the end justifies any evil means, that millions of peaceful lives had to be disrupted for impossible political dreams. You hinted you wanted to tell all, remember?'

'All right,' she snapped. 'All right. If you damned Westerners weren't so smug and arrogant about your own freedoms you might understand better how difficult it is for us . . .' She stopped talking and her shoulders fell in resignation. 'Yes, I am tired and weary of it all. The intrigue, the lying, the brutality. I've had too much. In the end you trust no one, not even yourself . . .'

Something in the utter desperation of her expression at that moment convinced him. 'I won't betray you, Georgina,' he said gently.

She looked up at him. 'The KGB man is not a defector. It is a trick?'

'What sort of trick?'

'He has said he wants to leave the country in a hearse which should be carrying Angela Magnusson's body, yes? They will substitute someone else. It is a plot.'

'Who?'

She paused, and licked her lips nervously. 'Lulinski.'

'Lulinski?' asked Robson in amazement. 'The chief Soviet negotiator in the SALT talks?'

She nodded, staring at the ground.

'Why the hell do they want to do that?'

'They wish to make it appear that the West is kidnapping Lulinski. They want to wreck the talks.'

'Who are "they"?'

She was staring wide-eyed over his shoulder, transfixed. 'Don't turn round!' She brought her eyes back to his face. 'Somebody's coming through the wood. Pretend we're lovers. Embrace me!'

Before he could move she flung her free arm round his neck and pulled his face down on hers. Their mouths met and he put both his arms round her. Her lips and cheeks were icy cold. He could feel the hardness of her teeth against his, between her lips. But all the while her eyes were open, staring over his shoulder and he could hear somebody coming quietly through the trees behind him.

The horse moved up close and reached out his muzzle curiously towards them. Robson felt its warm breath against his cheek. Georgina Morakova squirmed hard against his chest, twisting and moving until he could feel the heavy softness of her breasts under the riding coat. She was acting the part for all she was worth — but still watching intently over his shoulder. He pulled her hard against him.

'It's no good,' she whispered suddenly.

'Comrade!' The voice spoke from close behind him. She disentangled herself and turned quickly to face the other way. Robson looked round. The little waiter from the Lebed stood ten yards away, holding his right hand towards Robson. Because of the fur hat and coat he was now wearing, Robson didn't recognize him for a moment. 'You left these, Comrade. On the table.'

His thin face was expressionless. In his hand he held Robson's gas lighter and a flip-top packet of cigarettes. 'Take them and try a big bribe,' she whispered. 'He's a little crook at heart.'

Robson walked across, took out his wallet and peeled off two twenty-leva notes. The waiter took them without a word, his eyes still on the well-filled wallet.

Robson closed it and put it away. 'Not a word to my wife about this, Comrade, eh?' he said quietly. He gave the waiter a lascivious wink, clenched his fist and bent his right arm upward from the elbow. He took the lighter and cigarettes and slapped the Bulgarian on the back. 'Thanks. Not a word, remember.'

The waiter said nothing. He glowered at Robson, then took another long significant look over the journalist's shoulder at Georgina Morakova who was standing by her horse with her back to them. Robson peeled off another twenty-leva and handed it to the waiter in silence. As he tucked the note inside his coat, Robson suddenly grabbed him by the lapels and pulled him up on to his toes. 'Listen, Comrade, if you tell anybody about this lady or what you've seen here today, I'll come back tomorrow and batter the brains clean out of your nasty little head. Understand?'

The waiter, who was hanging helplessly inside his coat, nodded mutely. When Robson replaced him on the ground, he scurried off quickly along the path into the woods without looking back.

When he returned to her she stood staring anxiously after the waiter. 'He will telephone his report immediately. He will be more frightened of the "D.S." than he is of you – or your money. He is a known criminal who informs to keep himself out of jail.'

'But he doesn't know who we are!'

'We shall be recognized immediately from our descriptions. We cannot stay here long!'

'All right, talk fast,' said Robson. 'You were just about to tell me who "they" are.'

She pulled the fur collar of her leather riding coat closer round her ears. 'Not only was the move against Moscow twenty-five years too late, but it has come when the wild men of the Kremlin have become more powerful again!'

'You mean the hardliners? The anti-Brezhnev faction?'

'Yes. They are crushing our pathetic little bid for freedom and Bodinski is their man in Bulgaria.' Her face twisted in distaste. 'Extremists, blind dogmatists! They wish to smash the détente with the West. They believe history has now presented the supreme opportunity for the Soviet Union to complete the world revolution it began in 1917. They think they should now try to shift the frontiers of Communism across Western Europe.'

'Why?'

'Your enormous inflation in the West, your recessions, the success of communist-inspired strikes, Portugal, the oil crisis . . . They believe these are all signs that the classic Marxist-Leninist "revolutionary situation" is unfolding.'

'And how do they imagine planting Lulinski in Angela Magnusson's coffin is going to further world revolution?'

She breathed deeply before replying. 'When it is revealed the "treacherous" Western powers have tried to kidnap Lulinski, Brezhnev will be forced to withdraw immediately from the Strategic Arms conference and the forces talks in Vienna. His détente policy will be discredited. The "rebellion" in Bulgaria will help them overthrow him. Within a few days you will see the biggest shake-up in the Kremlin since Stalin's death and then the wild men will take over.' She leaned her head suddenly against the horse's neck and half turned from him as though in despair.

Robson stood watching her. Again he wondered whether she was acting the whole thing. 'Won't Lulinski be an enormous security risk in the West?'

She kept her back to him, twining her fingers in the mane of the horse. 'His brain has already been scrambled beyond repair by drugs. He will be a living vegetable by the time he reaches Athens.'

Robson moved quickly round to where he could see her face and took her gently by the shoulders. 'Tell me how you know all these things and why you are telling me.'

Her mouth twisted down at the corners in a sudden, bitter, half smile. 'Boris Bodinski keeps a mistress. For seven years I have lived a life of comparative luxury in an apartment that's normally reserved only for members of the Central Committee. I have my own horse, too, Pencho here, who is stabled at a state farm.'

'Congratulations.'

She tossed her head. 'I left last night. I slept in the loft above Pencho's stable.' She patted the horse's neck roughly.

'Is there a Mrs Bodinski?'

'Yes, but it makes no difference. I hate him now. I think I always did.' She breathed deeply and stared into the distance. 'I haven't slept with him for a year. I came to Sofia from Vratsa ten years ago, an ambitious Balkan peasant girl. But it was only ever an expedient to improve a dull existence.' She dropped her eyes to the ground and her mouth turned down at the corners again in an expression half fierce, half resigned.

'Where will you live now?'

She hesitated only briefly. 'That depends on you.'

Robson was taken aback. 'I don't understand.'

'I want to leave Bulgaria. *That* is why I am telling you all this. Help get me out!'

Robson nodded slowly, watching her face intently. 'Uh-huh, I see. The name of the game is becoming a little clearer.'

She dropped her head suddenly. 'I'm sick of the back-stabbing, the lies, the deceit. Politics, politics all day, every day.' Her shoulders sagged slightly, giving her a vulnerable defenceless look. She continued speaking towards the ground. 'I am a tough woman, you think, yes? You are right. But I am still a woman. I want to get married, have babies, before it's too late. I want to forget politics, and the hypocritical glorification of the working class.'

Her shoulders shook suddenly and he watched a tear fall from her chin on to the snow.

'With your job at the Foreign Trade Ministry you could have defected any time.' He kept his voice deliberately cold, impersonal.

She wiped the back of her hand quickly across her eyes. 'For the past year Comrade Bodinski insisted that I be allowed to travel only to Socialist countries. He had me watched day and night.'

Robson was still staring at her trying to read her face. 'The funny thing is I think that some of the time, Georgina, you are telling the truth.'

'Why only some of the time?'

'I don't know . . .' said Robson cautiously. 'I'm not sure. But I wouldn't mind betting you've already got some kind of risky plan worked out by which I might get you out.'

139

She turned away suddenly and put her toe into the near stirrup. 'If you don't trust me, then go! I still have pride. I won't plead with you!'

She swung on to the horse, settled herself straight-backed into the saddle, and turned the horse's head until it was facing down the clearing. 'The other thing I was about to tell you,' she said over her shoulder, 'was where Angela Magnusson is being held hostage.'

Robson ran quickly round to the front of the horse and caught hold of the reins close to the bit. He looked up into the haughty face of the Slav woman sitting calmly astride the horse. 'Where is she?'

She snorted contemptuously. 'Aren't you too worried about saving your own skin to be concerned with the missing daughter of the British Ambassador or the dangerous plans of madmen in the Kremlin?'

'Where is she?' Robson repeated the question in a tight, controlled voice.

The sound of a car drawing up at the Lebed restaurant a quarter of a mile away reached them on the still air. They heard the doors slam as the occupants got out.

Georgina Morakova looked quickly down at Robson. 'Do you want to help me?'

Would the risks be for nothing? Mightn't there be a definitive book to be written with her help on the Bulgarian rebellion? Wouldn't Vienna, where he was going to live *without* Beryl, be an obvious choice for her too? And with her inside knowledge, wouldn't she be an invaluable source of background information and interpretation on Eastern Europe?

He looked up into her level gaze for a moment. The leather coat suddenly stretched tight around her breasts as she half-rose and twisted anxiously in the saddle to peer into the trees. She turned back as his eyes were returning to her face.

'All right,' he said slowly. 'Against my better judgement.'

In the distance they heard the sound of footsteps hurrying across the concrete outside the restaurant.

'My car is at the farm. Go through the wood.' She pointed. 'The road is about a mile and a half away. I'll pick you up on the road in half an hour after I've stabled Pencho.'

He stood and watched her gallop away. From the lakeside path he could hear the sound of footsteps, growing louder. He listened for a moment then turned and began running fast through the thick snow towards the trees at the end of the clearing.

Twenty-Two

'The woman with the black horse was Comrade Morakova, I think.'

Zhermatov scowled as he listened to the whining voice of the waiter calling from the Lebed.

'The man was English, I think, but he wouldn't tell me whether he was a businessman or tourist. They were . . .' his voice died away, '. . . well they were . . . embracing under the trees in the wood . . . This is a good report, yes, Captain?'

'No, Comrade,' growled Zhermatov. 'You've told us nothing we didn't know already.'

'You will credit my account, yes? Ten *leva* you promised for good information, Comrade Captain, yes?'

'Not a single *stotinki*! Just think yourself lucky we don't pull you in for all those black market currency deals last summer with the tourists.'

The waiter was silent for a moment on the other end. Then he spoke again in a wheedling voice. 'So, okay, Captain. Then I don't suppose you would be interested in the men who came here following them. Goodbye, Captain . . .'

'Wait,' yelled Zhermatov. The veins in his neck and temples stood out with the ferocity of his shout. 'Who's following them, you dumb-headed little freak?'

'Just some men who came here asking me questions. But maybe it's nothing. If I get no credits, Captain, I won't waste your time.'

'Comrade, unless you tell me everything now, I will come out there myself immediately and wring your neck with my own hands. Then I will kick your stinking body into Pancharevo Lake!'

The waiter laughed a quick hysterical laugh. 'Just my joking, Comrade Captain. Honestly. I was going to tell you anyway about the Chinese.'

Zhermatov froze. His voice became a whisper. 'What Chinese?'

'The Chinese Comrades who were here just now. They asked me whether an English Comrade had been in. They said he was a visiting English Communist, a good Comrade, whom they wished to invite to a reception at their embassy.'

'Where are they now?'

'They have just gone out. They are hurrying into the wood where I last saw the Englishman and Comrade Morakova.'

Zhermatov exploded. 'You snivelling wretch. I suppose they offered you money.' He looked quickly at his watch and took a deep breath. It would take half an hour to get his own men out there. 'Listen carefully. Go immediately and follow them. Watch everything they do, and report to me as soon as there is anything to report. Do not let them out of your sight. And don't bother to conceal yourself! Let them know you are watching them. It might save a life. You understand?'

'Yes, Captain.' The waiter's voice was very worried. Reporting on the Lebed's customers was one thing, but following Chinese through the forest was another. 'Follow them and let them see me?' he repeated nervously.

'Yes, and if you do this job well, I will credit your account with one hundred *leva*. Follow them and don't lose them. If you fail, I promise I will arrest you and have you beaten to death in the darkest dungeon in Sofia. Now go!' Zhermatov turned and paced angrily across the Monitoring room, his brow furrowed deep with anxiety.

Deep among the trees Wang Chieh-ping slithered to a halt and held up his hand. His chest heaved painfully from the half-mile run through the snow. The scowling man who'd fallen a hundred yards behind panted up to him. 'He is heading for the road,' gasped Wang. 'We must have the car.'

He took a small portable walkie-talkie handset from his coat pocket and handed it to Wang. Wang repeated a call sign into it three times. Tsai Mei-li, waiting patiently behind the wheel of the Tatra in the car park behind the Lebed, heard the signal, took her set from the glove compartment and gave the answering sign. 'Quickly, take the car round on to the road from Sumako. Head towards Sofia again. We will be waiting.'

Tsai Mei-li acknowledged the message, started the car and drove fast out of the car park.

Whenever he stopped to rest, Robson could hear the two men plunging through the wood behind him. Because of the complete stillness among the trees, if he held his own breath, he could hear them, gasping as they ploughed through the thick snow. He'd zig-zagged off the path several times in an attempt to lose them. But he didn't dare go off it too far because he feared that if he lost the direction to the road, he'd miss the car and finish up stranded in the woods with his pursuers.

A half mile behind Robson, the little waiter was moving frantically through the forest, half trotting, half walking, sobbing to get his breath through lungs racked by the pain of the longest burst of running he had ever undertaken in his forty years of life. His agonized eyes searched ahead ceaselessly for a glimpse of the two Chinese. He knew Zhermatov didn't make idle threats. He wished for the hundredth time he hadn't taken the twenty *leva* from the Chinese.

But now he was sure his luck was changing. He'd taken a risk and stuck to the path. This was only because he didn't have the strength to strike off and battle through the deeper snow under the trees. He had simply taken the route his scrawny frame dictated and followed the sounds of the men he was chasing as best he could. Once to his dismay they almost disappeared away to his left. Then later they had crossed back and grew faint far off to the right. But on he jogged along the track, hoping against hope. And sure enough, the sounds were now returning ahead of him again along the winding path.

He slowed down to a fast walk. He was the only one among the four men who knew the forest. He'd followed courting couples this way on summer nights, after he'd finished work — it had often been worth a *lev* or two if one of them turned out to be married. The track, he knew, led only to the Sumako road and the trees stretched from the lake for several miles without interruption.

He rounded a sharp turn in the path, saw it was empty and moaning with the effort broke into a trot again. His head rolled from side to side as he ran. Because of the noise he was making himself, he didn't notice the two Chinese until they crashed out of the trees on to the path ten yards ahead of him.

Wang was so intent on following Robson's tracks that he failed to see the little Bulgarian. But his companion let out a yell.

The waiter stopped, dead. His instinct was to flee, but he remembered Zhermatov's order to let them see him. As a result of this inner conflict he stood gaping breathless and open-mouthed at the men he'd been chasing.

The scowling Chinese began moving slowly back down the path towards him, his hands held loosely by his sides. The waiter retreated a pace or two, staring stupidly and gasping for breath.

'Pu shih!' yelled Wang suddenly, seeing the man was defenceless. The big Chinese turned to look. Wang signalled angrily for him to leave the Bulgarian because of the time they'd lose, and he began running along the path again. The Chinese eyed the waiter malevolently once more then turned and loped away along the track after Wang.

The terrified little Bulgar stood trembling, unable to move. He watched until the Chinese had disappeared from view. His hand crept up to his mouth and he chewed indecisively at the stumps of his finger-nails. In the end he decided to risk the unknown wrath of the Chinese in preference to the certain retribution of Zhermatov and trotted forward again along the path moaning softly to himself on every outward breath.

Twenty-Three

Robson crouched low in the gully, gasping for breath and straining his ears for sounds of his pursuers. They seemed to be beating through the trees several hundred yards off to his left, close to the path. The rumble of another heavy lorry and trailer heading down from Sumako into Sofia grew louder.

The road was about a hundred yards in front of him. The sound of the first lorry climbing laboriously away from the capital towards the Rila Mountains five minutes before had been music in his pounding ears. He had turned immediately and run uphill at right angles to the path leaving it behind him, keeping low and staying parallel with the road. That way he hoped to meet the car as early as possible — if it hadn't passed already.

He had decided to stay and hide in the gully only after he'd fallen into it; waist deep in a drift, he realized he was out of sight below the level of its banks and stayed there, leaning forward in the snow until he'd regained his breath.

Now he began struggling bent double along the gully again, still keeping his head well down. If his guess was right he was only about a hundred yards from the road.

The little waiter paused behind a tree watching the two Chinese. They were searching the ground off to the right of the path for signs of tracks. He watched everything they did but, despite Zhermatov's command, he shrank back out of sight now whenever they began to turn in his direction.

They seemed to be arguing sharply, exchanging clipped, angry words. But they stopped and took cover behind trees themselves as the lorry and trailer heading down into Sofia, crawled slowly by on the icy road fifty yards away. The waiter made use of this opportunity to slip across the path and hurry into the protection of the trees on the other side.

When he peered out again Wang was pointing in the direction of the lorry and after another brief exchange of words the two men moved off slowly along the path towards the road. They'd obviously decided it was safer to wait for the Englishman to break out of the forest.

The waiter turned his head sharply as another distant movement off to the right caught his eye. At first he thought it was some small dark, furry animal scurrying between the trees, stopping, disappearing, then reappearing again. Then he realized he was watching the head of a man moving along a depression in the ground. He looked again carefully to make sure, then hurried on through the trees aiming to keep himself equidistant between the Chinese and the man they'd said they desperately wanted to invite to their New Year reception at the embassy.

Robson stopped fifteen yards short of the road and crouched motionless in the deep snow, listening. He willed his ears to hear the sound of the engine of Georgina Morakova's car, coming down the hill. But the road remained quiet. He took off his hat and cautiously raised his head above the lip of the gully.

What he saw made him duck down again immediately, as if he'd been stung. A hundred yards away the head and shoulders of one of his pursuers were visible, hurrying along the roadside towards him. In the distance the other man was moving off down the road in the opposite direction, searching the trees with his eyes.

Robson looked round desperately for cover. The man approaching would certainly see him when he passed the end of the gully. But if he climbed either bank he'd provide an easy target, too. So there was only one choice left.

He was scooping frantically at the side of a deep snow drift beside him when he heard the sound of a car coming down the hill. Although he'd been listening for it, its significance didn't register properly for several seconds. When it did, he stopped digging and held his breath.

The car was travelling very slowly. By the engine note he guessed it was in first or second gear. The road curved away to the right and Robson risked a quick look above the bank up the hill. He could just see the roof of the car moving down the far side, at about ten miles an hour.

He took another quick look in the other direction. The man moving towards him was only fifty yards away. That decided him.

He stood up, ran out of the gully and stopped in the middle of the road waving his arms above his head. The car came round the bend very slowly but Tsai Mei-li was so startled that she swerved the Tatra violently to avoid him and skidded across the road into the bank. He stared in amazement at her shocked Chinese face behind the windscreen. Then he turned to look at the man running fast towards him up the hill. For the first time Wang's distinctive narrow eyes and prominent Asiatic cheekbones became plainly visible.

Wang shouted over his shoulder and the other man turned and sprinted back towards them. Robson slipped and fell on the icy surface and was still struggling to regain his feet when Tsa Mei-li managed to free the jammed door of the Tatra. She got out and stood pointing frantically towards the bank.

Robson didn't turn back to see what had caught her attention. He got on to the soft verge at the roadside and scrambled up the hill towards the bend.

Wang Chieh-ping stopped in the middle of the road, reached into his overcoat pocket and dragged out a silenced Tsunyi automatic. He looked up, extended his right arm to its full length and took aim at the face of the little waiter peering out from behind a tree at the top of the bank. It was probably partly surprise and partly the residual effect of Zhermatov's furious order not to conceal himself from the Chinese that prevented the waiter moving back. He gazed mesmerized at the black mouth of the silencer pointing up at him from the road. As he stared he saw the Chinese man's arm jump as though it had been tapped gently on a vital nerve by a psychiatrist's reflex hammer.

The first sound he heard was the brittle 'crack' of a silver of bark being chipped from the trunk of the tree close to his cheek. It was also the last. His frail body was lifted up and toppled backwards into the snow by the force of the slug that changed direction only slightly after brushing the tree and entered his head at an acute angle under his left eye. It burrowed on upwards like a hot, angry maggot into the centre of his brain and he was dead before his thin shoulders hit the snow-covered ground.

Robson was staring round as he ran. He couldn't see what was happening back around the bend and he was wondering why the Chinese were not pursuing him. Georgina Morakova watched him running blindly up the hill towards her and if she hadn't braked sharply he would have run straight into the offside wing of the Volkswagen as it coasted silently over the brow of the hill with its engine switched off.

Robson turned his head just in time to avoid a collision. He stumbled round to the nearside, wrenched open the door and fell in onto the passenger seat. 'Reverse for Christ's sake,' he gasped. 'Turn round! Get us out of here.'

She took one look at him and started the engine quickly without question. She had fixed chains to the rear wheels because of the long, gradual climb out of Sofia and the car shot back off the road immediately, despite the covering of snow. She reversed confidently on the snowy shoulder of the road, turned neatly and eased the Volkswagen away up the hill. Robson twisted in his seat to stare out through the back window. Just before a turn in the road blocked his view, he saw Tsai Mei-li run round the bend into the middle of the road and stand staring after them.

147

They drove without speaking for several minutes. He watched anxiously out of the rear window while she gave all her concentration to pushing the Volkswagen as fast as it would go up the snow-covered hill. At the top she turned right into a minor road and followed it for a mile and a half before they came out on the main Samokov–Sofia road again. They'd passed the Lebed restaurant and were heading back towards the junction with the main trunk road, without any signs of pursuit appearing, before Robson spoke.

'Where the hell do the Chinese fit into this?'

'Chinese?' She sounded alarmed. 'Are you sure they were Chinese?'

He had pains in his lungs, pains in his legs and aching head from the strain of the chase. His whole body was bathed in perspiration inside his clothes.

'You don't spend half an hour getting chased around the woods and almost getting caught without getting a good idea who's doing the chasing. What do they want?'

'I don't know. I honestly don't know.' She bit her bottom lip anxiously as they drove on in silence.

He took off his hat, unbuttoned his coat, wound down the window of the car to breathe the cold air and lit a cigarette. But the smoke made him cough and after two inhalations he threw it away. The ache in his diaphragm had begun to produce a feeling of nausea now. He mopped his sweating face with a handkerchief. They were rolling along the wide E 20 highway into Sofia before he felt recovered enough to speak further.

'You got us out of that nasty little spot very well with your cool driving.'

'I'm sorry, Jonathan, that you had trouble because I asked you to come to Pancharevo. Has it made you change your mind about wanting to help me?'

He chewed over the new stage of familiarity they'd suddenly entered and eventually decided to let it pass without comment. 'Where's Angela Magnusson?' he asked finally.

'She's being held in a mortuary in the city until after dark. Then a hearse is due to deliver her in a coffin to the British Ambassador's residence.'

'Then what?'

'Three men will have arrived at the residence beforehand with a coffin containing Lulinski – heavily sedated, of course. The coffins will be changed, the hearse containing Lulinski will head for the border driven by the embassy chauffeur. The three men will stay for "an evening at home" with the ambassador and Angela until they are sure the hearse has crossed safely into Greece with its political booby trap!'

'Then all hell breaks loose!'

The engine of the Volkswagen drummed out its reassuringly steady rhythm and they moved on anonymously through the outskirts of Sofia, the chains on the rear wheels ringing and clinking on the hard, bare highway. The first tentative flakes of a new snowfall danced hesitantly in front of the windscreen then skittered away over the roof. Robson lit another cigarette and found to his relief that the walls of his lungs had recovered enough to allow him to enjoy it this time. He turned deliberately to study Georgina Morakova's profile as she drove. 'What's your plan for getting out of the country?'

'Simple.' Her face was utterly composed. 'Intercept the hearse before it reaches the residence and drive Angela Magnusson and ourselves south to the Greek border.'

'Of course! Why didn't I think of that?'

She ignored his sarcasm. 'That way I will get out, Miss Magnusson will be freed, and the vile schemes of Bodinski and his puppet masters in the Kremlin will come to nothing.'

'How exactly do we humble personages manage to outwit the combined strengths of the KGB and the Bulgarian Security Services – to say nothing of the political might of the Kremlin. Or is that too much of a simpleton's question?'

'With knowledge.' Her voice remained utterly confident.

'Oh?'

'My association with Bodinski has been very long and very close. I have been everywhere with him. My face is a passport to all doors. I am allowed access to all security areas without question and I have the knowledge to get us in where the Magnusson girl is held. With your help I can get her out. All you need is the uniform of the British ambassador's chauffeur, all I need is a passport in the name of Lady Magnusson to travel to the border.'

'The ambassador may not like chances being taken with the life of his daughter.'

'I will go to talk to him, reassure him – and get a uniform for you.'

'You *do* have it all nicely worked out.'

She pretended not to hear him. 'Meanwhile you can wait for me complete safety at an empty apartment to which I have the key in Ljuben Karavelov. Will you do it?'

He had been watching her profile with meticulous care throughout the exchange. No flicker of expression had moved her set features.

She leaned forward suddenly and turned on the car radio. Within seconds the voice of the Radio Sofia newsreader had provided the answer to her query.

Towards the end of the long item that was obviously about the opening of the Eleventh Party Congress he heard his own name followed by a torrent of fierce-sounding Slavonic vowel sounds. His rusty Russian allowed him to make out the sense of it.

'You were right. They've denied he's dead!' He sucked in an angry breath. 'And I've been made the bloody Aunt Sally.'

She lowered the volume of the radio and turned her head to look at him briefly. 'Yes. Did you get all of it? They have announced he has resigned through ill health. They are attacking your report without mentioning what it says as 'Western imperialist slander'. They've put a ban on all BAPPA correspondents entering Bulgaria for five years and they're also accusing you of spying for western intelligence agencies. A warrant has been issued for your arrest.' She leaned forward slightly to peer ahead through the thickening snow. 'I'm sorry Jonathan.'

Robson slumped back in his seat and vehemently repeated a string of short explosive curse words several times beneath his breath.

The second secretary from the Chinese Embassy stepped back quickly behind the curtain in the kitchen of the third floor apartment as the Volkswagen drew up at the opposite kerb in the cobbled street below. He remained standing close against the wall watching. Georgina Morakova and Jonathan Robson got out, looked quickly up and down the street, then bending their heads against the snow flurries, hurried into Block Entrance 97.

Without moving, the Chinese turned his head to check whether the orange Wartburg that had parked in a passageway on the other side of the street two hours ago was still there. When he saw that it was, he took a two-way radio from his tunic and spoke the embassy's call sign. 'Please inform Comrade Wang,' he said slowly, 'that address given by Jymeson woman correct. Robson and Morakova arrived 1500 hours at Block 97, Ljuben Karavelov. But advise Comrade Wang that it is inappropriate, repeat inappropriate that he approach area. Wartburg, registration S. 1678B with two men from Zhermatov's department arrived 1200 hours and still continuing close surveillance. End of message.'

He listened carefully as the embassy's radio clearer informed him that Comrade Wang was at present returning by road from Pancharevo and that he would be informed immediately.

The Chinese put his radio away, retreated from the window and picked up the long telephoto lens mounted on a low tripod that stood ready by the kitchen sink. He drew the curtains leaving a six-inch gap in the centre and adjusted the tripod until the lens was focused on the windows of a second floor apartment opposite. He peered through the lens but saw nothing in the empty unfurnished rooms.

He left the lens in position and, tying a handkerchief round his face, he walked quickly to the bedroom door of the tiny flat and opened it. The old grey-haired Bulgarian who lay bound and gagged on the bed stared mutely up at him. Satisfied with his inspection the Chinese closed the door again.

He went back to the window. He could see the driver of the Wartburg was speaking into the handset of his car radio. He took another look through the lens. Robson and Georgina Morakova were now just visible through the falling snow in the dim interior of the kitchen, talking together. He saw Robson turn and take a pen and notebook from his pocket, then using the kitchen drainer as a desk, he began to write.

While he was writing, the woman walked to the window. She thrust her hands into the pockets of her leather riding coat and stood looking down into the street. The Chinese straightened up

151

and watched her through the kitchen curtains without the aid of the lens. He saw her gaze take in the orange Wartburg but if she noticed anything special about it she didn't show it. Her eyes took in the windows of the building opposite but he remained motionless, as his training had taught him to do, and she clearly saw neither him nor his low-mounted lens behind the curtains of the tiny window.

'It's snowing harder now,' she said over her shoulder.

Robson grunted as he finished his note to Sir Charles Magnusson. He signed it, tore the page from the notebook, and slipped the latter between the pages of his passport. Then he walked to the window and looked out over her shoulder. 'You're sure this flat is safe?'

She turned and took the passport and letter from him. 'Absolutely sure.'

His eyes searched her face for a long moment. Then she suddenly smiled at him for the first time. 'You are still very suspicious, Jonathan, aren't you?' She tucked the passport and letter into one of her large coat pockets, then looked up at him again, still smiling faintly. 'Trust me.'

'I haven't got much choice.' His voice was suddenly bitter. 'Very bloody clever. Wanted on spying charges. I couldn't get far on my own, could I? Who helped you set me up?' He bunched his fists suddenly and brought them crashing down in exasperation on the metal draining board. 'Jesus Christ I must be in the terminal stages of galloping bloody insanity to hand my passport with an incriminating letter inside to the darling of the Bulgarian Politburo – then prepare to hang about in this empty freezing bloody flat like a sitting duck!'

She laughed out loud.

'What's so bloody funny?' he shouted angrily.

'Your face!' She moved closer to him, pulled off her glove and reached up tenderly to touch his face with her hands. 'Please trust me.' He didn't move but just stood with his hands in his coat pockets looking stonily at her.

'Look.' She turned to the cooker in the corner by the window. 'The electricity's connected here. I'll turn on all the hot plates. If you close the door it will get quite warm.' She twiddled the four switches. 'I'll be back in less than an hour. I'll buy us something to eat on the way back.'

She went out quickly locking the outside door behind her. Robson sat down on the only chair, pulled his coat collar up around his ears and stared out through the window at the falling snow.

For the next hour the only thing that the Chinese spy in the opposite apartment block could see was four red rings glowing brightly in the gathering gloom.

Twenty-Four

The man known, not unaffectionately, throughout the BAPPA organization as Sir Someone Barnes returned to the boardroom from lunch with his wife at the Connaught Grill in a bad frame of mind. They'd had another of their frequent rows and for the fourth time since Sunday she'd talked about wanting a divorce – this time loudly enough for people at the next four tables to hear. His lunch had also been interrupted by a telephone call informing him of the spy charges against Robson. His irritation showed clearly now as he straightened the reports and statements still cluttered around his blotter on the boardroom table from the morning policy session.

The rest of BAPPA's directors took their places around the table without looking at him. Most of them had lunched together in the executive dining room on the ninth floor of the building. Only the chairman and the vice-chairman, who was one of his closest friends, had been conspicuous by their absence.

Barnes cleared his throat noisily which, to the irritation of most board members, was the way he had always been accustomed to bring meetings to order, and looked out at them from under his grey bushy eyebrows. 'Before we begin our business proper, you've no doubt all heard about the trouble the agency's run into this morning in Sofia. I'm sure you will all agree with the action I've taken over the lunch hour of issuing a complete refutation of the espionage charges laid by the Bulgarians against our man, Robson. I've reiterated for the umpteenth time that our correspondents are, unlike their East bloc counterparts, always journalists and never spies. And I've stated that the correspondent concerned enjoys the full support and confidence of this board.' He cleared his throat noisily again. 'That's all we can do for now in my view, except await further developments.'

The men around the table, replete with an expensive lunch that had cost them nothing, received the statement without comment.

'And now,' the chairman continued, picking up a draft of points he wanted to make, 'I'd like to summarize my contentions of the last two days as to what the modern aims of an independent news agency like ours should be . . . If we are to compete with larger organizations like the Associated Press, Reuters and AFP I maintain that the highest priorities of our service should continue to be given to gathering hard, fast, factual foreign and world news — the policy in fact of the agency for the past fifty-three years . . .'

'Sorry to break in, sir!' A tall, thin, arrogant-looking man in his early forties who appeared anything but sorry for his intervention broke the chairman's flow. 'But did you actually say in your public statement on Bulgaria "unlike their East bloc counterparts"?'

The chairman's face coloured. He was both angry at being interrupted and astonished by the naked aggression of the question. He tried to think back to the angry scene with his wife and the interruption of it with the news from Bulgaria. Could he have let that indiscretion slip out into the statement he'd dictated from the restaurant telephone booth? He wasn't sure.

'If you did, sir,' said the arrogant-looking director drily, 'I would suggest, with respect, we shouldn't be surprised if we find ourselves banned not only from Bulgaria for five years, which is in my view inconsequential, but from all the other countries of Eastern Europe as well, not to mention Moscow itself. And apropos what you were just saying, that would be much more serious since it wouldn't do our ability to gather fast, accurate information from the communist half of the world any good whatsoever.'

The room was suddenly still. The director who had spoken, fully aware of the impact of his remarks, sat back easily in his chair, inspecting the carefully manicured finger-nails of his right

154

hand. The chairman to everyone's surprise stared down silently at his blotter.

'And do I understand, Mr Chairman, that you were actually personally responsible for the . . .' The director, paused, searching carefully for the right combination of wounding words, '. . . for the "reappointment on trust" of this man, Robson, who had proved himself, if my memory serves me correctly . . .' He paused again and looked quickly at the chairman to make sure his final dart was going home, 'to be somewhat "unreliable" in the past?'

When Barnes finally looked up at the circle of eyes staring steadily back at him, his heavy jowls were red and his whole face was shaking. His voice shook too, when he spoke. 'It is now clear to me that there is taking place in this room what in other places might be called . . . a . . . conspiracy. That is to say certain members of this board are placing matters of policy second to matters of personality.' He paused, looking slowly round at each of the directors in turn. 'It goes without saying, since I am the target of this vendetta, that I believe this to be unhealthy, negative and against the best interests of the agency.' His breathing became ragged and for a moment some of those around the table wondered idly whether they were about to witness a dramatic boardroom coronary.

'As you all know,' said the chairman, continuing with difficulty, 'I have devoted the best part of my professional life to building up the agency on the basis of its present policies. Therefore it pains me particularly to find myself . . . victimized . . . in my own boardroom by people, who having been appointed by me, are now engaged in a shameless scramble for personal prestige and authority regardless of its effect on the organization's fortunes.'

Barnes paused and held a hand to his forehead, covering his eyes as though he were in physical pain. 'In view of these sad, disgraceful and pernicious developments,' he said at last, in a muffled voice from under his hand, 'I wish it to be known that I have neither the spirit nor the desire to continue to lead the affairs of the agency beyond this meeting.'

He dropped his hand suddenly and looked steadily round the table at the men who had deposed him. All without exception avoided his gaze. He looked at them in silence for a long time with an expression of contempt growing on his face. He opened

155

his mouth as though to speak again, then suddenly he seemed to think better of it. Leaving his papers and belongings where they lay he rose from his chair and moved unsteadily towards the door. He opened it quickly and walked out and down the stairs. He walked down all nine flights and out into the pouring rain of Fleet Street by the side door. He would continue walking in the heavy rain for the next two hours, without hat or coat, not knowing where he was, where he was going, or where he had been. When the door closed behind him the men round the table avoided even each other's eyes and it was some long time before any of them spoke.

'Well in view of what we all agreed at Lorenzo's last week,' said one of the elderly directors whom the chairman had always thought to be amongst his most loyal friends, 'I propose that Arthur should take over the chair.'

The rest of the board murmured their assent and drummed the palms of their hands loudly on the highly polished table. The arrogant-looking director who had delivered the *coup de grace* stood up, smiled thinly at nobody in particular, and walked towards the chair.

'Thank you, gentlemen, for your confidence. I think we'll have a short adjournment to let ourselves cool off, shall we?' He didn't sit down. 'Meanwhile, my first act as chairman will be to get in touch with Personnel and tell them to inform Jonathan Robson as soon as he is contactable that his services will no longer be required by BAPPA. Is that agreed?'

'Agreed!' The answer came back in a ragged male-voice chorus.

Still smiling faintly at the room in general, he picked up one of the internal telephones on the table beside him.

At that moment Georgina Morakova was turning the Volkswagen ostentatiously in Ljuben Karavelov and heading off in the direction of the British Embassy residence. But before long she made a series of turns and headed back in the direction she'd come. Within minutes she came in sight of the high walls of the Vassil Levsky Stadium standing in an open area less than a quarter of a mile from where she'd left Robson. She drove round the stadium close to the curving oval of the banked terraces and stands. The dusk was closing in and snow still fell steadily. On the side of the stadium furthest from the road she passed the administrative buildings. But

Wednesday was the one day of the week when the whole stadium and its accompanying sports complex closed down and the offices stood silent and unlit. This was the reason why George Jymeson had chosen the back of the stadium as a rendezvous point. In the fading light Georgina Morakova saw his dark blue Ford Escort parked without lights close against the girder-work foundations of the tall floodlight pylon which stands outside the walls of the stadium bowl at its north-eastern corner.

She cut her own lights and engine and coasted in silently to park close by the British diplomat's car. Jymeson immediately got out, came round to the Volkswagen and opened the passenger's door. He carried a large brown paper bundle which he placed on the rear seat of the Volkswagen before getting into the passenger's seat and closing the door.

'Everything going all right? Swallowed the fable about the Lulinski kidnap okay, has he?'

She nodded without speaking or looking at him. She didn't look at Jymeson any more than she had to. She didn't like his thin gaunt face and the way his eyes always ran quickly down over her breasts and legs before he spoke.

'Thought that would do the trick. We chose a shudderingly real scenario to pitch him, what? My own pet idea actually . . . Got the letter?'

She handed him Robson's hurriedly scrawled note to the ambassador about their plan, and his passport. Jymeson quickly scrutinized what Robson had written. 'Yep, that should be all right.'

He took a large Manila envelope from inside his jacket and spilled its contents on to his lap. He opened an unsealed envelope bearing the embassy crest and skimmed through the words written on a single sheet above what appeared to be the signature of the ambassador, holding Robson's note beside it.

'Super, no problems. That answers all his points. Good guesswork on my part eh?' He turned to her. 'There's your passport in the name of Lady Magnusson but with your photograph in it. Had to be a forged one of course. There's a passport for Robson in the name of the embassy chauffeur — let's just transfer the photograph from his real passport . . . like . . . so . . . There's the ambassador's "letter" — Huh! Huh! — replying to Robson. Make sure he destroys that before leaving the flat. And his jolly old uniform and cap are in the brown parcel. Okay?'

'Thank you,' she said quietly.

'Keep him away from the radio, by the way. Lulinski's giving yer actual opening press conference in Geneva about now . . . You've memorized the account I wrote for you of your supposed meeting with the ambassador?'

'Yes.'

'Bit of luck Robson actually being at the residence when our so-called defector dropped in, what? Pure coincidence. Saved him checking your story out with the ambassador though, eh?' He looked her quickly up and down again. 'Nothing more to say then, except, the best of British luck.' He held out his hand.

She shook it formally. 'Thank you for all you have done for us.'

'Not at all. Sorry I couldn't do more, old girl.' He got out of the car quickly. 'Just hope it all comes off. My best to old Nick, anyway. Must dash.' He slammed the door, ran round to his own car, got in and drove rapidly out of sight round the curving wall of the stadium.

She waited five minutes, then drove to a nearby supermarket and spent another fifteen minutes buying food, drink and cigarettes. When she parked outside the flat in Ljuben Karavelov, both the Chinese in the flat opposite and the Bulgarian security men in the orange Wartburg logged her in by radio to their waiting superiors. As a result of the message, ten minutes later Wang Chieh-ping moved into an alley two streets away with his wife and the scowling Chinese in an embassy Mercedes.

When Georgina Morakova let herself into the apartment and opened the kitchen door, the heat hit her like a wall. '*Dobre Doshli!* Are you warm enough in here? It's like a furnace.'

Robson looked up at her from the chair where he sat with his jacket off smoking a cigarette. The flattened ends of six or seven others lay squashed on the floor by his feet. The four hotplates on top of the stove glowed bright red in the darkness.

'I didn't really expect you back. Did you see the ambassador?'

She put her armful of purchases down on the draining board. 'Yes. He agreed. He is a marvellous man, Sir Charles. He's making arrangements to deal with the men when they arrive and keep them there until Angela is over the border.'

She handed him the letter Jymeson had given her and showed him the passports. She unwrapped the parcel and pulled out the navy blue uniform and cap. 'See?'

He studied the documents and the uniform with care.

'Sir Charles asks you to burn that letter immediately.' She took it from him and held it to one of the hot plates until it flamed. Then she washed the black ash down the sink. 'Now you must eat and drink. You must be famished.' She poured a slug of dark cognac into a plastic beaker she had bought with the provisions, and handed it to him. He drank it at a gulp. She rinsed the beaker then filled it with milk from a waxed carton. He drank that straight off too.

'What time do we move?'

She glanced out of the window at the darkening sky. 'In about an hour.'

He watched her take off her leather riding coat and fur hat and shake down her hair. Underneath she was wearing tight twill riding trousers and a plain grey sweater.

'God, it's so hot in here, I don't know how you've survived.' She turned off two of the hot-plates, asked him to help her off with her riding boots and padded round the kitchen in her stockinged feet preparing the things she had bought. As she worked she answered his questions about her 'meeting' with Sir Charles Magnusson with a smooth assurance.

When Robson got up from the chair to switch on the light he moved across the room to stand in his way. 'Leave the lights off, Jonathan,' she said quietly. 'It might attract attention. We can see to eat by the street lights outside.'

She had bought a small camping frying pan and some plastic plates and forks at the supermarket. 'I hope you like Bulgarian Loukanka.' She cut up the flat garlic sausage into slices and dropped it into the pan with a tin of 'taskebap'. She heated stuffed green peppers in their tin and whipped up a couple of eggs in the plastic beaker.

Robson said nothing. He broke a thin loaf of bread apart with his hands, applied butter liberally with a plastic picnic knife and wolfed one crisp chunk down immediately. When she'd finished cooking, they ate the food and the rest of the bread off the plastic plates, standing silently side by side in the darkness at the draining board. They washed it down with a beakerful each of raw Bulgarian Mavroud. Then she rinsed the pans and beakers and boiled water to make coffee.

She gave him two packets of Bulgarian cigarettes she'd bought at the Supermart. When he'd lit one she hoisted herself up on to the draining board and sat looking down at him. 'Feel better now?'

He nodded. The light filtering in from the street through the condensation on the kitchen window left half her face in darkness. Her behaviour was in no way sexually provocative but now that the food and drink had refuelled his empty stomach and they had spent half an hour close together in the hot, dark kitchen he found himself becoming increasingly conscious of the heavy pout of her breasts beneath the grey sweater.

'What are you thinking? Are you worried?'

He looked away towards the window. 'Georgina, whatever else I may be, I'm not a fool.'

'What do you mean?' She drew hard on her cigarette, and in the reflected glow of it he saw the anxious frown crinkling her forehead.

'While you were gone, I tried to work out what the Chinese are after.'

'Yes?' She spoke quickly. 'What conclusion did you reach?'

'I suddenly remembered something that happened to me early yesterday morning in London — on the way to the airport. Some crazy bastard in a Volkswagen practically smashed me off the flyover road. I managed to avoid him. I thought at the time it was just an accident because of the bad road conditions.'

'Well?'

'I caught a glimpse of his face. I'm pretty sure he was Chinese.' She sat and stared at him.

'At the reception last night, I fancy one of the Chinese diplomats here was trying to listen to our conversation. And when I got to my room last night an American woman was dead in my bed.'

She still said nothing.

'You knew about that?'

She nodded.

'Zhermatov told you?' She nodded silently again. 'I think they were trying to kill me,' he said slowly. 'And what happened today in the forest confirmed it.'

She jumped down from the draining board and poured the boiling water onto the instant coffee in the beaker. 'You like it black?'

'Yes. So what I've been trying to work out is why they should want to do that. What motives could they have? While you were away I asked myself what I am now committed to doing. Trying to foil a Russian plot to wreck the Geneva conference on Strategic Arms and maybe the Vienna talks on Force reductions too.' He paused and took a sip of the scalding hot coffee and handed the beaker back to her. 'The Chinese have been obsessively warning Western Europe for a couple of years now about the danger from Moscow. They're obviously pretty frantic to prevent the Russians tying up their back-door defences securely in the West because that will leave them free to concentrate all their strength in the East on the Chinese front. Therefore, strange to say, Peking's motives coincide with the plans of what you call the "wild men" in the Kremlin. They both want to wreck the conferences – although for vastly different reasons!'

She drank some coffee looking at him all the time over the rim of the beaker.

'But if they have been trying to kill politically insignificant Robson of BAPPA since at least yesterday morning,' he said quietly, 'they must have known long before I knew myself that I was going to be forced into trying to break up the coffin party for Lulinski.'

He smoked in silence for a while. Then he stepped towards her and looked directly into her face. 'Which means there was a deliberate scheme set up specifically to trap me into doing this, with you as the bait.'

She dropped her eyes and sat staring into the beaker of coffee.

'The diversion of the plane from London to Bucharest, you getting on, sitting across the aisle from me. Was that just a coincidence? Or was it very high-level planning indeed. Then the set-piece crash landing and the disappearance of Angela Magnusson. Was it coincidence that we were both there? I suppose it's just possible, but I doubt it. And why me? Why me?'

161

She twisted the beaker of coffee back and forth in her hands, her head down, her long hair falling forward over her face.

'And yet the strange thing is quite a lot of the time, I believe you have been telling me the truth.'

'What are you going to do?' she said softly, still without looking up.

'I don't have many choices open to me. Thanks to you and those behind you, I am now a wholly driven man. Whoever dreamed up the scheme of giving me the tip on the Congress murder, when Radovanovic finally lost out, sewed up my fate very nicely with Bodinski's victorious Soviet opposition, didn't they? Spying charges? A twenty-year jail sentence would probably be the alternative if I decline to go along with whatever your tissue of lies turns out to be. That at least does seem to offer me a possible road of escape. Maybe not. But I can't afford not to take the risk. Very clever indeed!'

'I'm sorry.' Her voice came quietly through the thick fall of her brown-red hair.

'Why not tell me what it's really all about?'

A long silence greeted his question.

He considered her bent head for a moment, then dropped his cigarette end on the bare floorboards and squashed it with his foot.

'What are you going to do Jonathan?'

She looked up in surprise as he stepped towards her. He took hold of the bottom of the grey sweater, pulled it up roughly over her head, tugged her arms free and dropped it on the draining board beside her. 'I'm going to fuck you now, Georgina,' he said quietly.

She sat unmoving, her hands in her lap, looking at him steadily, with the same expression she'd worn in the plane when he caught her off guard. 'It's one of the few choices I have left now — or maybe ever — and I'm going to exercise it.' His voice was flat, unemotional. He reached behind her and unhooked her brassière.

She didn't resist as he removed it. 'It was part of the lure wasn't it, your sex appeal? All part of the plan, whatever it is.' He took the full round heaviness of both her breasts in his hands and spoke fiercely between his teeth. 'Whether you act, as you've

162

been doing all along, or whether you submit or whether you resist, is immaterial.'

Still she didn't move. She sat staring at him mutely for a moment. 'Jonathan,' she said softly, 'the next few hours will be very dangerous for both of us. You won't be alone in that.' She unfastened the waistband of the riding trousers herself and stepped down on to the floor.

He pulled her by her haunches hard against his groin. Her mouth tasted of coffee, garlic sausage and harsh Bulgarian tobacco smoke. He sensed the same kind of desperate ferocity in her that he'd felt when the waiter was approaching by the lake.

He dropped her leather riding coat onto the bare floorboards and they lay down. Her face was a luminescent white in the shadows but her eyes had a bright wildness in them as if she was enduring great physical pain. She shuddered as though from cold, although the room was stifling hot. 'Where it really matters Jonathan, I have told you the truth,' she gasped. 'I want you to trust me . . . you will understand perhaps . . . in Athens.'

The dark cloth of the chauffeur's uniform lying in its brown paper wrapper on the floor caught his eye and for a moment his thoughts returned to the ice and snow outside, the hundred-mile drive south to the border.

'Oh my God!' Her teeth fastened into the muscle of his shoulder and she began shaking uncontrollably. He realized suddenly that she was weeping desperately.

With a gathering swiftness thought and reason burned towards a bright void.

'For God's sake, stay,' she moaned through her tears. 'Stay inside me!'

PART THREE

Egress

Twenty-Five

The Chinese watching stolidly through his telephoto lens saw a hand suddenly rub a hole in the condensation which had obscured his view through the window for the past hour. He was just able to make out the figure of Georgina Morakova holding her left wrist to catch the light coming from the lamp outside on the pavement. She was obviously checking the time. When she disappeared from view he reported the sighting to Wang in the Mercedes two streets away.

In the locked Monitoring room of Section S. 14, Committee for State Security, Captain Zhermatov sat with his chin resting listlessly on his right hand. He was wearing headphones to listen to the voices of Jonathan Robson and Georgina Morakova in the kitchen of the empty apartment at Ljuben Karavelov. He passed his other hand wearily across his brow and glanced at his watch. Thirty-five minutes. He looked round at his young assistant who was watching him anxiously from his desk. 'It won't be long now!'

'You mean I will be able to go home soon to see my wife and baby, Captain?'

Zhermatov's grunt could have meant yes or no. He swung back to concentrate on his amplified headphones. The younger man continued to watch him uneasily.

Robson nursed the navy-blue uniform cap on his knee as she started the Volkswagen and moved carefully away from the kerb into the westbound traffic stream. He turned in his seat to peer through the back window. But the snow, the darkness and the heavy traffic made it impossible to be sure if anyone was following. The orange Wartburg let five or six cars slip between it and the Volkswagen before pulling out of the alleyway and taking its place in the slow-moving line.

The Chinese in the third floor apartment finished making his radio report as the Volkswagen went out of sight at the junction with Graf Ignatiev. Round the corner Wang Chieh-ping in the embassy Mercedes watched the Volkswagen go by, waited carefully until the orange Wartburg passed, waved two other cars in front then pulled quietly out and took up station a hundred yards to the rear.

The Chinese in the apartment carefully folded his tripod and lens, packed them into their purpose-built leather case and placed it by the door in the hall. Then he put on his dark glasses, tied the handkerchief round his face and went into the little bedroom. He took fifty *leva* in notes from his pocket and put them by the bed. Then he untied the terrified old man. He spoke quickly to him in broken Bulgarian, a mixture of threats and warnings, pointing repeatedly to the money. Finally he made an explicit gesture, drawing his finger suddenly across his throat, and went out of the room leaving the old man to struggle with the gag himself. He put on his hat and coat, took off the handkerchief, closed the door of the flat quietly behind him and walked down the stairs and out into the snow, still wearing the dark glasses and carrying the leather case in his right hand. Fifteen minutes later he was back at the embassy.

Robson looked at his watch. 'It's five to five.'

'Good, we are right on time.' She turned left across the southbound traffic stream on Dimitrov Boulevard and into the street leading to the State Security building. A minute later the orange Wartburg made the same turn. The Chinese followed, forty-five seconds behind.

Georgina Morakova pulled the Volkswagen off the street at the back of the grey, featureless headquarters building, switched off the engine and let it roll down a curving ramp towards the basement garages. She parked quietly in an outer bay and leaned across to open the glove compartment in front of Robson. She took out a Russian-made automatic pistol and slipped it into her coat pocket. She looked at him quickly. 'You are ready?'

He looked round the garage. There was no sign of any movement among the parked vehicles. He nodded.

She checked the watch on her wrist. 'They will just have sedated her and placed her in the ventilated coffin. She should sleep heavily for ten hours. She will know nothing of all this.' She took a deep breath. 'We have exactly four hours to get across the frontier. The Lulinski coffin is due at the embassy at nine.'

Robson got out, put the embassy chauffeur's cap on his head, straightened the navy blue raincoat and pulled on the button-up leather gloves. He followed her quickly between the cars to a heavy door. She took a bunch of keys from her pocket, opened it and motioned him into the maximum security bay. He stepped through and while she locked the door again he looked round at the surveillance fleet of twenty or thirty specially-equipped Wartburgs, Tatras and Volgas that were lined up there in neat ranks.

There was no sign of their drivers. Georgina Morakova held her finger to her lips and they stood listening. A sharp crack split the silence close to him, making him jump – then he realized it was the hot engine block of one of the cars cooling. From under the wings of several of the cars, melting brown snow-slush dripped quietly on to the concrete floor.

'Quickly, this way.' She brushed past him and led the way to a flight of steps in the corner of the bay. At the top she motioned him to silence and stood listening again.

When she was satisfied, she hurried down the steps and pulled out the bunch of keys once more. It was a double door, this time, leading into a white-washed passage. He followed her through and waited while she again locked both doors behind them. At the other end of the passage there were more steps leading down to yet another heavy door. When they reached it, she made silent signals to him that this was the last one. She unlocked it with another key and stepped confidently through.

The first thing he saw over her shoulder in the centre of the concrete underground chamber was the sleek gleaming outline of the black Zil hearse. Then she was walking confidently towards three men in heavy coats and fur hats who were clustered round a pine coffin on a trestle table by the hearse's rear door. As she walked, she flung her arms wide in greeting to a stocky, dark faced man with a drooping moustache, who turned first towards her. Gold glittered in the broad grin that lit his face.

'Kostadin!'

'Comrade Morakova! *Dobur vecher!*' He kissed her quickly on both cheeks. She accepted the embrace with apparent pleasure and waved vaguely over her shoulder towards Robson. 'I have brought the "chauffeur" to try the engine of the hearse.'

'*Molya, molya.*' He motioned Robson towards the hearse with his head and turned back to Georgina, grinning delightedly.

The journalist hurried round to the driver's seat and got in. He sat and pretended to check the controls, then started the engine, all the time watching the group around the coffin intently in the driving mirror.

The other two men who were tightening the four brass screw clasps on the coffin, stopped and looked up as the man she'd called Kostadin introduced her.

'My Comrade from Moscow, Yuri Pashov.' She shook hands with a sour-faced man who didn't smile. 'And Misha Abazhiev.' A young Bulgarian greeted her with a shy smile.

Robson saw a woman's coat was slung over the back of a chair. There was a suitcase and a pair of skis beside it. The case had gold initials — "A.M." — emblazoned on its side and a handbag lay on the table by a white cup that had lipstick stains on its rim.

The two men resumed screwing down the lid and when they had finished, looked up towards Kostadin.

'*Dobre, dobre!* We load the coffin now, Comrades.' He beamed at Georgina.

Robson left the engine idling and continued to watch the mirror. The three men slid the coffin clear of the table then swung it round and pushed it into the open doors of the hearse. Its base scuffed noisily along the studded floor. Robson looked out quickly through the windscreen. The long shiny nose of the Zil faced towards heavy metal doors painted pale green and mounted on runners in the concrete floor. Chains and pulleys hung at either side.

He checked the mirror again. The three security men were standing back, dusting their hands. Kostadin was pointing out quietly to Georgina how he had removed all the brass breathing studs from the lip of the coffin. She listened intently as the other two men swung the rear doors closed and secured them.

Robson, because he was looking in the mirror, was the only one in the stone chamber who saw the small door behind the trestle table open soundlessly. None of the three men looked round until Captain Zhermatov barked out a loud order to them from the doorway. Then they turned to see him holding a sub-machine gun, pointing at them in the firing position. They froze where they stood. Georgina Morakova immediately took two or three quick paces backwards, then turned and ran to crouch down at the front of the hearse.

Without another word, Zhermatov opened fire at the three men from a range of ten yards. The deafening clatter of the gun seemed to fill the basement chamber with an unbroken volley of sound. But Zhermatov in fact fired three distinct bursts of six rounds at each man. Robson was only aware, after the shock of the noise stopped, that they were no longer standing.

He turned in his seat to watch the fat secret police chief. He saw him throw the machine gun down on the trestle table and waddle quickly towards the chains and pulleys by the doors. Georgina rose white-faced from beside the radiator, hurried round to the passenger's door and got in beside him.

The chains squeaked noisily as Zhermatov yanked at them. The doors jerked slowly apart and it took a full minute before the gap was wide enough to allow the hearse through.

'Drive!' yelled Zhermatov finally and waved vigorously towards the dark tunnel.

Robson fumbled with the unfamiliar controls. He ground the gears twice before he found first. Then the complicated double-plated clutch made him stall the engine. Zhermatov screamed at him again. Georgina looked round anxiously at the three men lying on the concrete.

Robson found the gear at last and moved the hearse slowly forward through the doors and up the ramp. The chains began shrieking once more as the doors began to jerk closed behind them. He switched on the headlights and eased the long heavy vehicle slowly up the curving tunnel.

Twenty-Six

Zhermatov waited against the doors listening until the sound of the hearse's engine faded away up the ramp. Then he walked over to the bodies of the three men lying close together by the trestle table. He kicked the legs of the man called Kostadin and received a nervous gold-toothed grin from him as he got to his

171

feet. The other two stood up white-faced and brushed the dust from their clothes.

'Too bloody realistic by half,' grunted the man who had been introduced as the Russian.

Zhermatov's face darkened with anger and he glared round at each of them in turn. 'Get out of here – and don't let me see any of you ever again. Ten years ago I would have killed you all without a second thought. Now, I behave like a toothless old hag.'

They stared back at him unsure of his temper, not trusting his own self-deprecation.

'You and the men who pulled the Mausoleum stunt are the lucky ones.' His voice had sunk to a whisper. 'The charades for the British journalist are over. The bullets will be real now! You have to go. Others won't be so lucky . . . Get out! Go back to your villages. Stay away from Sofia until this madness is ended.' His lips retracted suddenly from his teeth. 'And if I ever hear that you breathe a word of this to anyone . . .'

He turned his back abruptly and picked up the machine gun from the table. The three men hurried out through the small door behind the table without looking back.

In the workshop adjoining the underground chamber the little carpenter still crouched under the workbench. He had fled beneath it when he heard the terrifying burst of machine gun fire. He'd heard too the running feet of the three men as they left – and envied them.

He strained his ears. The sound of Zhermatov's retreating footsteps reached him, followed by the hollow clicking of switches. Suddenly the lights in the tiny workshop went out. Surely he could not have forgotten he was there? Zhermatov's footsteps grew fainter, a door slammed. He listened agonized for several minutes. But the silence was as complete as the darkness.

Georgina Morakova wound down her window. She leaned out and inserted a metal template in the lock set in the top of a concrete post ten yards from the outer door of the maximum security garage. She twisted the template and the one-piece door slid up and over out of sight.

Robson let the clutch out too fast and stalled again. The hearse rolled backwards ten yards before he found the handbrake. Then he restarted the engine and eased the clutch back a millimetre at a time. The Zil glided smoothly forward under this treatment and the door fell silently into place behind them.

With the wheel locked hard over to the left to follow the tight curve of the ramp, they sighed smoothly out through the upper parking area where the beige Volkswagen stood inconspicuously among the other cars.

They came up on to the slush-covered street with a rush and the long, bus-like Zil almost ran away with him. He corrected the big wheel only just in time to avoid mounting the pavement on the far side.

Driving at a very cautious fifteen miles an hour, hugging the kerb, and staying in second, he turned right into Dimitrov Boulevard. Already his armpits and forehead were damp with sweat.

'Thank God there's only another hundred and twenty-five miles to go round hairpin bends and over snow-covered mountains.' He stared ahead obsessively at the screeching blue tram sliding along the slippery cobbles in front of his offside wing. The Zil was too wide to get between it and the pavement. He braked and stopped – this time without stalling.

Georgina Morakova turned to look through the glass partition at the coffin. Black curtains were drawn round the windows on three sides and it was barely visible from the driving compartment. She turned back and peered ahead through the snow. 'Keep straight on down Vitosha then go right at Evtimij.' Her voice was tight with tension.

Rush-hour crowds waiting at the tram and trolley bus stops stared curiously at the glossy black hearse with its curtained windows. The uniformed policeman directing traffic in Lenin Square halted three other lines to wave the Zil through.

As they ran on through the square Robson noticed a group of journalists, the *Times* man among them, standing at the top of the steps to the Balkan Hotel, talking and arguing animatedly together. He looked quickly back at the road and narrowly avoided a group of startled pedestrians. Because he was nervous

173

he steered unnecessarily all the way round the Russian Monument in the open plain on Skobelev Avenue when he could have cut straight across to General Todleben Boulevard that was going to take them out of the city.

The point duty policeman planted his hands on his hips and cocked his head at him in a theatrical mime of puzzlement. But probably because of his respect for the dead he didn't blow his whistle.

Two miles further on an empty tram swung unexpectedly across his path outside the Krasno Selo tramway depot and he slid the heavy vehicle sideways on, in a desperate skid along the cobbles to avoid it. The orange Wartburg following him, pulled up and waited a hundred yards back along the road while he restarted and got under way again.

The tall dreary cliffs of workers' flats in the Hipodruma Housing Area stretched the entire length of what was once the old Sofia race course. Eventually they gave way to villas and snow-covered gardens in the outer suburbs. The road began to rise and they climbed steadily through the foothills of Mount Vitosha with the long high hulk of the mountain itself standing blackly above the road, darker than the backdrop of the winter sky behind it. Some lights were already twinkling in the tourists' hotels and restaurants on its heights.

'We're being followed, you might like to know.' The traffic had thinned and Robson had been watching the Wartburg in his wing mirror.

'By what?'

'Looks like an East German job. Puce-coloured or orange.'

'Don't worry.'

He glanced sideways at her pale strained face. 'One of ours, is it? We getting a Zhermatov escort-bodyguard all the way?'

'No. Soon we shall be on our own.'

'Zhermatov only controls Sofia, eh?'

'Bulgaria is a tiny country but it is made up of many smaller "countries". At times of uncertainty like this local loyalties still run stronger than anything else. That's what "Balkanization" really means.'

They drove on in silence followed at a respectable distance by the Wartburg.

'When we reach Daskalovo we fork left. The other road to the right goes on through Kjustendil. After that we are heading due south all the way.'

As they approached Daskalovo, Robson saw a sign pointing back to Sofia. 'Twenty-four kilometres, eh?' he said reflectively 'Let's see, divide by eight, multiply by five! We've come . . . fifteen miles.' He was beginning to feel more confident about handling the long heavy vehicle.

'Careful, here is the turning.'

He slowed the Zil and slipped the big wheel through his hands turning gently to the left to avoid a skid on the icy road. Snow was still falling, but only thinly. He built up his acceleration again gradually watching the mirror on his offside wing all the time. He was about two hundred and fifty yards from the junction when he saw the orange Wartburg make the turn and settle down again at a steady speed in their wake.

Two minutes later Wang Chieh-ping braked the Mercedes down to thirty-five miles an hour as he ran into Daskalovo. He looked at his watch. 'We will keep to the fast road through Pernik and Kjustendil. It is forty kilometres further but that way they will not realize they are being followed. We shall be waiting for them at the crossroads at Stanke Dimitrov.'

The scowling Chinese beside him nodded silently. Tsai Mei-li sat quietly in the back seat, her woollen-gloved hands folded neatly in her lap. Her expression indicated that she automatically accepted her husband's decision as the best possible choice.

Higher up the Vitosha foothills heavy pine forests flanked the roadsides. The Zil slowed to a crawl through the deep shadows on the last steep gradient, then came out over a series of high steep ridges. The snow had stopped now and the skies were clearing. The moon hadn't risen yet but there was a brightness in the sky that reflected on the snow.

'I think we're just about to find out whether you were right about our "friends" in the orange Wartburg.' He watched in the mirror as the headlights that had stayed a steady quarter of a mile behind since the Sofia suburbs closed fast on them driving well out in the middle of the road.

The two men in the East German car didn't even glance up at the Zil as they went by. Robson slowed up and watched its tail lights

175

disappear round a sharp bend. They exchanged relieved glances in silence. The road was dropping away fast again, heading down into a broad cultivated valley on the edge of Bulgaria's prolific tobacco bowl. By the time the road levelled and straightened on the valley floor there was no sign of the Wartburg. Robson slowed right down and checked the mirror. The road was dark and empty behind.

He released a long outward breath through pursed lips. 'From his performance in that basement, I take it that my earlier guess that Zhermatov was Radovanovic's right-hand man is correct?'

'Yes. He is unpredictable, Zhermatov. He told me only that he would somehow arrange for us to leave with the coffin. Not how.'

'Does Bodinski suspect him?'

'Bodinski admires his ruthless efficiency. But he hates Bodinski. That's why he helped me. He is from the Vratsa region. Like Radovanovic and the two who killed themselves he was one of the famous "Gavril Genov" partisans. They fought as young men in the same detachment against the Germans – and the Bulgarian collaborators who tried to hunt them down. Like the others they were very angry when the men who had spent the war in Moscow – men like Bodinski – came and took over after 1944. Even today the partisan fighters still stick together.'

'And now they're dying together.'

She shook her head grimly. 'Yes. Zhermatov is now in great danger too. The purges have been going on all day. Bodinski has always trusted him but with his record Moscow will not allow him to survive.'

The Zil cruised along the wide road across the moonlit valley squatting broad and solid on the snow-rutted surface like a tank. Robson had at last found the way to the heart of its grinding gear box – double declutching. The unnecessary lessons drilled into him by bad-tempered instructors sitting in already-synchromeshed RAF Regiment Standard Vanguards on deserted airfields in North Lancashire twenty years before were at last paying off. The Zil loved it and purred smoothly now in response to his every gear shift.

The Sofia–Athens railway line that threads its way through the length of the same valley as the E 20 wandered over from the right to join the road. A long dark goods train, hurrying south, pulled alongside and gradually drew away from them. Robson watched it go. He was holding the Zil carefully to an unspectacular eighty kilometres an hour. Even so they went by a wobbling local bus packed to its steamed-up windows and towing a heavily laden trailer, as if it was standing still.

They ran on through the quiet village of Dolna Kikanja. Robson steered carefully around two peasant carts plodding slowly through the main street, one close behind the other. The two drivers appeared to be asleep, or drunk – or both. The horses were clearly used to being in charge. Out on the open road on the other side of the village Georgina Morakova lit two Bulgarian cigarettes and handed him one. He glanced sideways at her. The green glow from the large dashboard instruments reflected on her face. She was looking ahead through the windscreen holding the cigarette in front of her face, her lips pulled down tight at the corners in that peculiarly determined expression he'd first noticed in the plane. Her manner was detached, distant. The fierce, desperate intimacy of the empty apartment might never have happened.

'Georgina,' he said quietly, 'I'm a long way from being convinced that Angela Magnusson is really lying sedated behind our ears at this moment.'

She drew hard and long on the cigarette. The ash on its end glowed brightly into a red spearpoint.

He stared grimly through the windscreen. 'I wonder who's really being taken for a ride. Me? You? Whoever's inside it – or all of us?'

He waited a long time but she offered no reply.

'And who's really doing the driving? Just the Bulgarian moderates – or might they have had a little help from certain secret institutions not entirely unheard of in Washington and London?'

'Watch out!' She leaned forward suddenly to peer ahead.

They had rounded a bend and the orange Wartburg was pulled half off the road ahead of them with its lights out. Robson changed down, pumping the clutch fast and eased the Zil into the middle of the highway. As they went past he could see two men sitting motionless in the front seats. Robson checked his wing mirror as he approached another bend. But the Wartburg wasn't moving.

'What do you make of that?'

177

She turned to look through the glass into the dark curtained interior of the hearse again. 'I don't know.' Her voice sounded puzzled.

'Perhaps we should stop and open it up, Georgina.'

She turned to him sharply. 'What do you mean?'

'Unscrew the coffin. To see what's inside. Then we'll both know where we are.'

'No!'

'Why? Is it your own personal hoard of gold bars from the vaults of the Bank of Bulgaria, to fund your retirement in the West?'

She held her wrist against the light of the dashboard. 'It is already six twenty-five. And we are still fifteen minutes from Stanke Dimitrov – that's only one third of the way. We must cross the border by nine. We have no time to stop, Jonathan! It would be crazy!'

'Or it might be equally crazy to go on, not knowing.'

Her leather riding coat creaked as she shifted and fumbled in one of its pockets. From the corner of his eye he saw she was holding the heavy Russian automatic in her hand. She leaned forward and placed it carefully on the shelf below the windscreen. He spoke without taking his eyes off the road. 'That wouldn't be a subtle sort of threat, would it?'

The steady hum of the Zil's engine covered the silence between them.

'It is for our protection,' she said flatly.

He considered this for a moment. 'That's fine – except it all depends what you mean by "our".'

The orange Wartburg appeared abruptly from nowhere and overtook the hearse, travelling very fast. It skidded round a bend in front and disappeared. The moon was rising behind them now and as they ran on down the hill they could see by its light the high, snow-capped peaks of the Rila Mountains standing starkly above the distant tobacco factories and warehouses of Stanke Dimitrov. The icy stream of the Dzerman appeared from nowhere cutting sharply across the floor of the valley from their left. The road turned to meet it and as Robson slowed to negotiate the bridge the orange Wartburg appeared again – this time driving fast towards them. It came swiftly across the river flashing its lights. Robson braked. As the car slowed by them the driver lifted his hand briefly from the wheel in salute. Then he was gone, hurrying back up the road in the direction of Sofia.

'Does that seem to mean our shotgun's going home now?'

'Yes. I think he has been scouting both ways up and down the road. That flash of his lights means he has found no sign of pursuit, behind or in front.'

'I shall miss being followed. There's something comforting about it once you get used to it . . .'

The little carpenter only realized he had been asleep when he woke suddenly. He was surprised that he had been able to fall asleep in that cold, uncomfortable position on the floor under the bench. Then he realized it was the scrape of the key turning in the lock on the other side of the pitch dark cellar that had awakened him. It turned again, the door swung open and the shadows of two men fell across the small workshop with a square of yellow light from the adjoining cellar. He held his breath.

'Nobody in here.' The man, who spoke in Russian, began closing the door.

'Wait, Comrades, wait please!' The little Bulgarian shouted and scrambled out from under the bench. He was surprised when he saw that both the Russians, who wore civilian coats and hats, carried revolvers in their hands. When they turned to point them at him he wished he had stayed where he was under the bench. But he suddenly remembered his wife's advice and took no chances. He put both hands up straight above his head as high as they would go and stood there shivering slightly.

'What are you doing here?' The first Russian spoke Bulgarian now.

'I got locked in. I was making a coffin for Captain Zhermatov.' Words fell from his mouth in a babbling torrent. 'But I think they forgot I was here. Locked the door. Went away and I couldn't get out. I'm hungry and cold. I've been here all night, all day. And my wife will be very worried about where I've got to . . .'

'Coffin? For Zhermatov? But he's not dead.'

'No! I mean, Comrades, not *for* Captain Zhermatov. He *told* me to make it. I worked all day and all night. Secretly. Then it went out, I think, in the big hearse. An hour or two ago.'

'Who was it for then?'

'I don't know, honestly, Comrades, I don't know. It was a special one . . . it had cushions and air holes in it.'

The Russians looked at each other quickly. Then one of them put his revolver away and walked across to the shivering carpenter. He grabbed him roughly by the scruff of the neck and frogmarched him swiftly towards the door.

Twenty-Seven

Gordon Miller yawned and looked at his watch. Quarter to seven. He didn't enjoy the evening shift very much. He preferred days. He took another sip from the lukewarm tea he'd just bought from the trolley that trundled round every three hours between the rows of teleprinters.

The neon tubes buzzed annoyingly overhead. The glare seemed to bleach everything in the room after an hour or two. He picked up a wad of copy from the top of the pile in the wire basket, and ran his eye over the first sheet. It was from Geneva. He only had to read two lines to know that it wasn't worth the five hundred words that stupid bugger Finneran had wasted on it.

'*Superpower delegates clashed head-on again here today in another fruitless round of the Strategic Arms Limitation Talks*', he'd begun. '*At their ninth meeting in three weeks Soviet and American representatives . . .*' Miller scored out two whole paragraphs, ran his eye quickly down the rest of the page, then turned to the second sheet. '*The chief Soviet negotiator, Alexei Lulinski, this evening called a press conference in which he lashed out verbally at what he called the West's stubborn intransigence . . .*' Miller jabbed his pencil impatiently through the last half page. He wrote 'one hundred words maximum', circled it with a heavy black pencil and threw it to a sub-editor half way along the stem of the T-shaped table.

'A hundred of your most succinct words only out of that, Jim, please.' He spoke airily. 'Cut out all Lulinski's propaganda verbiage. And write one intelligent paragraph, which Finneran clearly isn't capable of doing, telling our thick-headed newspaper-reading public why the Russians won't cut back their missile numbers till the Americans grant them more export credits. Get the SALT cuttings up from the library.'

He hated copy-tasting. He would be glad when nine o'clock came round and Jock Baird pushed off home. Then he'd take over the desk as supervisory night editor. He looked across at Baird's empty chair. He'd been called upstairs an hour ago. Something, Miller presumed, to do with the Robson fiasco in Bulgaria. Instead of reporting the news the bloody agency *was* the news today. The London evenings were leading their front pages with spying charges against Robson and the fact that he'd disappeared after reporting the Congress murder. Big passport pictures of the correspondent that Personnel had issued were on both front pages.

Miller saw a story begin to chatter in on the Vienna line and got up to go across and see if Robson had at last turned up and filed a story from somewhere. But before he got there, the loud sound of banging from Jock Baird's desk made him stop and turn.

Baird, his face red and angry-looking, was opening and closing drawers, tossing some papers into his waste bin and stuffing others into his briefcase.

'What is it, Jock, old man?' Miller's voice was artificially solicitous.

'Nothing,' snapped the old Scot. 'Nothing at all!'

'Oh, come on, Jock, don't be coy.' Miller advanced towards him, scenting drama.

Baird stopped what he was doing, jammed his hands against his hips and glared at Miller. 'The chairman's resigned and the man popularly known as "bastard features" has taken over. BAPPA's having its balls cut off!'

'Really! Arthur Kennington's taken over, has he?' Miller was smiling despite himself. He'd played squash at the RAC by chance one morning last month with Kennington when their respective partners failed to turn up. 'But what's all this about removing our corporate scrota?'

'The agency's being . . .' Baird paused and his face went a deeper shade of red, '. . . streamlined and modernized. News reporting is to be cut right back in favour of fast commodity and stock exchange reporting from all major international centres.'

181

'Streamlined? What does that mean exactly?' queried Miller innocently.

'It's a euphemism for sacking bloody journalists, that's all. We'll have reporters only in a few big centres, like Washington, Moscow, Paris. I told Kennington straight – if the chairman's gone and the agency's just going to tot up figures, you can have my resignation here and now before you even think of sacking me. I'm a newsman, not a bloody stockbroker's clerk.'

'So, Jock, you were right on the button about the BAPPA power struggle. Just about as right as Robson was wrong about his punch-up between Radovanovic and Bodinski.'

Baird glared at him. 'Aye – and Kennington's already sacked Robson, the cynical bastard. If anybody wants me up to nine o'clock I'll be in the "King and Keys" getting thoroughly pissed.' He swung on his heel and marched out.

The sub-editors down the desk had stopped work and were whispering among themselves. Miller picked up an outside phone and called his wife.

'Janie?'

'Yes?'

'It's Gordon. Got a bit of news.' He turned his back on the subs and lowered his voice to a whisper. 'Jock Baird's just resigned, walked out.'

'Is that good?'

'Should mean an extra couple of thousand a year for me.'

'Do you think you'll definitely get his job?' She was whispering too.

'Yeah, I think so. Sir Someone Barnes has chucked in his hand too. And guess who's the new chairman – Arthur Kennington.'

'That friend of Daddy's you let beat you at squash last month?'

'Yeah.'

'Oh good . . . I say, darling, that's terrible, isn't it, about your poor man in Bulgaria. I heard it on the television news.'

'Bit of a fool apparently. Look, don't wait up. I might be late tonight, sweetheart. I'll probably have a little celebratory drink with one or two of the chaps before I come home. Byee.'

He hung up, picked up the pile of copy from his in-tray, took it over to Baird's desk, settled himself in the new chair and began wading through it with a new relish.

*

Robson saw the three Chinese in the Mercedes at almost the same moment that they themselves caught sight of the hearse. As he came carefully round a bend in the main road in the centre of Stanke Dimitrov, just short of the main square, his eye fell on the German car parked in a dimly-lit road leading off to the right towards the river. It was the Mercedes's sophisticated incongruity in the provincial Balkan town that hit him in the eye. Among the unlit cycles of the workers pedalling home from the tobacco factories and the local horse-drawn *britschka* leaving the evening market, the fact that its lights were correctly and legally lit set the Mercedes clearly apart.

Robson gave no sign that he'd seen it. He continued to keep the Zil well within the built-up area speed-limit of sixty kilometres an hour through the long sprawl of the town. Tinny little Soviet-built Trabants carrying local Party officials home to their waiting wives stopped hooting irritably at the throngs of cyclists and pulled respectfully aside when they saw the hearse bearing down on them.

He glanced in the wing mirror and saw the Chinese had pulled out on to the main road. But although clearly following them, they stayed well behind keeping a steady hundred-yard gap between themselves and the hearse.

'Hold on to your seat,' said Robson suddenly. 'I'm going to brake hard. We're going to play the part we've dressed for.'

He pressed his foot firmly and steadily on to the brake, bringing the hearse's speed down quickly to around eight miles an hour.

'What are you doing?'

Robson motioned backwards over his shoulder. 'I think three uninvited mourners have just joined us.'

The Mercedes, taken by surprise, braked gradually to avoid skidding. To stay behind it had to drop its speed to match the Zil's. Georgina Morakova wound down her window and poked her head out. A moment later she wound it up again and turned to him wide-eyed. 'It's the Chinese. Why are you slowing up?'

They were moving on towards the main square at a snail's pace, with passers-by staring curiously at what they obviously believed was a two car, funeral cortège.

Robson bit his bottom lip thinking hard. 'It might be better to have a confrontation here with an audience of thousands than out on the mountains ahead.'

He leaned over quickly and took the Russian automatic from under the dashboard. He pushed it into his right-hand coat pocket. She looked at him astonished. 'What are you going to do?'

He was looking from side to side through the windscreen. The evening market straggled untidily across the southern side of the square beyond the central State Dimitrov monument. On the eastern side of the square stood a large building with 'People's Theatre' picked out above its doors in red neon. He glanced quickly in his mirror then suddenly accelerated the Zil to the left and ran it on to the theatre car park.

He switched off the engine, pulled on the handbrake and reached for the door handle. The Mercedes was hovering indecisively in the square, its three occupants watching the hearse curiously.

'Stay inside! Lock all the doors. If anything goes wrong, try and drive the bloody thing to the frontier yourself.'

'What are you going to do?'

'I never make detailed plans. I'll improvise.'

'For God's sake be careful.'

'Perhaps *they'll* tell me what's inside the coffin.' He swung the door open, jumped out and ran into the square towards the Mercedes, waving his arms above his head.

Twenty-Eight

The wizened Bulgarian peasant-woman in charge of the evening market's 'Chicken Corner' pulled the heavy wool shawl closer around her ears against the chill wind. She knotted the string quickly about the legs of the scrawny-looking hen she'd just plucked from the squawking cage beside her and handed it to the Stanke Dimitrov housewife who'd selected it. As she took her money she pointed over the customer's shoulder towards the centre of the square. 'Something funny's going on there, d'you see? D'y' see?'

The housewife turned and looked at the man running towards the Mercedes waving his arms above his head. 'Foreigners!' She spoke tonelessly as if the one word explained everything illogical under God's heaven.

They saw the running man reach the car and bend towards the driver's window. The door opened suddenly and the driver got out. Both men, after exchanging quick words, began hurrying across the square directly towards the chicken seller.

'They're coming to buy one of your skinny chickens,' said the woman sourly as she took her change. She checked the coins suspiciously and held up the miserable-looking hen. 'If they knew how little flesh they had on 'em, they'd stay in their warm cars and save their money.' She sniffed loudly and strutted off among the stalls with her nose in the air.

'Maybe I can help you Robson,' said Wang sibilantly, as they pushed past the chicken seller.

Robson glanced at the baskets of eggs and wrinkled yellow cold-store apples heaped on the trays next to the chicken pen. The stall holders stopped serving, to stare as they walked by.

'I see, Comrade Wang, I've misunderstood you, have I?' asked Robson with heavy sarcasm. 'You've been trying to contact me for forty-eight hours to try to help – that's what your man was trying to do when he accidentally crashed off the ramp at Chiswick, that's what you were doing when you accidentally killed Gloria Zuckermann in the Balkan Hotel last night, and that's what you were doing when you chased me for two miles through the woods at Pancharevo this morning, is it?'

Wang stared straight ahead. He nodded and smiled, excusing himself with elaborate politeness among the crowds of Bulgarians thronging the stalls. He stopped to inspect a piece of pottery decorated with a brown and white wavy-lined pattern in which staring, disembodied eyes were the main motif. He held it up, as though for Robson's benefit. 'You are wanted for spying by the new régime here, yes?' He spoke so quietly that Robson had difficulty hearing what he said. 'You have to get out of the country . . . I suggest you leave the hearse and your companion here and I will take you over the frontier in the boot of my car – without risk, with full diplomatic immunity.'

Robson shook his head towards the vase. 'Those eyes, no good,' he said loudly. 'It would make you feel you were being watched all the time.' He took the vase from Wang's hands and peered inside it, leaning close to the Chinese. 'Why would you want to help me now when you've been trying to kill me for the past two days?'

Wang took the vase back, put it down and walked on, talking quietly out of the side of his mouth. 'You are a victim, Robson, aren't you? Or are you a very clever intelligence man who just makes himself appear to be a victim?'

'I'm a reporter.'

'Then you need somebody to help you. Somebody outside — to break the circle of those who are making a fool of you.'

'Who are they?'

Wang paused and looked round quickly. The pungent spicy aroma of frying *kebabcheta* sausage rose in clouds from a food stall where a long queue had formed. Wang looked round quickly again, then walked on. 'The Bulgarians, the Americans, the British.'

Robson noticed that Wang kept both hands in his coat pockets. 'Everybody except the Chinese and the Russians, eh?'

He ignored Robson and lifted his head to look upwards. A granite monument to the man who started a humble tobacco-growers' commune in the valley in the twenties and after whom the town was named towered up suddenly above the covers of the stalls. When he spoke the Chinese appeared to be appraising the statue. 'You believe that you are preventing a Kremlin plot to smuggle Lulinski to the West and so smash the détente policies of Moscow and Washington, don't you, Robson? That's why you got involved, isn't it?' Wang looked around him then hurried on again without waiting for an answer. They reached a quiet shadowy corner of the market and Wang stopped and turned to face the journalist, his eyebrows raised inquisitively. 'Isn't it?'

As Robson framed his reply a dark-skinned hand holding a wickedly curved scimitar flashed between them. They both turned. The grinning face of a gypsy wood-carver broke into a strangled laugh. He stepped back behind his dimly-lit stall and smacked the scimitar hard against the side of his own head. The thwacking sound that it made revealed that the weapon was carved from wood. The gypsy raised and lowered his heavy Chaplinesque eyebrows rapidly in a mime of amazement at his own skill in creating such a life-like sabre.

'Ten *leva*, Comrades,' he said in Bulgarian, holding the sword handle first towards Wang, then towards Robson. 'Ten *leva?*'

Wang shook his head at the gypsy and turned back to Robson. 'Isn't that so?' he repeated.

'Partly — but isn't that also why you and your comrades have been trying to kill me — because you think I might prevent the Lulinski plot working, because you want the Russians to fall out with Western Europe too, but for different reasons to the Kremlin hawks?'

Wang smiled uneasily as the gypsy danced between them again holding up an armful of wooden bowls, plates and elaborately worked boxes. 'Five *leva*, Comrades, *five leva?*'

Robson had to speak over his head. 'Comrade Wang, do you and Mao Tse-Tung know what or who is in the coffin?'

The Chinese waved the gypsy away but kept his eyes locked on Robson's. His face broke into a glittering, humourless smile, 'Yes!'

The gypsy, back behind his stall again, clapped his hands loudly to gain their attention. He held up two more carved wooden swords and pointed to a cast-iron rack of genuine antique sabres which they resembled. He held them side by side for comparison, grinning proudly, then grabbed the hilt of one of the real swords. He heaved at it and made as if to swing it wildly in their direction.

Robson and Wang took a step back but the gypsy staggered back theatrically, his fist empty, indicating in wide-grinning mime that the real swords were solidly welded into the heavy iron display frame.

'And are you interested in the coffin's contents?' Robson watched the Chinese's reaction carefully.

Wang shook his head. 'We are interested only in you Mr Robson.' The smile glittered again for a moment. 'What would you say if I told you there is no Kremlin plot. That it is a hoax.'

'What sort of a hoax? For whose benefit?'

Wang took a pace closer to Robson. 'That I will tell you only after I've taken you across the border.'

'And what happens if I refuse your kind offer of safe passage in your boot?'

Wang still had both hands in his pockets. He stared at Robson, his lashless eyes unblinking. 'Then we will kill you before you reach the border.'

The gypsy picked up his curved wooden scimitar, swished it about wildly above his head, contorting his face all the time into a series of bloodcurdling expressions.

'All right Comrade,' said Robson quietly. He put his hand into his coat pocket. 'Then you'd better start right now because I'm going over the frontier tonight under my own steam to get to the bottom of all this – and by tomorrow the story will be on the front page of every newspaper in the western world with you in one of the starring roles.'

The gypsy swung the scimitar in one last lunatic arc above his head, overbalanced and fell down out of sight inside his stall. Wang's lips parted in a fixed smile as he took a quick step towards Robson. The Chinese moved so fast that the journalist had no time to shift backward. Wang's right hand came out of his pocket jabbing upward with a short, broad-bladed knife that looked like a potato peeler. His left hand clamped the hand Robson had on the gun in his pocket and prevented him from removing it. Robson twisted and caught Wang's knife wrist with his free hand. They cannoned into the canvas front of the wood-carver's stall, sending a pile of wooden plates cascading to the ground. The gypsy rose, his face contorted with real alarm now, to stare at the two men swaying locked together against the front of his stand.

A group of Bulgarians went by the end of the row of stalls twenty yards away, pointing and laughing loudly, imagining the foreigners were joining in the gypsy imbecile's pranks.

Robson grunted and strained to keep the knife that was hidden between them from entering his ribs. Wang's grin had become a clenched-teeth snarl as he concentrated all his effort in his hands. Robson swung his right shoulder suddenly and forced Wang off balance. The goggle-eyed gypsy shrank back against the side of his stall as the two men staggered and stumbled through the gap in the counter, bringing down another stack of wood carvings in their wake.

In the rush Robson's right hand came free. He grabbed the Chinese by the collar, swung him bodily against the side of the stall and twisted quickly to force him down towards the ground. But there was suddenly no need. The Chinese had gone limp.

The grip on his own right wrist relaxed and the broad-bladed gouge knife clattered to the ground. Robson, startled, looked into Wang's face. His eyes were staring over his shoulder. His mouth sagged slowly open and his arms slipped and hung down loosely at his sides. He coughed once and blood began to run out of his mouth.

Robson stepped back, breathing fast. The gypsy moved up beside him, staring dumbly at his wrought-iron rack of display swords. The six-inch points that protruded beyond the racking were buried deep in the left hand side of Wang's back from shoulder to hip.

The gypsy was the first to move. He pulled a knife from inside his shirt, slashed a four-foot gap in the back canvas of his stall, scrambled through and ran. Robson stood rooted to the spot for a moment, still staring at Wang. Then he, too, bent double and ducked out through the hole.

The gypsy was already out of sight, lost among the carts and garbage at the rear of the stalls. Robson headed for the western edge of the square and cut into the cobbled side streets. Walking quickly he kept parallel with the square along its northern and eastern edges and four minutes later came into the People's Theatre car park from the rear.

He paused in the shadow of the theatre. The Mercedes had moved closer to the market but it was parked in a position where its occupants could still watch the Zil. Robson slipped quickly across the car park, bent double, keeping the hearse between him and the Mercedes. He moved round to the passenger door, reached up and knocked quietly on the window.

Georgina's face, pale and frightened, appeared looking down at him. She unlocked the door and he clambered in, still crouched low, beneath the level of the windows.

'What happened?'

He waved a hand at the dashboard. 'Start her up.'

She turned the ignition key and the engine fired first time. He let it warm up for a moment, hoping the exhaust fumes weren't visible from across the square. Then he straightened in the driving seat, pumped the clutch, found first gear and shot out of the car park on to the square. He swung the nose of the hearse south and accelerated away fast down the main road.

The heavy figure of the scowling Chinese immediately leapt from the Mercedes. He stood at the open door, looking first towards the market into which Wang had disappeared, then back towards the departing Zil. He was still standing indecisively in the middle of the road when the hearse went round a bend and out of sight.

Twenty-Nine

The air in the windowless Monitoring room was stale and heavy with the smoke from the Bulgartabak cheroots that Zhermatov had been smoking incessantly for the past two hours. He had flung off his coat and stripped down to his shirtsleeves for the laborious job of feeding the tall piles of papers from his filing cabinet into the shredding machines. Even so a sheen of perspiration glistened on his face in the glare of the strip neon lighting.

Trichkov was sweating too. His hair was plastered against his forehead and his shirt stuck to his back as he fed individual documents quickly into the second shredder, taking great care not to read or even look at their contents. He was grey-faced with fatigue and he yawned incessantly. He had almost reached the end of the files Zhermatov had handed him, when the radio receiver crackled and made him start. It came to life with the call sign of the Wartburg patrol on the E 20 highway.

He moved towards the radio but Zhermatov waved him back, waddled over and picked up the hand microphone himself. He listened with narrowed eyes as the Wartburg driver reported his position from Raika Daskalovo. 'No signs of pursuit of the Zil at any point on the E 20 Sofia-to-Stanke Dimitrov,' said the driver crisply. 'Please advise.'

Zhermatov switched to transmit. 'Abandon the car immediately. Crash it. And return to your homes on foot. Stay there for two or three days before reporting here for fresh duty. Understood?'

The voice of the man came back through the radio, puzzled but obedient. He knew better than to question Zhermatov's orders even when he didn't comprehend them. 'Understood, Captain.' Zhermatov replaced the microphone on its rest, returned to the shredder and picked up the last sheaf of papers lying beside it.

'I've completed destruction of the documents you gave me Captain,' said Trichkov hopefully. He had listened carefully to the instructions given to the E 20 patrol.

'All right,' Zhermatov irritably glanced at his watch. 'Then get out. Go home to your damned wife and baby.'

The young man ran for his jacket. As he put it on he turned to look at the bull-necked security captain bending over the shredder. Against his will he felt, for the first time, a surge of something approaching affection for the rough-mannered, peasantish man he had been closeted with for the last two days. He was on the point of asking him if *his* wife was waiting for *him*, then thought better of it.

He drew back the three bolts on the heavy steel door that had remained locked constantly for the past thirty hours, except when the older man arrived and departed.

'Say nothing of this assignment,' growled Zhermatov over his shoulder. 'Stay at home for a week and when you return say you've been ill. If you're lucky it won't be noticed in the confusion.'

'Yes, Captain . . . and thank you.'

He opened the door quietly and staggered backwards. The Russian stepped quickly across the threshold and struck him viciously in the chest a second time with the butt of his automatic rifle. Trichkov went down in a heap on the floor. Seven other KGB officers, all carrying similar weapons, crowded into the room. Three of them ran to Zhermatov and pinned his arms as he lunged towards his jacket and the belt containing his pistol holster. One of the two men who'd searched the basement cellars pushed the ashen-faced carpenter in front of him through the doorway. The little man's wrists were handcuffed behind him.

Trichkov was dragged roughly to his feet and hauled across beside Zhermatov and the carpenter. The Russians had not uttered a single word during the brief struggle and now the noise of men gasping to regain their breath was the only sound in the silent room. Two of the Russians took up guard positions on either side of the door covering the captives with their automatic weapons, and waited.

The sound of approaching footsteps grew louder in the corridor outside. A moment later Boris Bodinski stood framed in the doorway.

His small, restless eyes darted left and right, taking in everything quickly at a glance. Then he walked slowly across the room and stopped in front of Zhermatov.

'All right Uyri,' he said quietly. 'Where is the Zil?'

Zhermatov tried to spit in his face but Bodinski stepped alertly backwards out of range. 'You are too late, Boris, you treacherous bastard. It's across the frontier by now.'

The little pig-like eyes of the new First Secretary seemed to grow even smaller. 'You're lying Uyri. And you, above all others, shouldn't have forgotten that we have quick and efficient means of dealing with those foolish enough to be liars. Which route did it take?'

Zhermatov glared back at him in defiant, sullen silence. Bodinski looked towards the Russian who'd burst into the room first, and shrugged. 'He leaves us no alternative, does he? Take him downstairs.'

In the soundproof basement room, they strapped him to a table. An enormous Russian slipped his hand quickly inside Zhermatov's collar and ripped the shirt and vest from his chest in one movement. Then he took hold of the enormous waistband of his trousers and ripped them open to the crotch. He did the same with his underclothing then turned and nodded to the man who stood behind him holding the electrodes.

In the shadows against the wall, Trichkov and the carpenter stood handcuffed between four guards. They watched the man step up to the table. As he attached the electrodes to Zhermatov's testicles the little carpenter fainted and sagged to the floor.

Robson was driving the Zil as fast as he dared. The speedometer held steady on the hundred-kilometres-an-hour mark as the hearse ran smoothly along the flat road between the frozen cherry orchards and vineyards of the Blagoevgrad plain. In the distance dense black beech forests marched over the lower slopes of the Rila mountains.

He'd had only one really bad moment – on the steep gradients of the Belopole Defile as they wound slowly down into the mouth of the plain. Then, on an unfenced hairpin, he'd slid out close enough to the edge to find himself staring down a steep, boulder-covered scree as he wrestled with the hearse's heavy steering. It had taken all his strength to keep the front wheels from slipping over the crumbling edge of the road. After that he'd driven over-cautiously in first all the way down to the valley floor.

Blagoevgrad, named after the founder of the Bulgarian Communist Party, had caused them no trouble. The tobacco workers were already in their homes and the frozen streets of the town had been deserted. The only vehicle moving was the half-full Athens–Sofia bus pulling out of its last main stopping depot on its way north.

Now they were heading through the broadest part of the valley of the Struma. The road across it lay white and deserted under bright moonlight. The high rocky peaks of the Rila massif came into view standing out starkly against the sky to the east, as the road began to climb gently again towards the Oranova Defile.

'How are we doing for time?' Robson, who hadn't taken his eyes off the road for an instant since the People's Theatre, looked quickly at Georgina.

'It's almost eight o'clock,' she said anxiously, 'and we still have fifty miles to go.'

'Georgina,' he said slowly, 'isn't it time you dropped your pretence about having to be over the frontier by nine? Wang told me the Lulinski thing was a hoax.'

She stiffened. 'You would rather believe the Chinese than me?'

'He told me too that the British and the Americans were involved in this. Perhaps it really is time you filled me in on the background.'

'We must be over by nine.' Her voice carried a note of desperation. 'Our contact at Petrich can't wait forever! It's very dangerous for him to show us the unofficial crossing point. We are in solid Bodinski territory now! We can't just roll through the frontier point at Kulata like tourists. Besides Zhermatov cannot guarantee that things in Sofia will hold that long. Every moment counts, don't you understand?'

He shook his head. 'I'll just have to take your word.'

Her voice softened. 'For a few hours more only, Jonathan, I promise you.'

The black mountain slopes came rushing suddenly across the plain from either side, converging fast on the Zil. The Struma river, the railway and the E 20 highway were all bundled abruptly together like the wires in a flex in order to squeeze them through the long thin canyon between the two mountain ranges. They passed the signboard announcing 'Oranovski Prolom' and immediately the road began to climb steeply. Rock walls rose sheer on both sides, the river dipped in a rushing torrent to the narrow V-shaped bed of the valley far below and the railway track disappeared into a tunnel by the roadside.

As they neared the top of the first high spur, Robson caught a flash of yellow headlights in his wing mirror far back on the plain. They were moving very fast, about three or four miles behind them. He pressed the Zil forward along the winding defile, driving hard into the corners, braking steadily and accelerating fast out of the bends. Now that he'd got thoroughly used to the vehicle he found that although heavy it handled with a sturdy uncomplicated consistency, braking straight without dragging right or left and, because of the weight on its back wheels, responding firmly to the accelerator.

Gradually Georgina Morakova became aware of this new tension in his driving. 'What is it, Jonathan?'

'Headlights. Moving very fast behind us from Blagoevgrad.'

She sat forward in her seat holding on to the dashboard to steady herself with one hand as the Zil swayed and shuddered through the bends.

The little hot springs village of Simitli appeared suddenly before them in a hollow. There was no movement of people, vehicles or animals and they drove through its white silent streets without slackening speed. On the other side of the village the road climbed and fell, tracing an erratic route over the gnarled roots of the Krupnik massif that towered above them to the east. The railway dodged constantly in and out of tunnels on their right and the river roared below on the other side. The road snaked through the Kresna Gorge, twisting and turning back on itself sometimes, holding the speed of the long heavy hearse to an average of under twenty miles an hour.

Robson cursed the road constantly beneath his breath as he fought the Zil along, glancing every few seconds in his mirror. A metal girder bridge appeared suddenly and the river dashed underneath them and came up on their right. The road and the river swung from side to side shadowing each other closely and occasionally the road swerved out over the river itself on an overhanging cliff. Rock bays had been cut back into the side of the road farthest from the river to allow tourists to stop and admire the spectacular scenery in summer. The protective barriers, he noticed, were bent in places where they had saved vehicles from slipping over the edge.

Robson began watching them carefully as the Zil slid round the tortuous bends. Without warning, at a point where the barrier was already buckled outwards, he hauled the heavy steering wheel to the left, crossed the oncoming lane and ran into a bay in the rock on the opposite side of the road. He reversed and manoeuvred hastily until the Zil was parked hard under the lee of the rock, with its nose pointing outwards.

He pulled on the handbrake, switched off all the lights, but left the engine running.

She looked at him anxiously. 'What if they see us as they go by?'

'We couldn't have kept in front of them much longer. Wind down your window. Then get out of sight behind a rock at the back of this lay-by.'

She wound down the window, got out and ran quickly into the darkness behind the Zil.

A minute passed, and the only sound apart from the steady idling of the Zil's motor was the rush of the river beneath the overhang of the road.

Then he heard it distantly. The immediately-recognizable Mercedes engine was screaming and protesting in a high-pitched voice as the driver forced it rapidly through the corners, braking, and accelerating fast again with the bottom end of the gear box.

It slowed right down as it approached the loop of road out over the river. Then the engine revved loudly again as the driver put it into first before swinging out round the rock.

Robson waited with one foot on the clutch, the other on the accelerator, his hand on the handbrake and the lever in first gear.

As the Mercedes nosed round the corner, he switched his headlights suddenly to full, let up the clutch and shot out at right angles into its path. The face of the scowling Chinese behind the wheel lit up in alarm as the Zil's blazing headlights hit him. An instantaneous reflex swung his steering wheel right to take him out of the path of the hearse. His speed was down to about ten miles an hour on the corner and the metal crash barrier held him easily. But then the Zil with Robson's foot hard on the accelerator leapt across the remaining ten yard gap between them.

Its broad elaborate front fenders charged the Mercedes solidly amidships, shunting it sideways. The already weakened barrier snapped out over the river like a broken elastic band, leaving the Mercedes unprotected on the lip of the road high above the river. It balanced there for a moment, with its two nearside wheels hanging in space, then tipped slowly sideways. It turned end over end as it bounced down the cliff and hit the roaring, frothing river flat on its roof. Robson braked frantically and swung the wheel of the Zil hard to the right. The rear end of the hearse skidded slowly round until it banged noisily against the next unbroken stanchion. Then the engine stalled leaving him sitting at the wheel facing back towards Sofia, looking down through the yawning gap in the crash barrier at a dark, indistinct patch of turbulence in the river far below.

He turned his head as he heard the sound of footsteps on the road. Georgina Morakova opened the passenger's door and got in without a word. Her face was very pale but she didn't look at him. Instead she turned immediately and stared through the glass at the coffin. It hadn't moved from its moorings. Robson got slowly down from the driving seat and squeezed between the barrier and the hearse to look at the damage.

The offside wing was bent back so far that it was pressing on the wheel. He kicked at it violently for a couple of minutes until he cleared it. Then he got down on his hands and knees to see if the radiator was leaking. But there was no sign of liquid on the road underneath, probably due to the heavy ornamentation of the hearse.

He stood up and looked around. The road was empty in both directions. The river rushed on fiercely through its restricted bed and there wasn't a sound that nature wasn't making in the fresh, cold night.

He got back behind the wheel, restarted the Zil and turned its nose south again towards Sandanski and the frontier. As they set off a thick black cloud swept across the face of the moon and began once more to sprinkle snow on the mountains.

Thirty

The dark blue Ford Escort bumped slowly over the slippery cobbles towards the British Embassy residence. It stopped and parked at the kerb fifty yards short of the gates and George Jymeson switched off the engine.

'Why are we stopping here for goodness sake, Mr Jymeson?' Angela Magnusson's exasperation from the back seat was undisguised.

'Just be patient and hang on here a sec with my wife, Angela, there's a dear.' He spoke over his shoulder. 'I'm just going to have a very quick word in your father's ear about some embassy business. Then you'll see the back of Phyllis and me. Probably for good. All righty?'

He smiled round perfunctorily at the girl. His wife sat in the passenger seat beside him, staring stonily through the windscreen. Before she could answer he got out and hurried towards the residence gates.

Angela Magnusson sat primly back in her seat, more conscious than ever of her 'rank' as the ambassador's daughter now that they were in sight of the residence. 'What exactly did your husband mean by "for good", Mrs Jymeson?'

'We're expecting to leave for London first thing in the morning.' The older woman's voice was distant. Her face was pale and drawn and she still wore a flowered scarf around her head. 'My husband is being re-assigned unexpectedly.'

Jymeson ran up the steps to the porch two at a time. The door opened before he reached for the bellpull and Sir Charles Magnusson, stern and unsmiling, stepped aside for him to pass into the lighted hall. The ambassador led the way quickly towards the study without greeting his second secretary.

He lifted his left wrist, shot his cuff and checked his watch, as he walked. 'You'll have to be quick, Jymeson. You must be out of here by eight thirty. I have a very important appointment. I would have refused to see you at all at this time if you hadn't made that rather mysterious reference' – he stopped in the middle of his study and turned to face the younger diplomat – 'to my daughter.'

Jymeson took a deep breath and pursed his lips thoughtfully for a moment. 'What I've come to tell you, sir,' he said quietly, 'will at first astonish you, then no doubt make you angry. But it is good news and I think you can rest assured that the men you were expecting to arrive here at nine o'clock will not now be coming.'

The ambassador's eyes narrowed with suspicion. He turned his head slightly to the side, looking at his man sideways on. 'What do you know of this, Jymeson?'

Jymeson licked his lips quickly. 'Your daughter Angela is perfectly safe, Sir Charles. She is sitting in my car outside now with my wife. She has been with us for the past two days . . .'

'What the devil . . .' The ambassador stepped past him and moved quickly into the hall heading for the door.

'Please wait, sir, I insist, for your own sake.'

The ambassador stopped and turned sharply on him. 'You "insist", Jymeson? What the devil do you mean?'

The second secretary hurried on, his tone becoming apologetic. 'Let me explain, sir. I have been involved in an operation to protect your daughter since the crash landing. I collected her from the airfield with my wife and she has been staying at my house in perfect comfort since then. She believes this was at your request. Any over-emotional welcome would seem strange to her.'

The ambassador came back slowly into the room. His head came forward and his shoulders went back into an unconscious caricature of the stiff-backed military man he had once been. 'So she was never taken hostage at all.'

'No, sir.'

'Then what the devil's been going on?'

Jymeson swallowed hard. 'Those in London responsible for all this will no doubt be sending you a full detailed briefing at the earliest possible moment through the normal channels. It will be classified under the title "Cranbourne".' He glanced down at his watch. 'Within the hour, I should think now, you'll get a brief, sir, with a bit of luck.'

The ambassador's face darkened. 'You'll give me a bloody briefing right now, this minute. All that you know, Jymeson!'

'I've simply been following instructions, sir, you must understand that. All I am authorized to say as of now, is,' he paused and his eyes dropped for a moment, 'that it was, in its best construction, by nature of a protective operation that enabled a certain clandestine course to be pursued. Despite appearances, your daughter was never in any danger whatsoever, and it was felt that it was in the best interests of the integrity of your own personal office as Her Majesty's Ambassador to Sofia that you shouldn't be compromised by knowledge of it.'

The ambassador breathed quickly, clenching and unclenching his fists at his sides. He made no attempt to keep the sarcasm out of his voice. 'This "clandestine operation", Jymeson, is it now complete?'

Jymeson looked at his watch unnecessarily. 'Not quite, sir, no. May I suggest respectfully, sir, that we terminate this discussion until after you've seen Angela. She's pretty keen to see you again, of course. I suggest you explain as I did that the inconvenience to you both was due to the exigencies of the service . . .'

The ambassador cut him short, his voice heavy with displeasure. 'Jymeson, I'll want to go over this with you very fully later . . .' He began moving towards the door.

'I'll look back in about an hour if you like, sir. Perhaps London's reply will have arrived in the Communications Room by then. Things might look rather different then, if you'll forgive me for saying so.' He paused. 'There is just one thing, sir. To protect ourselves fully, we should report to the authorities here in Sofia the theft of our embassy chauffeur's uniform. I'll explain fully later but with your approval I'll do this so that the embassy is absolutely in the clear.'

The ambassador stopped in the hall, still barely able to control his anger. 'Very well, go ahead and do what you must.'

'And sir, one last thing. I shall, of course, be offering my resignation from the embassy staff immediately as no doubt you would want. I have booked seats for my wife and myself on the first London flight tomorrow morning.'

199

'Good,' said the ambassador grimly. 'That's your best news to date.' He walked quickly down the hall to the door.

Jymeson caught him up at the car outside. The ambassador opened the rear door and greeted his daughter with a quick peck on the cheek. 'Hello, my dear. Nice to see you back. Had a good holiday?'

She flung her arms round his neck. 'The holiday was super, Daddy – but I've been so bored since yesterday . . .'

'I'm sorry about that, my dearest. I can't explain now but you know how stuffy this dashed job of mine can be.'

She pouted playfully and hugged him again.

In the office of the First Secretary two miles away on the second floor of the Bulgarian Communist Party Centre, Boris Bodinski sat motionless behind a large empty desk. His elbows rested on the spotless white blotter and his loosely-clenched fists supported his square-jowled head. His eyes stared unseeing across the room at the pine-panelled walls. The silence of the room was broken by a loud 'click' and without looking up Bodinski knew that the minute hand of the electric clock on the wall had moved on to four minutes past nine. He glanced at the green internal telephone which he had separated from the other telephones on the desk and placed in the centre of the blotter, as though willing it to communicate with him. The minute hand broke the silence five more times at regular intervals before the telephone buzzed quietly. He lifted it quickly to his ear. '*Da?*'

'Zhermatov took a lot of breaking', said the voice at the other end. 'We had to . . .'

'Just the facts – quickly.'

'The E 20 to Greece. Blagoevgrad, Sandanski turning off the main highway at Marikostinovo towards Petrich where they will try to cross illegally through a farm produce checkpoint. Robson, a British journalist, is driving the hearse. They left at five o'clock.'

Bodinski had already picked up one of the other telephones on the desk. He dropped the green one back on its cradle without a word as the switchboard operator came on the line. 'Get me three separate calls category "Absolute Priority" to headquarters in Petrich, Marikostinovo and Sandanski. Put them through in precisely that order on lines four, five and six.' He put the telephone down and replaced his elbows on the blotter. He looked back quickly at the clock. His brow furrowed briefly as he calculated times and distances. Then he checked the clock again.

It was eleven minutes past nine.

Thirty-One

'Why don't we just bluff our way through the Kulata checkpoint? We've got passports, haven't we?' Robson leaned forward as he spoke to switch on the wipers. The pinpoints of snow speckling the windscreen were maturing into large flakes. They'd left the Kresna Gorge well behind now. The valley and the river had widened and the road itself had become a gentle downward slope.

'It's impossible. The frontier is normally open only from sunrise to sunset. But even if we try to get through there, the risk of discovery would be too great.'

The Zil's headlights picked out a yellow and black name-sign announcing in Bulgarian and English that they were approaching the village of Marikostinovo 'famed for its mineral baths'. But its streets were now completely devoid of mineral bathers and all other signs of life. A signpost in the village centre pointing south said: 'Kulata 8 kilometres'.

Robson pressed the accelerator a shade nearer the floor. 'My arithmetic tells me that we're five English miles from the frontier. On this road that would be less than ten minutes.'

She looked at her watch and drew in her breath sharply.

'What is it?'

'It is already nine thirty.' She peered ahead through the thickening snow. 'Slowly! I think the turning to Petrich is just around this bend. The road will not be good. The going will be rough from here.'

Robson had the Zil in second and he slowed right back into first when he saw the sign. It was leaning drunkenly at an angle. The post seemed to have snapped and it was propped against a wall at the side of the road. Snow obscured part of the letters of 'Petrich' but it said clearly enough that the town was twelve kilometres away. He pulled round into a narrow track that immediately began to climb steeply between high narrow banks.

'The Greek border curves northwards towards this.' She pointed through the windscreen. 'It is only a mile or two over there. Tulbokov will show us.'

'Tulbokov?'

'Our contact. Arranged by Zhermatov.'

'You said we were going to use an "unofficial" crossing. How "unofficial" is it?'

The Zil began to labour as the slope grew steeper. Then at the top of the long incline it dropped suddenly away and Robson had to change down rapidly to prevent the heavy hearse from running away down the hill.

'It is a small commercial checkpoint used only in summer. For transporting melons, cherries, that sort of thing, from the collective farms to markets in Greece.'

'There'd better be a bloody Greek taverna on the other side, that's all,' growled Robson. 'I'm dying of thirst.'

The road dropped steeply again and he crawled down it cautiously in first. The Zil rumbled and shook over the uneven surface.

'These are the foothills of Mount Belasica. It straddles the frontier.'

The Zil skidded suddenly in a rut. It cannoned hard against the right hand bank and Georgina Morakova turned to look anxiously through the glass partition at the coffin.

'Still there is it?'

She glared at him without speaking and turned back to watch the road.

Robson peered at the neatly banked snow on either side. 'You know, this road, bad though it is, looks as though it's been recently cleared by a snow plough.'

'It was also arranged by Zhermatov. Tulbokov lives at the farm on this road. He agreed to clear it and the track to the crossing point for us – after dark tonight.'

She leaned towards the windscreen. 'We should come to the farm soon.' They drove for five minutes more in silence. Robson could feel his chest tightening with tension. His back was stiff and his head had begun to ache with the strain of concentrating on the Zil's headlights. His legs ached too from the uninterrupted physical effort of controlling the big unfamiliar vehicle that had begun five hours and a hundred and thirty miles ago in Sofia. The jolting ride along the hilly rutted track seemed to be requiring as much effort yard by yard, as the miles had demanded on the E 20 highway.

A dark cluster of low farm buildings showed in the headlights below them as they came over the crest of another hill and swung down into the valley. Georgina Morakova touched his arm and pointed. 'That is where we are to meet Tulbokov. Can you manage on sidelights from here?'

Robson switched off the headlights and drove slowly down the incline.

At the bottom he swung the hearse through a gap in the stone walls, drove across the yard and crunched to a halt in the fresh snow beside a barn. He switched off the engine and windscreen wipers and they sat for a moment in silence watching the snow settling against the windshield. As their eyes grew accustomed to the darkness they were able to make out the dark shape of Mount Belasica looming behind the farm buildings. Nobody emerged to greet them.

Robson was the first to put into words what both of them were thinking. 'Why are there no lights?'

'I don't know. Tulbokov should have been waiting for us.'

'We're an hour late, aren't we?'

'Yes, but he lives here with his family.'

Robson looked out at the dark, silent buildings. 'I'd better go and take a look.'

He got out and crossed the yard. The snow was settling fast and it was too dark to see whether the vehicle tracks in the yard were fresh. He tapped on the farmhouse door and waited.

The only sound in the farmyard was the wind howling down from the mountain. He tried the door handle and it gave under his pressure. He stepped inside.

Georgina Morakova watched from the hearse, holding her breath. She saw the shadowy outline of Robson disappear through the doorway. Several times during the next few minutes she saw a flicker of light through the windows of the lower rooms. Then a shadowy shape emerged from the door and hurried back across the yard. The door opened, Robson got in and took a deep breath.

'What did you find?'

'Nothing. Absolutely nothing!'

'Not even any furniture?'

'Plenty of furniture! But no people. No lights either. I had to use my cigarette lighter. A half-finished meal on the table, red embers in the grate, a child's bed upstairs, slept in – still slightly warm – but empty.'

She was silent for a moment. Then she shuddered suddenly. 'We're too late.'

Robson searched round the shadowy buildings bordering the yard with his eyes.

'What can we do?'

He looked at the anxious white blob that was her face in the darkness. 'Turn back?'

'No! It would be suicide.'

'Not for you. You can go back to your "grace and favour residence" in Sofia, can't you, and pretend you never left?'

She turned her head to look back into the coffin compartment although it was too dark to see anything. 'Turning back would be death for me, Jonathan,' she said in a fierce whisper.

He sat back in his seat. 'Do you know the way to the frontier crossing point without Tulbokov?'

'No.'

Then an obvious thought struck him. 'We can find it ourselves! It's been marked for us! We just look for the snow ploughed track!' Then an even more obvious thought struck him. 'And they'll be waiting for us there, of course.'

He looked at his watch. It was nearly ten o'clock. 'The other alternative is to stay here in this hearse in this farmyard on the slopes of Mount Belasica for the rest of our lives.'

Her hand was on his arm again in a mute appeal.

He sat thinking for a moment without looking at her. Then he switched on the ignition, started the Zil's engine again and flicked on the lights.

She removed her glove quickly and her hand covered his on the gear lever.

'Jonathan . . .' She hesitated and leaned closer to him. 'Thank you for all this. Please remember what I'm going to say now.' Her voice died away and she half-glanced over her shoulder at the rear compartment. 'No matter what, Jonathan, I'm glad you made love to me . . .'

He squeezed her hand quickly, pushed it away and put the Zil in gear. He swung round the yard and back onto the road. He put the headlights up to full and accelerated, skidding across the icy ruts along the narrow lane.

The snow-ploughed route was obviously the first junction they came to, running off south at right angles to the road. The snow fell heavily through the twin beams of the headlights but the ruts of other vehicles were clearly visible. The Zil rocked and bumped over the unmetalled road, jolting them violently in their seats.

He switched out all the lights suddenly and ran on in total darkness. But there was no sign of a light anywhere ahead and he put them back up at full beam.

The track ran round the side of the mountain that rose abruptly to their right. The ground fell away sharply to the left and he had to drive slowly to keep the Zil from skidding off the steeply cambered road into the deep snow. Without the clearing work done by Tulbokov's plough it would have been impossible to drive the Zil along there at all.

The track dropped down through a clump of fir trees heavily laden with snow and a hundred yards ahead the headlights of the hearse suddenly picked out the fence of the border, a group of green painted huts and a red and white diagonal-striped barrier across the road.

'That's what we came a hundred and thirty miles to look for, isn't it?' he said quietly and eased back on the accelerator.

'Give me the gun please, Jonathan.'

He took the automatic from his pocket and handed it to her.

Thirty-Two

He let the Zil slow to a crawl. The red and white striped barrier pole looked like a flimsy wooden construction. But impenetrable gates of heavy steel laced with chain-link mesh stood closed behind it. The vehicles that had made the tracks in the snow were nowhere to be seen. Presumably they'd been parked out of sight behind the small customs sheds.

He looked at the steel gates again. Crossing here with the hearse was clearly out of the question. For a moment he wondered what chance he would have if he jumped out and ran. Leave the hearse, Georgina and the coffin and all the bloody imponderables and just bolt for it over the gates? The Zil dawdled on even more slowly as if sharing Robson's indecision.

A white flare fired from a pistol soared into the sky abruptly from behind the customs sheds. It sizzled upwards through the falling snow and exploded into a white suspended blaze that lit the area like neon. Two men in army uniform ran out from behind one of the huts and kneeled on either side of the track, their machine guns pointing at the Zil.

Two other soldiers moved out quickly from the other side carrying lanterns. They waved them in an arc above their heads as they ran shouting towards the slow-moving hearse. In their free hands they carried pistols.

'Don't stop, Jonathan!' Her voice was a scream.

He saw her raising the pistol towards the windscreen pointing it towards what now looked like a garishly overlit film set gradually filling with armed men. Another white flare wiggled up into the snowy sky to add new brilliance to the scene.

His foot went down hard on the accelerator. The back wheels spun ineffectually for a moment and the Zil slid slowly sideways towards the edge of the road. Then it took off forwards, moving directly at the running men.

The two machine guns opened up simultaneously and their first burst hammered into the bodywork on its nearside wing. The top of the windscreen exploded inwards on them with the second burst showering glass on them like confetti. Then the gun in Georgina's hand roared deafeningly close to his ear as she fired back in the direction of the crouching soldiers.

The two men with lanterns flung themselves sideways into the roadside snow as the Zil bore down on them. Their first volley of revolver shots smashed the side windows of the coffin compartment. Georgina Morakova turned to fire through her open window at the man on her side as they went by. Twenty yards from the barrier Robson stood on the brake with all his strength. The hearse turned its slow clumsy length sideways on and began sliding broadside towards the red and white pole. He waited until he was fifteen yards from it then flung the wheel across the other way and squashed his foot back on to the accelerator.

Bullets from machine guns tore into the body of the Zil, raking along its sides and smashing through the rear doors, as the back wheels spun wildly searching for a grip. The carpet of splintered glass from its windows crunched beneath the tyres as they finally got a tractive hold and shot the Zil over the lip of the road. It careered nose-first down the steep slope, sliding in the snow like a great, ungainly black sleigh. Robson swung the wheel desperately left and right trying to keep the nose in front of the heavy tail-end that was trying to overtake.

The chain-link mesh border fence turned down the slope, curving slightly to the north on a converging track with the Zil. Robson cursed the hearse frantically at the top of his voice as he wrestled with the wheel, trying to get the nose straight before they reached a thirty-yard wide ledge in the hillside that preceded a sheer drop into a gully.

Gradually the Zil responded and he brought its front end round ten yards from the lip of the ledge. He pressed the accelerator flat against the floor and aimed the broad front fenders at a point in the mesh fencing midway between the twenty yard support posts. The engine was roaring and the rear wheels spun wildly in the thin snow of the rocky slope as the Zil flung itself bodily into the fence.

The wire mesh bulged, resisted then parted and went flat under the wheels, ripping itself from its supports. But the Zil was only half way through the fence when it came to a shuddering halt, snared in the steel mesh like some great, black whale in a giant drift net.

Robson revved the engine furiously but the Zil was stuck fast. The group of soldiers began slithering and sliding down the slope towards them. A machine gun at the top of the hill opened up at the trapped hearse but was silenced almost immediately by a shrieked order from an officer leading the men down the bank in its direct line of fire.

Robson glanced round at the soldiers and revved the engine once more at full pitch. But still the hearse wouldn't move.

He slipped the gear lever out of first and into reverse and tried the accelerator again. The engine roared, there was a fierce sound of ripping metal and the Zil jerked free of the restraining mesh and shunted backwards into Bulgaria.

Robson slammed the gear lever back into first and drove the accelerator pedal down to the floorboards again. The back wheels of the hearse gripped on the steel mesh covering the snow and the whole hearse shuddered as it shot clear of the broken fence.

The ground on the other side was strewn with rocks and two of the tyres shredded immediately to ribbons. Jammed in first gear the Zil careered wildly across the open ground in its death throes. As it went, its engine screamed in frenzy as if the hole in the border through which it had escaped was an exit from hell.

Thirty-Three

The lights of several vehicles at the top of the slope on the Greek side all came on at the same moment. But Robson didn't stop. He kept the Zil trundling along a rough path across the hillside, still heading south and away from the frontier wire. Then a third tyre blew and twenty yards further on the Zil ground to a halt with steam hissing from its empty, punctured radiator.

He slumped forward on to the steering wheel, exhausted. He lay with his head on his arms and felt the blood running into his mouth from wounds in his face.

He looked up when the door at his side was opened from outside.

'You all right, old man?' The voice spoke BBC newsreader's English. 'You've made a dreadful mess of this old bus, haven't you?'

'Look after my passenger, I think she's hurt,' said Robson dully.

The man who'd spoken went away and a moment later the door on the other side opened. Robson was vaguely aware that several

208

other men had come up behind him.

'Oh dear. Oh deary, deary me!' said the English voice as though from the other end of a tunnel.

Robson raised his head. 'What is it?'

'I'm afraid Mrs Radovanovic is dead.'

Robson watched the man drop her limp wrist back onto the seat. He wore a navy blue balaclava helmet and a camel-coloured duffel coat. Behind him a patrol of Greek soldiers in winter equipment ran by towards the hole in the fence and took up guard positions.

'Mrs Radovanovic?'

'That's right old man.'

'But this is Georgina Morakova!'

'Well yes, that's true. That *was* her maiden name until she married Nikolai secretly a couple of months ago. She was originally Bodinski's bird of course but decided – rather unwisely now don't you think – to switch nests. You'd better let the Doc have a look at your face hadn't you?'

'From Vratsa!' said Robson half to himself. 'Yes, of course, bloody Vratsa!' He didn't finish the sentence. He put his hand to his cheek where it was smarting and pulled a long splinter of blood-covered glass from the flesh under his right eye.

The man in the balaclava turned away. 'Well let's take a look and see how the merchandise has fared.'

A man in the uniform and cap of a British Army major had come up behind him with a Greek civilian who carried a doctor's bag. 'Ask the Greek colonel to have his chaps work on those rear doors with a tin opener would you? I want the lid off that box smartish.'

The officer hurried away. The crowd of men gathering round the hearse seemed to be ignoring Robson. He climbed down unsteadily and stood alone in the snow by the driver's door letting the large wet flakes fall on his upturned face.

A tap on the shoulder made him turn. Robson looked at Bradley without surprise. 'Sorry Jon.'

Robson said nothing.

'Washington wasn't really involved. I was just a weather eye.'

'You don't even have the bloody grace to look embarrassed.'

There was a loud clang as the rear doors were forced open by a Greek corporal with a crowbar. Two soldiers pulled the coffin half out of the Zil and began unscrewing the brass clasps. Bradley pushed a folded copy of the *Herald Tribune*, Paris edition, into his hands, pointed wordlessly to an item he'd ringed at the foot of the front page and walked away to join the group at the rear of the hearse.

As he waited for the lid to be unscrewed the Englishman fitted his forefinger idly into a bullet hole in the wood on the end of the coffin and whistled a tuneless version of 'Annie Laurie'.

Robson glanced at the newspaper in the glare of the headlights from the top of the hill. '*Woman journalist found dead in Vienna hotel room,*' said the headline. '*Mrs Zuckermann seemed to have died from natural causes and foul play is not suspected,*' said the one-paragraph story.

Robson wondered dully how Zhermatov had managed to move her so far, so fast. He dropped the paper on to the driving seat of the hearse and went round to the back. He peered into the hole in the front of the balaclava. 'Who are you?' he asked bluntly.

The narrow, haughty features framed by the wool gave the impression they were constantly suffering fools, not gladly, but because there was no other choice.

'Isn't your name Carruthers?' said Robson, suddenly, peering closer.

The man studied the journalist's face intently for a moment then put his hands behind him and rocked back gently on his heels. 'Let's just say I'm from London, shall we?'

He turned suddenly as the lid came off the coffin. He put one knee inside the back of the hearse and levered himself up to look inside. 'Mmmm. A shame. Just as I feared. Still warm, though.' He turned to speak over his shoulder. 'Take a quick look at him Doc will you, just to make sure.'

He climbed down into the snow again, dusting his mittened hands together. 'Pity. We've never had the First Secretary of a ruling Communist Party defect before. Would have been a nice coup.'

Robson stared at him. 'But Radovanovic was shot at the Congress.'

'Quite right Robson, quite right, as indeed you said in your admirable piece. But only "shot" in the broadest sense, not killed.' The balaclava bobbed around as its owner rocked on his heels again. 'Shot by his chum Zhermatov with blanks and with a Hollywood butcher's blood bag under his shirt. The medics standing by would have been fixed. Their PR is getting more sophisticated in Eastern Europe, these days. Nice little subterfuge eh? So his cronies could get him out of the hall and through a loophole in Bodinski's net y' see.'

'Shit!' breathed Robson.

'You lent the whole thing a bit more credence with your world scoop of course.' The man patted him patronizingly on the shoulder. 'Smart move on their part, that.'

The Greek doctor climbed down out of the hearse and nodded to the man in the balaclava.

'And his wife?'

The Greek nodded again and trudged away up the hillside towards the cars parked around the deserted customs sheds. The Englishman turned back to Robson. 'Like to have your face done in my car up there? You can have a cup of tea too. Got a flask in the boot.' He stepped away up the hill without waiting for a reply.

The doctor swabbed his face and stuck some plaster on the cuts as Robson sipped a plastic cup of lukewarm thermos tea, sitting in the passenger seat of the car. Through the windscreen he watched the Greek soldiers winching the Zil up the slope with a breakdown truck.

He screwed the plastic cup carefully on the flask by his feet and turned on the man beside him. 'So there never was any plot to mess up the SALT talks, no Lulinski kidnap?'

'Lulinski gave a press conference in Geneva this afternoon, old boy. Sounds as though somebody's been pulling your leg a fraction.'

Robson clenched his fists and took a long breath. 'So you and Radovanovic and Zhermatov fixed the fake crash landing, the mock shoot up at the Mausoleum, the whole damned . . .'

'Don't worry yourself too much with the details, Robson,' said the man in the balaclava soothingly. 'It's all over now isn't it?'

'I suppose he asked for asylum first? Why the bloody hell didn't we grant it?'

The man beside him sighed with mild exasperation. 'Too risky old boy. Cross up HMG too much with the Russkies. Bad for trade, and the détente thing. You're right, though, he did come to us through the Sofia embassy three weeks ago and said could we be standing by to help him out if things went wrong.' He sucked in breath noisily between his teeth and shook his head. 'Had to give him the thumbs down. Sorry nothing doing! The F & CO couldn't get involved in that sort of hanky panky.' He put his hand inside the helmet and scratched his head distractedly. 'He was lucky that you came along and offered to help him out in the end. Don't blame yourself. Nearly got away with it. Damned bad luck really.'

The hearse came slowly up over the edge of the road looking crumpled and sorry for itself.

'Three weeks ago,' said Robson quietly. 'That's just about the time I sent my courtesy telegram to Sir Charles saying I'd be coming to the Congress for BAPPA. So that's when you began to hatch this . . .' The man beside him didn't appear to be listening. 'You bastards, you rotten, fucking bastards!'

The man in the balaclava turned and raised an eyebrow at him in admonition. 'Steady on Robson. Sir Charles knew nothing of this. You've had a hard night. Need a spot of rest, don't you think?'

'I'll rest when I've written this story!' Robson realized suddenly he was shouting and lowered his voice. 'I'll plaster it and you all over the front page of every bloody newspaper in the world tomorrow morning.'

''Fraid not, Robson.' The man touched his pursed lips with the finger-tips of both hands. 'Can't be done. When you get back to civilization you'll find there's been a D-notice slapped on all this. Mum's the word.'

The snow was reaching blizzard proportions outside the car. The man in the balaclava started the engine and turned on the heater. 'Getting chilly now isn't it?'

Robson slumped lower in his seat.

'Oh and before I forget, your man in Athens asked me to give you this if I ran into you.' He handed over an envelope.

Robson began opening it but a loud clanking sound made him look out through the windscreen. He saw the Greek border gates swinging open. A dozen soldiers were manhandling the broken hearse along the sloping track towards them. They put their shoulders into it together and the Zil gathered momentum. It lumbered slowly through the gates and on down towards the Bulgarian checkpoint where the gates now also stood open to receive it.

Robson turned to stare at the man beside him.

He was studiously pouring out the last drop of cold tea from the flask. He spoke without looking up. 'Not much use to us in that state, are they? Don't let it worry you. Not worth it. Much tidier to let 'em have 'em back. No publicity.'

Robson opened the envelope and read his dismissal notice sent by teleprinter to the Athens office by the new chairman of the board, Arthur Kennington.

'Not bad news I hope,' said the balaclava man blithely.

'The sack.'

'Oh dear, what a beast.'

There was silence in the car for a while.

'Still I do hear you're renowned for being what's termed in popular parlance today "a survivor". Isn't that right?'

Robson didn't reply. Instead he sat staring dully out through the windscreen. Large wet snowflakes flopped against the outside like sodden fragments of rag. Several minutes passed inside the car in complete silence. Gradually his view of the bleak hillside was blotted out.

'Tell you what,' said the man from London brightly, 'why don't you wait a year or two, change all the names, places and dates and things and write it up as fiction? Make a rattling good tale, wouldn't it?'

Anthony Grey
A Man Alone £3.50

The seven stories which form the basis of this book are selected from thirteen written in confinement in the heat of the Peking summer of 1968. . .

The complete isolation that journalist Anthony Grey experienced when he was held hostage in China for two years (the full story is told in his bestselling book, *Hostage in Peking*) might have stopped his urge to write. But Grey used his creative ability in new ways over this period; indeed writing stories was perhaps the only thing that kept him sane.

These stories, smuggled out from his Peking jail – and by turns entertaining, abstract, philosophical – reflect the oblique perspective from which, for those interminably long months, 'a man alone' viewed the world.

'The subjects are varied, the approach imaginative, and descriptions graphic. What is more a sharp vein of humour runs through the book' THE TIMES

'Whether as literature or a sanity-preserving record, these compositions will rightly fascinate thousands of readers' THE SCOTSMAN

'Both readable and revealing' FINANCIAL TIMES

The German Stratagem £3.50

Every year three tax dodging multimillionaires hold a vital business meeting in no man's land: a plane flying high above the Atlantic. Until, that is, they are betrayed in the crossfire of East-West intelligence. . .

Their one ally is a newspaperman hiding his cowardice behind a veneer of cynicism — but not his desire for the beautiful and arrogant daughter of one of the trio.

The headlines announce a new financial crisis in the West. In reality, a bitter ideological war is raging. It is anyone's guess who will survive the fallout.

'Blackmail, seduction, hostage taking, hijacking. . . the story just races along. . . Bond at his toughest would do very well for the hero' EVENING STAR

'Anthony Grey's first novel is a slick, modern politico-thriller. . . the total effect is one of considerable entertainment' BRISTOL EVENING POST

Previously published as *Some Put Their Trust in Chariots*

Peking £3.99

A long terrible night was ending. And amidst the horror and despair
was a passion that would rise from the ashes of turmoil. From the mill
towns of the north of England in the decade after the First World War,
Jakob Kellner brings crusading zeal to a once proud China — besieged
by a crippling malaise that Christianity can no longer salve. As the
marchers gather in southern Hunan, he becomes entangled in a love
that will outlive a nation's shattered dream.

With *Peking*, Anthony Grey enshrines in towering fiction the turbulent
half century of conflict, struggle and idealism which marks China's
historic revolution. From the self-sacrificing beginnings of the Long
March to the human suffering at the core of the Cultural Revolution,
this is a novel of heroism, rivalry, love and forgiveness — an epic
masterpiece to mirror the vastness and grandeur of China's compelling
history.

'Gripping fiction . . . part epic, part blockbuster' THE TIMES

Saigon £4.99

Joseph Sherman first sees Saigon in 1925, as a wide-eyed fifteen-year-old on a family hunting expedition. For five decades he returns again and again, drawn back as much by the land's strange magic as by Lan, the Vietnamese beauty he can never forget. He is there when the hatred of a million coolies rises against the French, when the Foreign Legion fights at Dien Bien Phu, when military 'advisers' fire early shots in America's hopeless war against the red tide of revolution, and as the last US helicopters flee the fallen city.

'Anthony Grey is not just a man of steely courage, as his survival through two years in a Peking prison demonstrated. He is one of that rare species – a born storyteller' DAILY MAIL

All Pan books are available at your local bookshop or newsagent, or can be ordered direct from the publisher. Indicate the number of copies required and fill in the form below.

Send to: **CS Department, Pan Books Ltd., P.O. Box 40,**
             Basingstoke, Hants.   RG21 2YT.

or phone: 0256 469551 (Ansaphone), quoting title, author
             and Credit Card number.

Please enclose a remittance* to the value of the cover price plus: 60p for the first book plus 30p per copy for each additional book ordered to a maximum charge of £2.40 to cover postage and packing.

*Payment may be made in sterling by UK personal cheque, postal order, sterling draft or international money order, made payable to Pan Books Ltd.

Alternatively by Barclaycard/Access:

Card No. ☐☐☐☐☐☐☐☐☐☐☐☐☐☐☐☐☐☐☐

Signature:

Applicable only in the UK and Republic of Ireland.

While every effort is made to keep prices low, it is sometimes necessary to increase prices at short notice. Pan Books reserve the right to show on covers and charge new retail prices which may differ from those advertised in the text or elsewhere.

NAME AND ADDRESS IN BLOCK LETTERS PLEASE:

....

Name ———————————————————————————

Address ——————————————————————————

————————————————————————————————

————————————————————————————————

————————————————————————————————

3/87